Listen to the Child

Elizabeth Howard

Published by Hookline Books
Bookline & Thinker Ltd
7 Regent Ct., New St
Chipping Norton OX7 5PJ
Tel: 0845 116 1476
www.hooklinebooks.com

A CIP catalogue for this book is available from the British Library.

This book is a work of fiction. Names, characters, places and incidents
are either a product of the author's imagination or are used fictitiously.
ISBN: 9780993287480

Cover design by West Coast Design
Printed and bound by Lightning Source UK

As Constance ran out into the rainy night, the wind whipped her cloak around her thin figure like a winding shroud. She tugged at it, anchoring it firmly against her thin chest, letting go only as she tripped over a hard bundle which cried out in pain.

Constance knelt down, her dress and cloak soaking up rain from a puddle. The heavy wind made the gas lights flicker, but a short lull allowed her a glimpse of a small face glistening in dampness. "Lawrence! You're supposed to be in bed."

The boy swallowed a sob and then spoke with a fast rhythm that once started couldn't be stopped. "Miss, I was waiting for my father. He said he'd come back for me, but it's been weeks. He's never left me this long. I don't want him to come while the home is closed for the night – he might go away again." Lawrence paused briefly as he read Constance's face for trouble. "I was only watching for him, Miss. I didn't mean to do anything wrong."

Constance pulled the boy to her and then dabbed his face with a dry part of her cloak, but the heavy rain quickly undid her work. "Lawrence, you must learn patience. Your father has to find a job, and then he has to pay off his debts and find a home where he can raise you. Only then will he be in a position to take you away from here." She rubbed a tear that hovered at the tip of his chin. "All that can take a very long time."

Lawrence sobbed. "How long?"

"Only Our Lord knows the answer to that question."

The boy's swollen eyes threatened to erupt once more. Constance pushed gently at his shoulder. "Let's go back inside. Miss Winifred will find you a cup of hot broth and we'll get you into a warm bed."

Without waiting for agreement she ushered the nine-year-old back up the steps to the heavy door that guarded the Home of Industry. It was locked for the night, but Constance pounded heavily.

Winifred's stout figure peered out cautiously.

Constance pushed Lawrence forward. "I'm sorry, Winifred, but I found this young man outside. He thought his father might come and fetch him tonight, and I found him waiting in the gutter. I think he needs dry clothes."

Winifred eyed the boy's wet nightgown, which hung below his coat. Lawrence's right foot, shorter and thicker than the other, looked ruddy and chunkier than usual.

Lawrence caught Winifred's gaze and pulled his clubbed foot under his gown.

Her gaze interrupted, Winifred pulled a hefty key from her pocket and ambled toward the provisions room.

Constance ladled hot mutton broth from the stove and then watched the boy as he sipped. He didn't palm the entire cup and risk burning his hands like the other kids did. Instead, Lawrence held the handle of the mug in a perfect pincer grip.

"Lawrence, I'm sure your father misses you."

The boy looked down into his broth, giving only a light nod.

"You know, Our Lord works mysteriously, and there are always reasons for our difficulties." Constance put a hand on his shoulder. "Your life, Lawrence, has been a privileged one compared to many children, and maybe it would be good for you to share some of your fortune."

Lawrence didn't feel any fortune. His old life felt like a distant story he'd once read: Living in Prickwillow House and being cared for by Mrs Williams, the cook, Martha, the housemaid and Mr Johnstone, the tutor – his own tutor. But that was before his father lost it all playing cards.

Constance sipped her own broth and then placed the cup on the table for Winifred to wash. "Lawrence, how would you like to help the other children with their reading and writing? You know we don't have many children as skilled, and you could be of great use teaching letters. You could be my assistant in learning."

Lawrence sat up a little straighter. He missed his lessons. Schoolwork at the Home of Industry was mostly copying words onto a slate. He wanted to write, put his thoughts down onto paper, pour out all the sadness he'd felt since his father left him in this orphanage.

"Miss, it would make the time pass faster, wouldn't it?"

Constance patted his dark hair. "A busy mind is a happy mind – make that your motto. We can start in the morning."

Winifred came in with a dry nightgown. Lawrence took it and climbed the stairs to the boys' dormitory. He balanced cautiously so his clubfoot caused only the barest perception of a limp.

The elderly matron sat down, her thighs falling heavily onto the wicker weave chair. "You know it's the ones with hope who have the hardest time settling in – those parents with their promises that don't mean nothing are a waste of good air." She picked up her knitting. "You know he's a bed-wetter, that one."

Constance's eyebrow's shot up at this news. The Mission Board liked cleanliness.

"Don't worry, the boy's a real gentleman. He came and told me was afraid of 'disgracing himself'. Those were the words he used – 'disgracing himself'. He said it had happened at his father's friend's house and he asked if he could sleep on the floor. Of course, I gave him a waxed sheet and told him I'd waken him during the night with the others."

Winifred routinely rose during the night to relieve her own bladder. While up, she would rouse the known wetters. But that didn't protect the beds of those orphans who had only occasional accidents.

Constance said goodnight to Winifred for the second time that evening and hurried, head bent into the wind. By the time she neared Great Eastern Street, her cloak ties had worked loose, and the dark wool flopped against her like wet linen. Nearby an omnibus spilled the last passengers from the West End, while at the end of the street a paper boy called out for sales: "Gazette!"

The omnibus passengers scurried for home, their heads bowed to the wind. The boy held the wet newspapers tight to his chest as he chased after a portly gent carrying a leather bag. "Please, Sir, it's only a farthing!"

His words flew into the wind as the man hurried on.

The boy turned and ran quickly after the main stream of passengers hurrying toward Bishopsgate. But the wind and rain drowned any desire to put a hand in a pocket and fumble for a farthing.

The boy yelled, his voice burying into the wind: "Suez Canal opens – journey to India cut by half."

Constance watched as he pursued a stooped couple who shook their heads at his approach. He turned and kicked angrily at a puddle, making the water splash up into his face. Constance stepped towards him holding out a farthing.

The boy looked down at his newspapers now limp with rain and pulled one from the back where they were driest. "Sorry, Miss, they're all a bit wet." He took her coin and looked at it. "Does you only want one?"

The wind whipped so that Constance was pulled sideways. "I don't believe there is any point in my buying two."

The boy pocketed her money in his undershirt and scanned the road for more custom. The omnibus passengers had all disappeared.

"How many newspapers do you have left to sell?" Constance asked.

"A dozen! Four more if I'm to earn what they cost me." He looked at her hopefully. His nose was twisted and unnaturally large for such a small face.

"Have you eaten today?" she asked

"I aint a beggar. Me ma can feed me."

Constance took a small step back. "Then good luck with selling your newspapers." She walked into the darkness, stopping only when she was around the corner and could peek back at the boy who stood alone in the gaslight.

His lonely figure turned so the wind and rain blew onto his back. He waited several minutes, but with the last bus from the West End gone he knew his customers had all retired for the night. He walked slowly despite the wind pushing him forward.

Constance turned the corner and followed him off the main road and toward Field Street where they left the gaslights behind. The streets narrowed to alleys and became drenched in darkness. She walked with one hand on the walls to guide her, stopping at dark corners to listen to the boy's footsteps. Candlelight from the occasional window allowed Constance to hurry and not lose the boy in darkness.

In daytime Constance might have recognised the landmarks they passed. The pawnshop that looked poorer than any shop in the east end, and the cheap bakery with bread too tough to digest. It was rumoured that the undertaker next door sold sawdust to the baker to bulk up his dough.

As they turned into a tight lane, the stench of sewage forced Constance to shut her mouth tight and breathe only through her nose. Sewage squelched underfoot, and she had to lift her loose skirt.

Constance's hearing was trained on the boy's squelched footsteps as they hurried across the sodden ground. She stayed close as he turned onto the stairs of a steep close. She ignored the sound of curses and slaps coming from one of the rooms as she followed the boy. Tall buildings like this could house twenty families in twenty different rooms and she couldn't lose him now.

His footsteps sounded up the full five storeys. Constance hurried upward then knocked lightly on the first wooden doorway in the narrow attic.

The door swung open and a woman smiled, her sagging bosom uncovered for business. But her gummy grin fell to a glare as if Constance was the devil himself. "Get away, ye do-gooder. I know what would do you some good." Her mood changed quickly with her joke and she laughed hoarsely before flinging the door shut.

Constance, her heart racing from the chase and from her mistake, turned to the other room. There was no door to knock on, just a drape of fabric hung from timber.

Her voice sounded quiet. "Hello, I am from the Home of Industry and I wonder if you might need any help." She paused and heard voices – a child then a woman. "I spoke with your son tonight; I know he didn't sell many newspapers."

After a brief silence, Constance pulled open the curtain. A meagre candle gave a waxen glow to a room crowded with tiny boxes stacked wide and deep. In their midst sat the newspaper boy with other children in a circle on the floor. A pot of glue lay in their centre and, over it all, was a mother whose hands were black with sores.

"You are matchbox makers!" Constance said.

The mother nodded before lifting sandpaper sheets to paste onto a readymade box. "And we're behind on the rent." She pasted a sliver of sandpaper with a balding brush and then pushed her thumb tightly against the rough paper, scraping further at her sores.

She slid another sheet of sandpaper forward for pasting and reached for the next box made by her children.

The stacks of boxes prevented Constance from moving further into the room. She gazed at each child's face, seeing their white skin and pinched, tired eyes. The matchbox maker's curse had rested on the smallest child, whose small face rested on a hunched back.

Constance spoke quietly: "How much does the dealer pay you?"

The mother looked up briefly. "Never enough!" She returned to pasting sandpaper strips onto boxes. "We pay tuppence a gross for the wood, then he pays us tuppence-halfpenny for a gross of boxes. But we can make sixpence a day when we're all at it."

A cold draught blew through the room, and Constance looked up to see a hole in the roof that had been badly patched.

The mother nodded towards the newspaper boy. "We thought it would be good to branch out a bit, not rely so much on one industry." She gave a sarcastic laugh. "Didn't do us much good tonight though – lost on them papers." She glanced at her son. "Move them boxes onto the bed, George, so the lady can come inside."

As the boy gingerly lifted a stack of boxes, the mother apologised for the lack of heat. "We burned the door for firewood."

Constance sat down. "I followed your son because I saw all those unsold newspapers and I wondered if he'd had anything to eat."

The mother shook her head. "None of us have, but we don't depend on any charity. We work for ourselves – keep away from the workhouse door." She looked up quickly. "You're not from there, are you?"

Constance shook her head hurriedly. "I'm with the Home of Industry. We believe in dignity, hard work, education and the blessings of Our Lord."

"What about food?" The mother asked.

"Yes, yes, we have that. In fact, I can bring you some if it's not too late in your evening."

The woman gave a lopsided grin. "When your belly's empty, it's never too late in your evening."

Constance stood. "I'll be back as quickly as I can. My mother's house is not far."

She stepped back behind the curtain and then remembered the warren of dark alleys. "But I'd like to find my way back. Could the boy come with me as a guide?"

The mother stopped pasting and stared at Constance, gauging her. "George is a good fighter and will tear at anyone who tries to take advantage of him."

Constance caught her suspicions and stood a little straighter. "I am a Christian. I will ensure the boy comes to no harm. Please, you must trust me. Some in your neighbourhood already know me. You can ask – my name is Constance Petrie."

The woman assessed her as if storing up a memory for future use.

Constance followed George through the network of narrow streets until they reached the gaslights of Shoreditch. The rain had stopped but the wind still sent the light flickers leeward. Constance asked the boy about his father.

"Lost at sea, Miss. The shipping company says he's dead, but they've never found his body so my ma says he'll come home one day. She says he was always a fighter."

His pace hurried as he tried to lose the memory of his mother's shrieks the day the shipping agent visited them. She'd screamed that they'd all end up in the workhouse. After the shipping clerk left, she'd run from the house taking baby Tommy with her. Rose and he had chased after her, losing her in the alleys, but they'd come out at the riverside to hear the wailing cry of his mother as she loaded rocks into her pockets and down into the baby's nightgown. He'd tried to pull the rocks back out while pulling his mother away from the river, but she'd tugged and twisted free and took off along the bank. George had called on folks to stop her, tugging at the arm of a gentleman. But the man had pushed him off. "That'll make two less rats on this riverside."

George could still hear the man's voice, his slow articulation of the words.

Thankfully, two women tackled his ma, one grabbing baby Tommy so his mother was forced to chase her through the alleyways and think about what she'd been about to throw away.

7

A cold sweat erupted on George's brow. He and his sisters could have ended up so completely alone.

Constance quickened her pace. "How long have you been selling newspapers?"

George looked up at her, his nose seemed even more misshapen than before. "Just the winter, Miss. But I think I'll leave it now until the summer. On good nights, you can make sixpence; but in bad weather like this – well, tonight we lost money."

"How about matchbox making, how long has your family been doing that?"

"Since news came of me dad. His pay always came from the shipping company and we always had food. But after they said he was missing, well, there was no more money from them and we had to move. We used to live in a big room, Miss, near Bethnal Green. Me dad was a weaver then, but the machines put him out of a job." He kicked at a stone. "Now, we're behind on the rent again."

Constance led him across the road toward the only door with a candle at the fanlight. After only a short knock the door was unbolted. An older woman, taller than Constance, opened the door.

"Connie, where have you been in this weather? I was beginning to think I should go out and find you." She glanced at the boy beside her daughter. "And I see you've brought a visitor."

Constance pushed George forward then hurried past him toward the kitchen. "This is George. I brought him so we could find our way back – his family haven't eaten today. Is there any of Geeta's stew left? What about bread or soup?"

Helen pointed George to a bench in the hallway and followed her daughter down the steps and into the kitchen.

Geeta, the maid, rose wearily from her bedding near the range. Helen tapped her on the shoulder. "Lie down, Geeta, I'll see to this."

As the small Indian woman lay back down, Helen took a leg of ham away from her daughter and placed it back on the roasting jack.

"Constance, you can't keep doing this!"

"What?" Constance had moved on to the bread bin.

"Trying to feed all the starving of London. We live only on what your father left us."

8

"And we've never starved," Constance said with a vague smile.

"No, we haven't. But we give a lot to the poor already."

"And there are still children out there who go hungry."

"And, Constance, we can't possibly feed them all."

"Mother, she is a widow, like you, but has five or six children – I couldn't count them all in that tiny room. They haven't eaten today – I didn't even ask about yesterday. They didn't have heat either. They've already burned their door for firewood."

She wrapped a hunk of mutton in a muslin cloth. "Can you imagine the difference this piece of meat will make to them? For us it's just one meal that we can easily replace with a bit of cheese and pickle – but for this family, it's a feast."

Helen wanted to remind her daughter that the meat, cheese and pickle were bought from their carefully managed budget. But she knew that words made little difference when Constance was like this. She watched her daughter wrap the remainder of the day's bread and all of tomorrow's loaf in another cloth then followed her out to the hall.

George sat where he had been left, still wet and shivering from cold.

Helen handed him a wool wrap hanging from a hook. "This'll keep you a bit warmer on the walk home."

He wound the brown knit around his shoulders then looked up with an embarrassed smile. "Thanks, Ma'am."

Helen peered at his nose. In the bold gaslight of the small hallway it looked positively twisted. "Good gracious, child, what happened to you?"

"A fight, Ma'am. A man, a thief, tried to take me newspaper money, and we had a fight. He was bigger than me – grown up, like. He got the money and left me with a bloodied nose. That's when we got behind in our rent. Ma says if that hadn't happened we'd be fine – probably would have had a bit of bread today, maybe even some fat for broth."

Constance emptied the coal scuttle into a sack, sending coal dust out across the floor. Helen took a deep breath but said nothing. She lifted her own cloak from its peg.

George led the way, his footsteps fast at the prospect of taking meat and bread to his family. Constance was quiet, but Helen knew she was thinking, planning. As they hurried down Bishopsgate, hearing grunting heaves from a couple in a shallow doorway, Constance was stirred to speak: "How many spaces do we have in the Beehive?"

"Spaces in the Beehive? Why? None. We never have spaces, as you well know."

"Could we squeeze in this family? I think there are about five children."

"Constance! We have a waiting list."

The boy looked up suspiciously. "What's the Beehive?"

Constance patted his shoulder. "Don't worry, it's not a workhouse."

*

George awakened to feel his sister's feet poking his arms while the arched and bony spine of his brother jutted his ribs. A small smile played on his face as he thought about the bread and mutton he'd eaten before bed. It was more pleasure than he'd felt since, well, since his da's pay stopped coming.

Outside he heard the faint call of the baker's boy hawking buns. George smiled a little more. Usually that cry sent his empty stomach into cramps, but not this morning.

George rolled over to see his mother already at work pasting strips of sandpaper to box ends. She liked to work in the early morning while he and his brother and sisters lay in bed. She said she could spread out the freshly pasted boxes, giving them space to dry.

Mary Trupper swept her brush across ten small strips of sandpaper. She pressed hard against the roughness, pushing against each box for several moments, eroding further at the worn and putrid skin of her fingers. Around her a mat of freshly pasted matchboxes spread across the dusty floor.

George squirmed out from between his brother's back and his sister's feet. "Ma, leave it a while. I'll take over."

"No, you paste that lot over there, and maybe we can get them done before everyone's up, and then we can all work on folding the boxes today. If we can put together two extra gross today and tomorrow, and eat only the food those do-gooders brought us, then we can get the rent up to date. We just have to work hard."

George thought they worked hard every day. He knelt down to paste the strips of sandpaper. He and his mother worked in unison, George using the pasting brush while his mother stuck down strips, pressing hard so they wouldn't fall off. She kept this job for herself. She didn't want to see her children's fingers as torn and painful as her own.

Rose woke first but stayed in bed so her mother and brother had full use of the floor. Maggie and Junie rolled over and leaned sleepily against their big sister. Only Tommy slept heavily, his spine curved so far forward that his head pitched permanently toward his toes.

"His poor back," Rose said as she stroked her fingers through her brother's matted hair.

Mary nodded toward the matchboxes that lay around her. "We all need to work or there's no rent or food. I don't know what else we can do."

"But he never straightens up anymore."

"Look, girl, don't make me feel guilty. It's just unlucky that his young life has been mostly work. The rest of you had more of your father's care and money, so be grateful." Mary pushed even harder at the sandpaper. "I really don't know what else to do. We need all of us to work, otherwise we can't live. It's this or the workhouse and if we have to go there we may as well pitch ourselves into the river right now."

George stopped pasting and stared at his mother, remembering the sight of her putting rocks in her pockets at the riverside, baby Tommy already weighed down with a rock wrapped in his gown.

"But maybe we're asking Tommy to do too much," Rose said.

Mary sent her oldest daughter a warning glare. "I suppose some of us could work the streets like our neighbours."

Rose reddened, and Mary paused momentarily from pasting. She knew she shouldn't take her anger out on the children. Threats only made everyone feel worse.

"How about some of that good food?" she asked.

Tommy stirred as at the word "food".

Mary left the cheese wrapped up in the muslin bag and cut the remains of the mutton into six uneven slices. The older kids, George and Rose, received the thicker slices; while the middle child Maggie got a slighter smaller piece. The youngest, Tommy and Junie, were awarded the slimmer slivers. Mary herself took the shavings of meat left up from slicing. She wrapped them in a chunk of bread and let the first bite soak appreciatively into her mouth. It wasn't just the juice of the mutton giving off a heavy meaty flavour, but the bread dough was light with none of the sawdust or weevils found in bread that came from the bakery down the lane.

The children ate fast, and Mary relaxed a little in their contentment. They'd all slept on full bellies thanks to the do-gooders. The two women had promised to stop by in a few days. The younger one talked about a beehive. She said it was where they could all work at making matchboxes and that it was comfortable with proper seating, good light, fresh air, meals and lessons for the children. But Mary was suspicious of the price, probably a share of profits. She couldn't afford to give a cut to anyone.

She turned wearily to look at the stack of flattened woodcuts. If they could just move faster at turning these into boxes, they could catch up on the rent.

She clapped her hands. With full bellies and some warmth from the coal the do-gooders brought, they should be able to work harder than normal. "George, Tommy and Maggie, you get started on them boxes. Rose, you work with Junie. She isn't getting the hang of them corners. There must have been more than ten boxes of hers we couldn't use yesterday and that's money."

Junie's right hand moved instinctively toward a dirty rag doll that lay nearby. Her fingers clasped the worn cloth, bringing it up to her face as her skinny thumb slotted firmly between her thin lips.

Rose clasped the rag doll impatiently and pulled it from her sister. "Honestly, Junie, that's going to have to be put away while we work. It always gets in the way."

The young girl gave a puzzled stare, her thumb fixed firmly in her mouth.

"You'll get it back when it's time for bed," Rose said. "Now dry that thumb and get it ready for work."

Mary sighed. "Honestly, I think our Junie will be better off in service. If we can get her a scullery maid's job – maybe those two do-gooders know of someone who will give her a chance."

"Ma, she's only seven," Rose said.

"I know, but it's best to start young in them jobs. Lots of time to learn and, in a few years, maybe she'll work up to the cook's job. People like that never go hungry." Mary stacked the ready-made boxes against the wall. Mr Robert would pick them up in the evening, count them and pay only for those that were perfect.

Tommy stood, his rounded back making him too short for his sharp face. "Ma, can I go and get water? The taps might be open."

Mary peered into the jug by the stove. A small pool lay at the bottom. She poured it into a mug to be shared among them and handed the jug to Tommy. "George, you go with him. But don't be long out there. We need plenty of boxes made if we're to pay the rent."

Tommy's bent frame, liberated by movement, hurried through the curtain. George hurtled ahead, taking the stairs two at a time. On the floor below, Tommy slowed to stare cautiously at a battered door. The last time he'd passed, the Irishman there had sent a gob of spit that had stung his eye. It could have been an accident, but Tommy had felt the man's cursed glare.

He watched to see if the door handle turned, and then ran to catch up with his brother.

Upstairs in the small attic room, Mary and nine-year-old Maggie bent thin wooden sheets so they were pliable. Junie watched vacantly as her mother's scabby fingers bent a crucifix-shaped woodcut and moulded it into a box.

"Now, Junie," Rose said, "we'll make the sleeves. You'll get on faster if I bend the lines, and you fold."

Junie took the shape from her sister and her thin fingers began to shape a sheath for the matchboxes. The four figures worked on the cold wood floor. Little light penetrated the deep alleys and even less made it through the small hole that served as a window. In the corner of the room a toilet bowl gave off a stench.

Mary gave it a brief glance. "Rose, empty that pot out the window."

"Ma, we can't. We have to wait for the sanitary cart."

"To hell with the sanitary cart, it stinks in here."

"Ma, the sanitary man said it's for our own good. He said throwing shit into the street causes disease."

Mary rolled her eyes. "What does he know?"

Outside, George and Tommy stood at the well. Ahead, along the line, they could hear shouts and arguments until words spread towards them. "There's not enough water – the pump's closing early."

George's full belly gave him more energy than usual, and he ran forward. With the water jug under his arm, he plundered through the crowd until he reached the pump where four women pushed at each other as they all aimed to catch the last of the water in their own jug.

The fray gave George his opportunity. He aimed low, catching the stream of water as it missed the brawling women's jugs.

"Could you do mine when you're finished?"

George glanced up to see his neighbour Beryl. He passed her his half-filled jug and took hers.

"Hey, you!" the sanitary man yelled. George readied to run with Beryl's jug and hoped she would take off with his.

The sanitary man pushed toward Beryl, his face red with anger. "I know you with that devil mark."

Beryl's face glowed red, turning the mole on her cheek purple.

The sanitary man glowered over her. "Where's your mother? I've been hearing things about her."

The young girl stepped back, shaking her head.

The red face followed. "I've heard she's got the sores and is spreading disease. Tell her I'm after her and if she don't show up clean then it's the Lock Hospital for her. And there'll be no work there – not unless she wants to take money from them that's scabbier than she is."

He stepped back and followed his apprentice who was pulling a woman with bleeding sores on her face toward a cart.

Beryl's legs shook as she hurried away with George, the two children carrying each other's water jugs.

"I need to find me ma and tell her the sanitary man's after her," Beryl said.

George handed Beryl her jug. It wasn't as chipped as his. "What will she do?"

The girl's eyes were wide, and George guessed that with the mother off the street Beryl would have to take extra customers.

Tommy had stayed at the street corner. The three children took their pitchers of water up the stairs, and then Beryl went in search of her mother. She knew the sanitary man was right. She'd seen her mother's sores. Now she needed to get her indoors and out of sight. No one who went into the Lock Hospital ever came out.

She hurried down Houndsditch, through Aldgate and into the Whitechapel market searching for her mother's large red hat with blue feathers. Traders hawked jellied eels, mouse traps, pea soup, offal, flowers, furniture, second-hand clothes and pies. At the corner of Goulston, Beryl crossed the road to avoid a thin man selling brown envelopes containing photographs. He'd offered Beryl work, but she didn't want to show herself to all those people. It was bad enough having one man at a time groping at her.

Across the street, one of her mother's friends held two men in her arms. All three, soused with gin, reeled from wall to wall. Beryl crossed to ask if she'd seen her ma. Pearl looked over her head like she wasn't there. Two customers meant double pay and she didn't want to have to share.

But Beryl pulled on Pearl's arm so she couldn't be ignored.

"No, I ain't seen your ma. I'm busy with my own doings," and Pearl pulled her customers after her.

The younger of the men turned to wink at Beryl. She sent him a scathing stare even though he looked cleaner than some she'd had to deal with.

Beryl hurried on, looking for signs of her mother's red hat. At the corner of Brick Lane, near a penny theatre, she caught site of the blue feathers through the crowd. She hurried toward a large canvas painting with a naked fat lady whose arms and legs looked stuffed with sacks of flour. A black dwarf with a massive erection had been painted next to her.

Beneath the poster, Beryl's mother's breasts were bared, but her dugs were puny compared to the woman on the canvas.

A skinny man took Beryl's mother's arm, but Beryl grabbed her other hand and pulled her away. "Ma, you need to stop work. The sanitary man's after you."

The skinny man arched his brows and hurried on. Jean shook her daughter off and called out after him. "She's not serious. She's just trying to take me business. Five minutes, mister, and I'll have you smiling like a swaddled babe."

The skinny man didn't glance back.

"Ma, you need to come home. He's threatening to give you an inspection."

Jean Brown's breath was heavy with gin. "I'm clean as a whistle. I know that sanitary man. He's just after a free turn. I'll see to him later."

"Ma!" Beryl stopped to think of an argument that might scare her mother. "He knows about your sores."

Jean looked around quickly to see if anyone had heard. She clenched her jaw and spoke through her four remaining teeth. "I have no sores. Now mind your own business and get some work." She stood back, her voice not so threatening. "Look there, over that road, Pearl's corner is free and with that public house there's no end of business."

Beryl's stomach sank.

Jean held out the gin bottle. "Come on, now. This'll help."

Beryl played her only card. "I'll go to work if you go home and stay out of sight."

"I don't need to, I told you, he's only after a free turn."

"Ma, we can't take any chances. If you go to that Lock Hospital, you'll never get out and then what will happen to me and Ruby?"

Jean reluctantly tucked her sagging breasts inside her gown and tied up the neckline with a bow. "I suppose I should keep out of sight for a while. But this means you have to be out earning every day."

Beryl took the gin bottle from her ma and swallowed hard. Her throat burned but she knew she'd soon feel a haze that would make everything distant no matter who she endured. As she crossed Whitechapel she glanced around to see who would be her first customer of the day.

*

Constance tapped her feet on the wooden floor. "Mother, I don't know why you're doing this."

Helen glanced up, her face flushed from pummelling dough. "I'm doing it because last night you gave away all our bread."

Constance pulled a long face. "Well, we could just buy bread like other people."

Helen glared at her daughter. "I hate shop bread. It's full of things that shouldn't be there – and it's not healthy to have all those people handling your food before it reaches the table."

"The Good Lord says we have to make do with what's available."

Helen sighed and placed the newly formed dough on a tray.

Geeta knelt on the floor scrubbing the range, a pot of black lead and a brush beside her for polishing. Helen lifted the black lead, afraid it might tip onto her carpet, and placed it carefully on the hearth. "Geeta, if you could put the bread in the oven when you're through?"

The young girl smiled, showing teeth beautifully white against her dark skin.

Pastor Beckett had found Geeta after she'd shown up hungry and scared at a church and wouldn't talk for days. Eventually Helen managed to understand her oddly accented English and found out that she'd travelled to London with an English family, who had employed her as a nanny. But the Parker family had been met by Mr Parker's mother, along with the old nanny who had cared for Mr Parker as a child. Geeta had been dismissed at the dock side, her single bag beside her and five shillings of pay. She had been robbed while trying to find a room at an inn and had wandered around Wapping Wall for three days, too scared to talk to anyone. It was the music that had attracted her to the mission. She said it sounded like the church the Parker family went to in Simla.

Pastor Beckett had brought Geeta to the Home of Industry, even though it was obvious that she was too old for the orphanage. After hearing her story Helen offered her a job as their housemaid, even though she couldn't really afford it and she and Constance had grown used to managing without help.

The small woman worked hard, especially at cooking. Helen taught her reading and scripture on Sundays, and Geeta saved all her pay for the voyage back home.

Constance watched impatiently as her mother wiped her face free of flour, pulled at the knot on her apron and threw on her cloak.

Outside the younger woman's feet moved as fast as her speech. "That family we visited last night, the youngest is already hunchbacked from work. We should try and find space for them in the Beehive – make them a priority or they'll be sure to end up in the workhouse. We really need another Home of Industry – we could easily fill it."

She paused to watch a small boy hawking fried fish and only moved on when she saw him make a sale. "Annie MacPherson said some wealthy church members might be willing to fund a second home." Constance moved fast, calling to her mother over her shoulder: "Just think of it, we could give more children the space to work safely and they'd have food, scripture and schooling. Think of the joy we could bring, Mother."

Helen glanced upward as though beseeching help. "What would give me joy would be to see you married."

Constance turned abruptly so that her mother stumbled into her. "Mother, look at me. I'm plain. In fact, I'm more than plain, I'm ugly. And in addition to that, I'm poor. I'm also twenty-four and far too old for any man to even consider as marriage material."

A few people in the street stopped to watch the two women for a possible confrontation. Helen dropped her voice to a whisper. "Constance, you are not ugly, old or too poor for marriage." Her voice rose just a little in tone. "What you need to do is to slow down so that a man might have a chance to get a better look at you."

Constance began walking again. "I don't want some man to get a look at me. I am happy with what I do each day – working at the Home of Industry with you. I see the children come to us, their faces all sharp and shrivelled but then, after a few months in our care, they grow softened from regular food and hope for a better future. I have the Good Lord with me every single day, and I am happy in his work."

"But I don't want you to grow old and lonely. When I'm no longer here, a husband would be a good companion."

"Mother, for companionship, I have the children at the Home of Industry."

Helen sighed. "Well, I just wish your brother were here. At least he had friends who might show an interest."

Constance walked faster, moving ahead of her mother. Mathew had left for Africa three years ago with 600 Bibles and a mission to take The Lord to the heathen. Constance herself would have loved such a mission.

All that faded from her mind as they entered the Home of Industry where Winifred and a crew of older girls were serving porridge to three hundred orphans. Annie MacPherson nodded a greeting from her office near the front hall. Constance stopped, hoping to exchange more words with the great woman, but Miss MacPherson's head was already bent over her papers.

It was Annie MacPherson who'd turned 60 Commercial Street from a disused warehouse into the Home of Industry. She'd pursued all and any businessmen who professed Christian belief and persuaded them to give money for the orphanage and workplace. Some of the wealthy had given easily; but others had had to be shamed into donating with repeated visits and lengthy descriptions of the poverty, grime and sickness that saturated London's East End.

Constance had watched Annie MacPherson drown all stubborn argument by pushing her earnest assertions on the rightness of employing and educating the poor. Some of her words still played in Constance's ears: *"All will benefit when the children are able to work securely. All, even the benefactors, will be saved by the Lord."*

Constance wished God had given her such power of speech. All she could do when asked to speak at mission meetings was blush and stutter, and she hated herself for it.

She left the great lady at work and hurried to help with breakfasts. Lawrence sat at the end of his row of fifty children, his porridge bowl already empty. "Miss," he called out to Constance as she passed. "Please, Miss, do you remember your promise?"

Constance's mind went blank. She searched the boy's face for a clue.

"The reading and writing, Miss. You said I could help the others instead of copying onto my slate."

19

Constance smiled at the memory. "Of course, Lawrence, remind me when we're upstairs in the classroom, and I'll give you someone to help."

Lawrence turned to the boys who sat around him. "See, I told you I was going to be an assistant."

A bell sounded the end of breakfast and the children filed upstairs to class. Helen climbed the steep stairs to the classroom. The orphans had two hours of writing Bible passages and the rest of the morning was spent in vocation classes. The boys learned either carpentry or valet skills so they could work in service or trade, while the girls received instruction on cookery, laundry and sewing in preparation for positions as maidservants.

Outside the home, three hundred matchbox makers queued at the front door for breakfast. After eating, they would work in the Beehive, a large airy hall that was well lit and lined with high tables. At the end of each day, they had a hot supper and received lessons in reading, writing and scripture.

Constance followed the orphans to her classroom and sat at the piano. With the first note, the children rose from their benches.

"There is a better world, they say,
Oh, so bright!
Where we can find the Lord
And he will help us everyday,
And never let us fall."

When the song ended, Constance told them of Jesus, the five loaves and the two fishes.

"Children, this story teaches us to have faith. We must believe. The Lord will always provide. He will never leave us hungry."

She wrote across her board and bid the children copy her.

My little children, these things write I unto you, that ye sin not.

Lawrence's hand rose immediately.

Constance nodded permission for him to speak.

The boy stood, wobbling a little as his clubbed foot caught on the leg of his stool. "Miss, may I help the younger children with their writing?"

Reminded of her promise, Constance led him to two small boys. She pointed to the taller one. "John sometimes forgets which side of the slate to begin his words, and Peter often puts his letters backward. They will both be grateful for your help, Lawrence."

He grinned widely and, as the others worked, he pointed John to the left corner of his slate and watched his two charges as they wrote the first words of the phrase.

In the next room, Helen's pupils, older than those in Constance's class, copied down the Ten Commandments. Two boys, the only black children in the classroom, leaned toward each other as they wrote.

"Henry and Horace, I've asked you before to separate." Helen approached two small boys sitting on either side of the aisle. With a tap from her hand, they stood in the aisle while Henry and Horace reluctantly parted to sit in the newly vacant spaces.

"You must mix with the other children," Helen said as she walked up the aisle.

Henry and Horace exchanged wary looks. The children around them shared grins as Helen expounded on Thou Shalt Not Steal.

"Oooww!" Horace called out as fingers tugged heavily on his hair.

Helen glared at the boy then noted his moist eyes and realised he was a victim rather than a perpetrator.

She glared at the children around Horace then spotted tufts of black curls under a seat. Helen sharpened her eyes on Horace's neighbour. "William! Why have you chosen to disrupt our lesson in this way?"

The boy stood, his head hanging from his neck so that none of his face could be seen. "Miss," he shrugged.

Helen moved forward so she looked down on the boy's drooping neck. "This is my commandment. That ye love one another, as I have loved you."

Silence settled across the room.

Helen stepped back only a fraction. "William, you shall make Horace's bed each morning for the next week, and offer him what he wishes from your evening meal. I hope he shows you more grace than you have shown him. Sit down."

William sat; his head still bent so far forward it almost reached into his lap.

Helen returned to the front of the class. "Now, children, we will return to the Commandments."

*

Teaching tired Helen and she let her mind drift during evening prayer. As Minister Beckett intoned God's help, she thought about her son Mathew out among the heathen. She missed him every single day and worried about the dangers he faced. Even his homecoming worried her as she fretted that he might be a stranger after so many years in a foreign land. She'd always felt closer to her son than her daughter. Mathew had been such an easy baby who slept well – compared to Constance who was always awake, always looking for activity. The memory of him, his wide smile and easy laugh, made her feel soothed and lifted as Minister Becket's tones filled the room.

"We must be strong in spirit and deed. For the lowly children who inhabit our streets have abandoned all hope. Their parents, of frail constitution and too weak to deny the life of sin, are leading their innocent ones into lives of degradation, drink, debt and debauchery. We ask your help, Lord, in rallying our cry of 'Resist!' to the parents of these innocents and in gathering the strength to lead the poor children to lives of wholesome fortitude."

"Amen!"

The call from the floor jolted Helen's thoughts back to the gathering of Church Governors. She looked around, hoping it was going to be a short meeting, and smiled when she saw a young man across the aisle.

She nudged her daughter and whispered. "Robert Morgan, his father is editor of *The Revival*."

Constance gritted her whisper. "I know!"

"He's not married," Helen said quietly.

Her daughter gave a low glower and then turned to give all her attention to Minister Beckett. He had lifted his shoulders to reach as far as his five feet four could stretch and spoke as though he were still in lyrical prayer. "Our temperance mission reports forty-six new pledges signed the last week."

"Amen!" called out the congregation.

"Our Brother Landen reports that he has met with five Parliament members to discuss compulsory school attendance. He said he has firm offers of support from four."

"Amen!" This response more muted.

"Brother Johns reports that he is to join the home secretary to discuss child prostitution, while Brother Anderson said he is getting close to an agreement from three large factories on better conditions for workers."

"Amen!" This time almost a cheer.

"Now, may I ask that we listen to some words from our dear Sister MacPherson." The minister stood aside as a small but sturdy woman took her place at the lectern. For several moments she looked silently across the congregation as though measuring them for good deeds. When her voice came it was full and sure.

"My dear friends, as you well know, these streets are saturated in deprivation and sin; and while many of us work tirelessly to overcome the problems of poverty, it oftentimes seems that the very gates of hell have opened around us. More and more families pour into these overcrowded streets. They come from the northern factories now taken over by machines, they come from the famine in Ireland and those seeking food and work, and then there are those who flee wars overseas and seek a little peace. We welcome them all. But their arrival creates a greater cesspit of vice. Even our police dare not travel alone, and strangers who wander here are kidnapped and robbed. Many of us grow weary of the fight that such desperation and poverty brings. I myself have lain at night wondering how we can move forward in this battle, how can we rise against such odds."

She paused to scan her audience, gaining assurance that she had their attention. "But, friends, I believe I have found the answer. I have found it in a place that no one has yet looked. I have found it in a land that offers great bounty of rich farmland and the opportunity to work hard, feed hunger and be free from sin. Dear friends, there is a land far away that we might see as a promised land. This land we know as Canada, and it is here that the degradation of overcrowded poverty will be vanquished and the vast sins that surround us will be conquered."

Constance sat upright, peering over the head of the man in front so she could hear news of this promising land.

"Yes, Canada – that far-off place that many of us have heard of but few have ever given much thought to. In this new land are good Christian families anxious to open their homes to those who might also reap the God-given benefits of this richness. These families will offer warm homes, good food and safe shelter to our indigent youth. In return, these young men will have to work hard, and they will be richly rewarded, growing bountiful in spirit and independent in work. So greatly do I believe in the rightness of this move that I have selected one hundred boys from the workhouse, from our Home of Industry, and some I have plucked from the depraved streets that surround us. Canada, this vast land of rich opportunity, will be their salvation."

"Amen!" rang heavily around the hall.

Annie MacPherson smiled. "I am well heartened by your endorsement because we leave these shores in six months. In the meantime, we need money for transport and supplies. In addition, I am looking for good women to sew the boys' uniforms – for they cannot arrive in the promised land wearing rags – and I would like someone to beg or borrow one hundred satchels that the boys might use for their meagre belongings."

Voices rose from the congregation.

"I can provide the bags," called out an elderly man who stood and leaned heavily on a stick.

"My wife will take up the sewing," shouted a hefty man whose wife, Helen knew, had six children to care for.

Annie MacPherson sent her assistant Ellen around the hall to write down a list of names and what they could promise.

Helen steered Constance out into the street before she could put forward any pledge of goods or work. "We have enough to do," she said quickly.

"But, Mother, I would dearly love to assist Annie MacPherson. Is she not such a wonderful woman? Who else would have thought about Christian families in Canada? You know I truly believe she has found the answer to our prayers. Taking orphans to Canada will not only provide good homes for our orphans, but it leaves room here for more children to come into our care."

Helen sighed. "It may leave us space to take more into children the Home of Industry, but I take pity on the poor children deposited with strangers so far from home." Her eyes watered a little. Her own son was twenty-three, and she worried that he had found cruelty so far from home.

"But, Mother, the children will all have good homes. For you know how thorough Miss MacPherson is – I am sure that she will inspect each and every house herself."

Helen slowed as they neared their front door. "These poor waifs have little experience of the world, and I do not believe it is our Christian business to take them so far from the only home they've ever known."

"Mother!" Constance glared. "Do you not trust our dear Sister?"

Helen pulled out her key and unlocked the door. "It is not that I don't trust Miss MacPherson. I believe she will do her best for each child. But the sheer number of children – one hundred of them – means she cannot ensure each home is a good one. When it comes to receiving free labour, some families might lie."

Constance hurriedly took off her cloak. "Miss MacPherson will see through any lies."

Helen rolled her eyes.

"It's true! She will not let anything bad happen to her charges."

Helen shrugged off her cloak and hurried into the parlour where she poured a tall brandy. She sat back into her armchair and took a long sip, feeling its warmth draw down into her chest. She sighed as a stillness settled across her shoulders. "Constance, please ask Geeta to prepare just a little bread and cheese for supper. It has been a long day, and I am too tired to sit at the table."

Constance gave her mother a hard glare.

Helen took another long sip of her brandy and ignored her.

Constance stepped closer. "You know, if you weren't so keen on your nightly brandy, you might not feel so tired each evening. It is that drink that drains you of life in the evening."

Helen took another long sip from her glass, deliberately ignoring her daughter.

Constance moved forward, near enough to snatch her mother's glass from her hand. "Drink is bad for you – you know that. Everyday we see the degradation and misery it brings on the poor."

Helen smiled stubbornly. "Constance, I work hard. At the end of each day I take one brandy. As a result, I sleep well and work hard again the next day. There is certainly no sin in that. I'm hardly out in the street rollicking drunk."

"But what kind of an example are you to those who let drink ruin their lives? We ask fathers, mothers and children to sign the pledge. Those who are serious about change do so, glad to put their lives on the Christian path. What would these newly devout say if they knew that one of the church's leading Sisters had a brandy habit?"

Helen sighed. "I think the people you talk of have enough problems of their own without worrying about an old lady and her daily glass of refreshment."

She reached out to take her daughter's hand, but Constance pulled it away.

*

Junie folded the matchbox frame, pulling too hard at the edges and snapping the thin wood in two.

Mary fired a glare. "Damn, Junie. You'll have us in the workhouse."

Junie's head bowed and her hand searched blindly for her rag doll. As her fingers eased around its familiar fibres, her mother snatched it away.

"Honestly, I think we need to get you something else to do, maybe selling newspapers when the weather turns fine."

George's voice rose fast. "But, Ma, that's my job."

"I know, but Junie's no good at matchboxes, and newspapers might be her game until she's big enough ..."

Heavy footsteps outside the curtain made Mary stop and listen. But all she heard was the sound of the Irishman's whistle downstairs, a mother yelling at her kids, while outside the heavy din of the street created a steady noise.

Again, a heavy cough cleared a male chest. Mary thought of her husband, and her heart raced with the notion that he might be home. She watched the curtain for movement. Instead, a pounding thud hit next door.

"Come on out, Jean Brown. I know your game."

Mary's chest fell, but she listened in silence.

The voice dropped in tone. "A quick look at your sores is all I need. I can't let you go taking the disease to any Charlie who chances your way."

He pounded the door again then stopped to listen for noise. The residents in the stairwell and along each passage had all fallen silent, even the whistle player.

"There's no escape now – I know where you live."

After a long pause, his footsteps sounded down the stairs. Mary let out her breath as the whistle resumed its air.

Mary shook her head. "What a neighbourhood! And the landlord's the cheek to charge a shilling in rent."

But footsteps coming back upstairs caused the family to fall silent again. This time the feet were lighter and stopped outside their curtain.

A voice called out. "It's Constance Petrie here to visit."

The young woman parted the curtain, and Mary noticed the plump linen sac she carried. Mary waved her hands toward the bed and beckoned her to sit.

Constance perched herself at the edge, taking care not to get too close to the rags that acted as blankets. "I bring you some very good news," she said.

The family eyed the linen bag, and Mary could smell fresh bread.

Constance smiled at the small faces before her, and then turned to Mary. "I have somewhere for your children to work – somewhere clean, with good air, proper tables and chairs, hot meals and some scripture and learning at the end of the day."

Mary's eyes turned dark with suspicion.

Constance leaned forward, dropping her voice. "At the Home of Industry – it's where children make matchboxes and get a decent pay for each day's work."

Mary's voice turned sharp. "And what do you get?"

Constance sat more upright. "We have the satisfaction of giving your children an education, teaching them scripture and bringing Jesus into their lives."

"But what else do you get?" Mary asked.

Constance looked puzzled. "What do you mean?"

27

"What's your cut?"

"We get nothing from their pay. The children will still receive tuppence halfpenny a gross."

A suspicious frown stretched Mary's face as she calculated the pay.

Constance stood, knowing she needed to defend herself. "Wealthy benefactors who care about the poor of this city pay for our building and its costs. We have space for three hundred children. There's always a waiting list to get in, but we've got more places because some of our children are going to Canada."

"What's Canada?" asked Mary, thinking of the workhouse.

"It's a huge land across the great ocean where Christian families are keen to take in poor orphans and give them a good, clean living."

At mention of the ocean, Mary thought again of her husband and wondered if he lay at its watery bottom or if he'd made a new life somewhere far away.

"What do they do there?" George asked.

Constance smiled. "They do whatever their guardians want them to do."

"Like slaves?" Mary asked.

"No, like sons!" Constance was anxious to turn the conversation back to the Home of Industry. "Anyway, on Commercial Street, we have a huge room known as the Beehive where children work on matchboxes. They start the day with a warm breakfast, receive a good lunch and dinner and then, before leaving at the end of the day, they are taught reading, writing and scripture." She looked at Tommy, whose neck twisted upward so he could see her. She reached down to pat his head. "And little ones with illness can get help and exercises so they grow up healthy."

Mary rolled her eyes. "Sounds too good to be true!"

Constance drew Tommy to standing and gripped his small hand, pushing it toward his mother. "Look at his hands stiff with cold and paste – at the Beehive, he'll work in warmth."

Mary reddened and looked away before turning back to Constance with another obstacle. "And what am I supposed to do if they're all at your Beehive all day?" Mary asked.

"You can work here alone or find other employment. But we do ask you to come to our Mothers' Meetings two evenings a week."

Mary's eyes narrowed.

"Don't worry, it's for scripture and reading and writing. So you can learn with your children. The women all seem to enjoy it."

Mary's lips tightened as she scrutinised Constance, looking for a sow's ear. She wanted to trust her, but it all seemed too good to believe. The young woman was keen to help, but maybe too much so.

George leaned closed and whispered. "Ma, say 'yes'."

A high-pitched lilt sounded from the Irishman's whistle on the floor below.

Mary leaned forward, her gaze firmly on Constance. "Our rent here is a shilling a week. For that we need to make forty-eight gross of boxes and still earn enough money for food, paste and twine to tie up our boxes. Are you telling me that you can give my children education, meals, employment and, with me working alone here, we can still earn enough to pay for rent and food?"

Constance smiled her reassurance. "Other families have. In fact, they often do better because, with the children fed and content, they work better."

Rose and George's voices joined together as if in song. "Let's do it, Ma."

"Please!" said Junie, Maggie and Tommy.

Mary's heart raced in fear. Her gaze took in each of her five children. For three years she'd managed to keep them out of the workhouse. They'd been close to its gates, closer than ever recently. She looked down at her fingers, swollen and crusted with sores. Even she wasn't as fast at work as she used to be.

"Please, Ma," whispered George again.

Mary looked at his ten-year-old face – thin from lack of food and his nose battered after he'd been robbed for newspaper money. "When do they start?"

The children let out heavy breaths of relief, and Constance gripped Tommy's hand in her own.

Mary's face grew grim. "I tell you, if my kids end up worse off than before, I'll be after you and I won't stop until I see you dead."

Constance was afraid to give a reassuring smile for fear of inciting Mary Trupper's suspicions. "They will be better off, I promise you."

But as she slipped from the Truppers' room she grinned with elation. Her mother might nag about finding a husband but surely, thought Constance, marriage cannot bring more pleasure than helping the destitute.

On the landing, two young girls stared at a notice pinned to their door. They gazed without moving, and Constance guessed they couldn't read. "Do you need help?"

She leaned over their heads to read the message.

"What does it say?" Beryl asked.

"Well, it's from the Sanitary Office and says, 'Notice is hereby given that Jean Brown should cease whoring and attend the London Hospital on Whitehall for testing of venereal disease within ten days or an order shall be made forthwith for her to be forcibly removed, tested and, if shown to be diseased, be placed in a Lock Hospital until clean."

Beryl leaned against the wall and closed her eyes.

"Is Jean Brown your mother?" Constance asked.

Beryl nodded.

"And your mother – is she at work right now?"

Beryl opened her eyes. Tears flushed forward. Her mother had promised. She said she wouldn't even go out. But where was she?

"Look, I can help you," Constance said.

Beryl shook her head and hurried to move past Constance while tugging Ruby behind her.

But Constance blocked the way. "Does your mother send you out to the same type of work?"

Beryl's eyes shut tight. She nodded briefly.

"And your little sister?"

Beryl's head shook, and she whispered between tight lips. "Not yet."

"Look, maybe we can help at the Home of Industry. There's a short waiting list but we could eventually train you both as housemaids. Many of London's finest homes take our girls." As she said this, Constance knew it would be difficult. All the children in training were either abandoned or orphaned, but these girls had a mother.

Beryl's head continued to shake. "Ruby's too young to be a housemaid."

"And she is much too young for the line of work you and your mother are in." Constance's thin hand reached out to Beryl's shoulder. But Beryl folded as if reaching to the floor and then darted under Constance's arm and into the room, pulling Ruby behind her. The door pounded shut behind them.

Constance rapped for it to be opened. "Please," she called out, "60 Commercial Street. We can save you from your mother's sinful life."

She heard a heavy piece of furniture scrape across the floor until it reached the door and she realised she'd been shut out.

*

Annie MacPherson looked up, her piercing eyes drawn slowly from her sewing and onto the two women who whispered in the corner.

"Ladies, I must remind you that we have one hundred boys leaving for Canada tomorrow, and the caps you are sewing are a vital part of their uniform."

The two women returned their eyes and hands to work.

Constance put the jacket she'd been hemming onto the desk. "Finished!"

She stepped before Annie MacPherson. Her small stature appeared girl-like compared to Miss MacPherson's matronly figure, although only two years in age separated the two women. "What next?"

Annie MacPherson gave her a quick glance. "Could you count the canvas satchels – make sure there are one hundred and ensure each bag contains a change of personnel linen, a towel, tin can, bowl, mug, knife, fork, spoon, a pocket knife, a Bible, two sheets of writing paper and a pencil."

Constance hurried next door to the Beehive. The children who worked there had left for the night, but their tables were stacked with rough serge jackets, corduroy trousers and scarlet scarves. A train of two hundred sturdy boots lined the wall, growing slowly larger in size, while on the table lay a stack of caps. Constance

31

counted fifty-four. The widows' sewing class had to make forty-six more caps before they went home for the night.

Constance's feet ached from standing in the classroom all day. She slipped her feet from her boots, enjoying the feel of the cold wood floor through her stockings. Quickly, but with care, she worked her way through the canvas bags, checking their contents and matching missing items with the mix that lay on a central desk. She was tired, her mother had already left for the evening, but Constance wanted to be sure that when Miss MacPherson and her one hundred boys set out for St Pancras in the morning they were properly supplied.

In the sewing room, twenty widows bowed their heads at sewing. One old lady was so short-sighted that her nose risked being pricked by the needle.

Miss MacPherson took away the cap the woman was sewing and handed her five beret pieces that needed only long-stitched tacking.

"No, no," said the old lady.

But Miss MacPherson shook her head. "Minnie, you'll go blind."

The other women sewed quietly until one, bigger than the others, broke the silence. "Miss MacPherson, this Canada place sounds very far away. I mean, how much do we really know about it?"

Annie MacPherson didn't look up from her sewing. "Canada may be distant, but it is a fine land and makes up a large part of our Queen's empire. Indeed, it is as British as Westminster or Bethnal Green."

"But how do we know our kids will be well cared for – I mean it's not like it's local folk they're going to. I mean, if something isn't right, it's too far away for the family to go and sort them out."

"You must remember that the children I am taking with me don't have any family to protect them – no one to sort things out! But instead of leaving them here in these dangerous streets, we're giving them a chance to improve their lives with hard work in a land where their labour will be valued."

The woman was silent for a few moments. "But how will you choose the families? How do you know you're not giving a child to someone who's evil – like those who might sell a child's body for the teeth and hair? We've got plenty of them sorts here."

Constance had crept into the room and watched as Annie MacPherson drop her sewing onto her lap.

"Sadie, I will only release children to those who come to me with a letter of reference from their preacher. I will ask each family questions on their habits and ensure that they are of good church-going stock. Trust that after taking these children so far across the ocean, I am not likely to let them slip into the hands of evil and vice."

Sadie sat back into her chair, her own sewing on her lap. "But you've got to admit, it'll be easy to lie. I mean, those folks might want a free servant to do all their work and all they have to do is persuade a preacher you don't know, maybe even pay him to write a letter saying they go to church."

Miss MacPherson sat upright and peered over the heads of the widows in the front row to direct her words firmly at Sadie. "I will ensure that no child leaves my side, until I am sure their new guardians have the right character. Each family must promise that they will feed, house and care for the child as though he were their own. In addition, they must agree to give the child an education and send the child to church each Sunday. We will release no child until those conditions are agreed to."

"Besides," Constance blushed as she heard her own voice – she hadn't intended to speak – "how can you ever doubt that sending these boys to learn new skills in a land crying out for labour could be anything other than a good thing? These people need hands to work, not bits of hair or teeth from a cadaver."

Sadie looked from Miss MacPherson to Constance and then bowed her head back to her sewing.

Miss MacPherson gave Constance a small smile, and Constance blushed even deeper.

*

The women all worked into the night, with the widows leaving the sewing class well after the midnight bell. Annie MacPherson and Constance took a short break for meat broth and then turned their efforts to lining up each child's belongings, making brief repairs, polishing boots that were less than shiny and placing labels on each child's belongings.

They finished shortly before the morning bell wakened the orphans and while Miss MacPherson changed and packed her own bag for the journey, Constance guided the boys through dressing and breakfast. Excitement meant that few of the children could eat.

"There'll be no more of this porridge for me in Canada," said a tall boy with a handsome head of fair curls. "It'll be bacon and sausages when I get there."

"No, you'll still have porridge – all respectable people have porridge in the morning," said his dark-haired friend.

"I'm going to raise pigs – the best meat in the world, that is," said the handsome boy.

"I don't know about raising pigs – but you might turn into one," laughed his friend.

"Boys, eat up – you have a long journey ahead of you," Constance told them.

The rustle of Annie MacPherson's heavy gown silenced all the boys. "Children, I hope you have eaten your fill for the omnibus has arrived to take us to the train station."

"I've never been on an omnibus," whispered one boy.

Annie MacPherson gazed at the room and waited only moments for silence. "Now, boys, we must behave with dignity and decorum. People will be watching you all through this trip – waiting for the perfect opportunity to call you rascals and thieves, and we must not give them that opportunity. You are ambassadors of the Home of Industry, and you must behave with all decorum."

She raised her hands, slightly bidding the boys to stand. They moved with only a little scraping of stools and followed Annie MacPherson out the door.

Constance watched the boys file quietly down the hallway and tailed them outside where they squeezed onto the omnibus. Annie MacPherson's assistant Ellen Bilbrough arrived accompanied by Minister Beckett. Constance wished desperately that she were going along on this grand journey. Ellen Bilbrough was Annie MacPherson's oldest friend, but she had little experience of working at the mission. Why had she been chosen? Where was Ellen Bilbrough last night when she and Annie MacPherson worked through the night? It didn't seem fair. Just like Mathew going off to missionary work among the heathen in Africa while she was left home with mother. Constance felt her stomach cramp with what she knew was envy.

Her lip quivered and she knew she was growing petulant. "Grow where you are planted," Minister Beckett had told her when she had grown surly after Mathew's departure.

She stood a little straighter and looked around for sight of the church's brass band. Surely, they would arrive to give the group a grand send-off. Instead, Minister Beckett arrived to lead a short prayer. The children on the bus bowed their heads while the four adults on the pavement blocked the passage of clerks and shop assistants hurrying to work.

"Three curses at you," muttered one man forced to step through the horse manure that littered the road.

"A most charitable gentleman," Annie MacPherson muttered at the end of the prayer.

Constance grinned.

Annie MacPherson glanced at the omnibus. "Well, we must be off. I will write once aboard the ship – but the letters won't be mailed until we land in Quebec."

Minister Beckett bowed his head again. "May the Lord be with you."

Annie MacPherson ushered Ellen Bilbrough onto the bus, while tears crept into Constance's eyes.

Minister Beckett touched her elbow. "Please don't cry, Miss Petrie. This is the Lord's work. It is His grand path and we must do nothing but follow."

Constance nodded. She remembered his words – she would grow where she was planted.

"Besides," Minister Beckett stood up a little straighter, "with these children off to the promised land, we now have room in the Beehive for other children in need of work and care."

Constance smiled through her tears. This was most definitely true.

*

.

35

Winifred watched the Trupper kids file into the Beehive, their eyes wide as they took in the vast room and its broad benches. The tall space made their thin, bent bodies grow straight as though released from confinement. Rose, the oldest, led her siblings to a corner bench where they could work together. The two younger girls stayed close to her side while the boy eyed the kids at the neighbouring bench. His splayed nose made him ugly, but he seemed respectful enough. The younger brother was upstairs being fitted for a back brace to straighten his spine.

They were a lucky lot, thought Winifred. There had been nothing like the Home of Industry when she was a child. After her mother died from fever, Winifred had wandered the alleys down by the riverside, stealing a bit of food when she could, and then she'd been taken in by Bessie Brown. The house had been crowded, but the young Winifred had learned to pickpocket. She'd grown quite deft and easily earned enough to make Bessie happy. The more you earned, the more food the old woman dished out to you and, on really good days when you picked a healthy purse, then Bessie made sure you had a bed by the fire.

But as Winifred grew, it became more difficult to get close to the purse. Many gentlemen thought it was some other business she was after. Winifred had taken her first customer when she was twelve. After that, all the money went for gin. It had seemed easy at first – good money and some laughter. But it didn't last. She was beaten up by three lads who'd done their business and wouldn't pay. They left her bleeding from knife wounds. She'd have died if the missionaries hadn't found her and brought her to their house. And they didn't turn her out at the end of the night. They put her in a bed, fed her soup and watched her recover. Of course, she'd listened to their stories of Jesus and the Lord. By the time she was well, she was more than ready to sign the pledge and join them. She still blessed that beating and had no doubt she'd be dead and burning in hell if she'd carried on with her old life.

Of course the missionaries didn't always know what they were doing, sometimes they saw things a bit too black and white, but their blessed hearts were in the right place.

She watched the children get down to work, and then took up her knitting.

*

Upstairs, Tommy shivered as cold hands pulled on his shoulders while an icy metal rod pushed against his spine.

"Stand straight!" the nurse told him.

Tommy stood as upright as he could, but what he really wanted to do was crumble and cry. George and his sisters were downstairs making matchboxes, and although Tommy hated the work, hated the thin slices of wood, the heavy smell of the paste, the rough sandpaper that scraped at his skin, at least down there no one would poke and push at him without telling him what was going on.

He stared at the line of leather vests hanging on the wall, metal rods creeping out from their lining, while along the floor stood leg braces, all upright like stiff boots. During breakfast, Tommy had seen a few children in the Beehive wearing them, all walking as though their legs were frozen.

The doctor pushed his cold fingers onto the thin muscle across Tommy's shoulders. "I think a four-inch brace to begin with."

The nurse lifted one of the smaller leather jackets from the wall. She pushed Tommy's arms through its sleeveless holes. The weight crushed Tommy's shoulders and he staggered a little.

"Now, you must wear this all the time, even at night, if we're to get that back of yours straightened out." Her breath smelled sweet from something Tommy couldn't name. She buckled the jacket across his chest. "Now, I know it's heavy, but if you want help then you must be prepared to take your side of the burden."

The vest crushed his chest, leaving him too leaden for breath. He blew air out from his lungs and then sucked it back in.

"I know it's uncomfortable," the doctor said. "But you will get used to it. Now, how old are you?"

Tommy took another breath then pushed out the words. "I'm four."

Dr Colpress patted the vest but Tommy felt nothing. "Well, maybe by the time you're eight, we'll have you out of this."

Tommy followed the nurse from the room. The jacket rubbed into his back bones, forcing him to push back his shoulders or face pain. At first the stretch of his shoulders felt good, but within minutes the weight exhausted him and all he could do was slump forward, making the jacket's coarse seams rub against his spine.

"Stand straight!" the nurse told him again.

Tommy pulled his shoulders up, but by the time he reached his brother and sisters the weight crushed him so heavily that all he wanted to do was cry.

He looked at Rose for help and saw her eyes moist with pity. Tommy couldn't stop himself any longer and began to bawl. "Please take it off, Rose. I hate it, please take it off."

Rose pulled him into a hug but felt only the rigidity of the leather. "Oh, Tommy, it's for your own good."

The boy wailed louder, and other children in the room stopped work to stare. Winifred put down her knitting and beckoned a boy follow her. The pair stood in front of Tommy.

"Now, me lad, what's your name?" Winifred asked.

Tommy burrowed his head into Rose's abdomen, crying heavily into her dress.

"Now look here, there's no point in feeling sorry for yourself. This jacket will help, and one day you'll be glad of it."

Tommy burrowed further into Rose's dress, his sobs causing the vest to rise and fall.

Winifred motioned for Rose to stand. The girl hesitated, and then stood, forcing Tommy's small face, wet with tears and snot, to look up. He curled his hands into his eyes in an effort to stay hidden.

Winifred took one of his hands and held it in her own. "Now listen, lad. We aren't about to take that jacket off no matter how much you cry because it's to help you."

Tommy glared as the tears ran freely down his cheeks.

Winifred pulled the other boy forward. "Now, see this lad here. When he arrived, he had your problem. All he could see were his feet. Isn't that right, Jack?"

The boy nodded, and Winifred pushed him in a quarter turn. "Now, look at him, a back to make his mother proud. And it's all because he wore that jacket like he should and didn't go crying to take it off."

Tommy peered through his tears. The boy stood straight, looking out across the room.

Rose crouched down in front of her brother. "See what this jacket can do? It will really help you stand straight."

Tommy looked again at the boy and, automatically, his shoulders pulled back to relieve pressure on his spine, but again he felt his shoulders crushed under the jacket's weight. "I'll try," he said puffing up his chest so he could stand straight and upright.

*

Winfred tallied the children's matchboxes at the end of each day. Between them the Trupper children made ten gross. George puffed up with pride; this was more than they ever made at home. At this rate they'd soon make enough for rent and food.

His mother still had her doubts about the Home of Industry and even that morning had suggested they stay home to work. "We can't trust these people. They must want something from us," she'd said.

George had stayed silent as Rose argued that they be allowed to give it a try. If they didn't like it, they could leave. Mary Trupper said nothing, but her last instruction to her children was to run if anyone asked for their thumbprint.

In the classroom Miss Constance talked about a man with an odd name, but George loved the story she told about him feeding a whole town on a few loaves and fishes. Constance wrote on a large blackboard while the children recited the words and copied letters onto a slate.

Suffer little children to come unto me.

It seemed cruel to ask the children to suffer, but George thought Miss Constance must know what she was talking about. Tommy was certainly suffering. George watched his little back tilt up and down as he pushed against the weight of the jacket.

"Children, Our God, who is rich in mercy, loves us," Constance told the class. "He gave his only son that we might live."

George raised his hand as he'd seen other children do when they had a question.

"Yes, George," Constance called out.

He stood, as he'd seen others do. "Miss, I know I'm just new here, but is this God and our Queen relatives?"

A giggle rose from the class.

Constance suppressed it with a firm stare. "No, George. God is our everlasting Father in Heaven; while the Queen is our monarch here on earth."

"So which one rules, Miss?"

"Our Lord rules, George, as you will learn when we go on with the lesson."

"But Miss, where does he live?"

"George, Our Lord lives in the hearts of those who will let him in."

"So, how do you let him in, and if you don't let him, does that mean he doesn't rule you? And who's this other guy you've been talking about? Is he a king?"

Children around the room grinned at each other.

"George, I've been talking about Jesus, the son of God."

"So does the Queen rule him?"

Constance sighed. "George, I think we need to have this talk later. We can't hold up the rest of the class."

George sat down more confused than when he started. Where did the Queen fit in with God and his son? He still didn't know.

*

George wasn't the first child in the Home of Industry to puzzle over the relationship between Queen Victoria and the Lord. Constance had talked to Minister Beckett about the problem and he'd advised her to continue with lessons and the children's questions would ease as they grew more familiar with the stories.

But Constance wanted more. She wanted the children to know the Kingdom of Heaven and how it could live in your heart. She wanted the children to feel the exaltation and happiness that came from knowing that nothing here on earth could hurt you when you were in the good Lord's hands.

As Minister Beckett's voice uttered words of salvation, Constance thought about the children in the Beehive and how their faces had grown soft and round with food and care. George had lost his rough edge, and his sisters had been heard to laugh as they worked. Constance felt her spirit grow light as Minister Beckett's voice called on the congregation to stay faithful to God.

"Amen!" came the response.

Constance opened her eyes to see Minister Beckett lean over the lectern.

"As you are all well aware, our dear Miss MacPherson left several weeks ago, taking one hundred boys to Canada. We ask you all to keep our dear Sister in your prayers that her mission will be accomplished."

"Amen!" came with nods of assent.

Minister Beckett spent some time unfolding his tiny spectacles and resting them on his sharp nose.

"I have received several letters from our dear Sister, the first mailed as soon as the party stepped down from the boat, and I would like now to read it to you:

"My Dearest Friends,

You may have imagined our first night was rough. I send you a few lines to assure you that all is love, even to the small details.

Many a faithful prayer has been made for a prosperous voyage, but when my boys told me how ill some of them had been during the night, and how they had held little prayer meetings, crying to Jesus in the midst of what to them seemed like a storm, I rejoiced.

With the exception of two, all are on deck now, as bright as larks. They have carried up poor Jack Frost and Fred Miller. It is most touching to see them wrap their friends up in rugs. Michael Finn, the Shoreditch shoeblack, was up all night caring for the sick boys. He carried them up the ladder on his back. Michael Finn and I have exchanged nods at the railway corner for five years. It is great joy to give him such a good chance in life. I will write again when we reach land.

With the love of Our Lord
Annie MacPherson"

Talk in the audience was fast and excited. Minister Beckett held up his hand again. "I can assure you, our brethren, that the second letter from our dear Sister brings even more blessed news:

"We have been so well received here. In Quebec, the agency gent would willingly have kept all one hundred boys there, but we left him with eleven and brought the rest onto Montreal. There, too, people were anxious to keep all of them and said, if it were made known, in three days we should not have one remaining. As it was, we left twenty-three and all in excellent situations. Then we left eight at Brockville and another eight at Kingston before continuing our journey through towns on route to Toronto.

Canada is a land rich in work, and I have found the farmers here are keen to serve our mission. Many a farmer's son does not take up the plough or hoe, but instead turns his attention to business or goes west to find his own land. As a result, these hard-working farming men are bereft of youngsters to teach, and our young inmates are keenly taken up.

I write this to you as evidence of our success and to point the way forward in our mission. All who labour in London must be tired of relieving misery from hand to mouth, and also heartsick of seeing hundreds pining away from want of work when on the shores of Canada the cry is heard, 'Come over and we will help you.' We must seek out those in need and we should build a golden bridge where the poor and needy can step across the Atlantic to this Promised Land.

Amen, my fellow labourers, Amen.

Many in the congregation made hearty calls of "Amen!" But Constance stood, her hands clapping in hearty applause.

Helen shook her head. "Constance, please sit! It is orphans taken to a strange land that you are applauding."

But Constance kept her eyes on the letters Minister Beckett held in his hands as though they were missives from the Dear Lord himself.

Minister Beckett flapped his arms in an appeal for calm. "Please, but with the good grace of God, we have even better news from our dear Sister."

As the noise quietened Constance sat and turned to her mother with a joyful grin. "See, Mother, we must have faith in Miss MacPherson."

Helen kept her lips tight as Minister Beckett held out yet another letter from Annie MacPherson.

"You will be pleased to hear that our dear Sister MacPherson now urges us toward a bold step and asks us to gather even more of our children that they may be saved by passage to this new pasture."

Helen sat upright. Constance gave a small smile, pleased to see her mother show enthusiasm.

Minister Beckett's voice rose. "Our Sister declares that she can find homes for thousands of our children with the good people of Canada."

Helen's face grew pale and she raised her hand to speak.

Minister Beckett nodded his assent.

Helen stood, her voice shaking a little. "My Brother, I am happy to hear news of Miss MacPherson's success with this mission, but surely we should wait to ensure the first group of children are successful in their new homes before we begin sending more children."

The minister's mouth moved in a silent stutter, and Helen took the opportunity to outline her objections.

"Taking children from our streets and setting them down with neither kith nor kin in a foreign land is a radical proposal. I believe we must wait and closely examine the results. In the meantime, we should apply our charity more vociferously at home. With more money from benefactors we could fill several more Homes of Industry with hard-working children who are keen to learn."

Loud and low murmurs spread through the hall, but Helen was unsure if they were in agreement.

Minister Beckett raised his arms, knowing he needed to reassure his flock. "Brothers and Sisters, time is precious and while we might spend years reading reports of our success in Canada – hearing how the children's limbs grow on good food, their minds develop with scripture and schooling, their futures expand with new horizons – we are condemning those children left in our overcrowded streets to lives of degradation, temptation and evil. Left at home in sinful streets, more children will grow to become unemployable, untrained, unsteady drunks who themselves will have children whose care will fall to charitable societies such as ours. Already in our city streets, the children of drunkards are receiving an education that make them fit only for prison or the penitentiary. The ranks of illegitimate children continue to grow as the sins of the parents crush the waifs and strays.

"Brothers and Sisters, we must be strong. This is not a battle for the faint-hearted. We must have courage to try new paths that may look unsure, but may lead to salvation."

Several voices called "Amen", and Minister Beckett's voice grew more confident.

"Miss MacPherson suggests we prepare one hundred more boys to leave next month. She says she can find guardians who will care for them in Christian homes. The older among them will receive a small stipend to save for their future release as adults. With this, she suggests that they might buy land further west where it is cheap and become farmers in their own right. With this plan we offer the lost children of our desolate city hope for a new life – a good life."

Helen felt her brow grow warm, and she stood without seeking permission to speak. "But is it fair to send children to foreign lands so far away that they are unlikely to ever set eyes on their kin again?"

Constance gave her mother a darted glare.

Minister Beckett mopped at the sweat on his brow. "Sister, I would like to remind you that Canada is not a foreign land but simply a part of Britain where the Britisher can have access to the richest parts of the earth. I will agree that this is a radical proposal. No one else working in these overcrowded streets has ever proposed sending starving urchins to a land where food, work and Christian homes are abundant. But, I repeat, we must be brave. The problems that surround us here cannot be corrected by a few meals and some schooling. We must embrace even that which makes us uncomfortable. For what is our discomfort compared to a new life for a hungry child?"

This "Amen" sounded louder than ever before, with Constance's voice calling out more vehemently than any other.

Helen flushed, her voice wavering against the crowd. "But it just doesn't seem right. There is something barbaric about taking children so far from their families."

Constance spoke without standing. "Mother, we must keep an open mind. You said yourself we cannot feed all the starving in London. This is an opportunity to help them feed themselves."

44

Minister Beckett held up Annie MacPherson's last letter. "I can do nothing more than let you hear the words of Sister MacPherson herself. As you all know, our dear Sister is knowledgeable about these London streets, she knows these children and is fully acquainted with the difficulties that lie here. I would like to read the last letter we received from her:

My Fellow Labourers,

God shines on all who does his work, and he has surely shone on our mission to this land of abundant opportunity. Our work is giving great sustenance to these good people. We are giving the Christians of this land objects to work their love upon.

Everywhere we visit, food is brought out by farmers. Such abundance could almost be declared a sin unless it were shared. And these good people are keen to share.

In one small town, a distant community heard about our business and a farmer was deputed by his neighbours to come for seven boys. We could only give him five.

Of course, then came the painful leave-takings; and to see great lads of thirteen and twelve sobbing was no easy work for my clinging heart; but He who scatters disciples and went on lonely pathways knew our need, even at this time.

So, I declare our mission a success. Our agency, even on the business principle of supply and demand, has met the full approval of Canadians. We must bring out more.

Several in the audience stood to applaud. Constance joined them, her head high in approval.

Helen sagged in frustration.

*

Beryl stepped back as the plump man grunted to his end. She dropped her skirt and held out her hand. "One shilling!"

The man, still breathing quickly, ignored Beryl as he tucked his shirt in his trews. Finally, he looked at her hand and his flushed cheeks rose in a grin. "Now, come, my little lady, surely sixpence is the going rate in this part of town."

Beryl held her hand even higher. "One shilling! As we agreed. You said I was worth it because of my youth."

The plump man felt for his purse and then paused. His pudgy fingers reached out and pointed to the mole that patched Beryl's cheek. "Young you might be, but that dark blemish spoils any good looks. And, for that, I think I'm due a discount."

Colour rose through Beryl's face, but she kept her outstretched hand still. "I didn't hear you complain before the job was done. Now pay up – one shilling!"

He leaned forward as though to whisper. "Give me another when I raise myself in a short while, and I will quite declare you full value."

Beryl lifted her hand high to deliver a hefty slap, but the man grabbed it in his pudgy paws.

"Come, little one, do not disrespect your elders." He pushed her hand down toward his crotch.

"No!" Beryl pulled back, but the man held her tight, levering her wrist downwards. But a sudden movement from behind felled him sideways. George dropped to his knees so that his gnarled face with his flattened nose peered closely at the man. "Giving her some trouble, are you?"

Beryl stepped closer. "Refused to pay. He said he wanted another round."

George glanced quickly behind him to where his sisters and Tommy stood and then glared back at the man. "Now, pay this girl or we'll all kick you so hard it'll be a long time till you'll be wanting anyone near you ever again."

The plump man let out a sigh and shuffled his hand toward his pocket. George stood, ready to kick if he tried any funny business.

A shilling rolled toward Beryl. She picked it up and grinned at George. "Thanks – you can let him go now."

She skipped toward Rose, Maggie and Junie, while George took Tommy by the hand.

"Devil kids!" shouted the plump man as he picked himself up. "I was robbed. She wasn't worth a shilling."

A few passers-by glanced at him but most smirked and hurried on.

Rose nodded toward the shilling held tight in Beryl's hand. "So, is this your rent money?"

Beryl shook her head. "No, that's paid for this week, and I've earned enough for bread and some mutton for stew. I just wanted a bit extra. Ruby likes a cake. And I want to buy some liniment for me ma – you know, for her sores and that."

Junie's eyes grew large at the idea of a cake. She'd seen them in the baker's window, watched them being handled so carefully by the sales assistant.

"So, you think your ma might get better with some liniment?" Rose asked.

Beryl shrugged. "It's worth a try – might get her back to work faster." She glanced down. "Besides, I don't like this work. I'd like to find something with you – at that big house. Do you like it there?"

Rose nodded. "They teach us letters – and give us stories."

"Told us about a man who was dead and then he was alive – they're magic people," Junie said. "Miss Considerance said he could do anything he wanted."

"Her name is Miss Constance," Rose and Maggie said together.

Beryl sighed. "You're so lucky – and you're learning to read?"

Junie nodded. "But we have to work first – as hard as we ever did at home."

"Well, it's bound to be better than this." Beryl kicked at a loose rock on the road and thought of an earlier client who'd taken her from behind.

"Your ma's not thinking of bringing little Ruby into the business, is she?" Rose asked.

Beryl shook her head quickly. "No – no, I'm working enough so she doesn't have to. It's just ..." She shrugged, feeling suddenly tired.

Rose put her arm around Beryl. "Let's go home. You're ma will be glad to see you."

She ushered the girl toward their lane, feeling so glad she only had to fold matchboxes for pay.

*

Belleville
Hastings County
Ontario
Canada

 Dear Miss MacPherson,

 We met following your exciting talk on child immigration to our fair town. I am happy to say that all eight of the youngsters you deposited with our citizens are fitting in mighty well. So much so that, as Warden of Hastings County, I would like to offer you a house to assist you in your work.

 Marchmont is a large dwelling in a residential neighbourhood close to the centre of town. We would like to suggest you might use it as a distribution home for the children you bring to our fair country.

 Should you accept this offer of a permanent residence in Belleville, our county council would pay the rent of the house with no stipulations on your charitable work. I am sure you understand that the success of your visit indicates our need for new workers, and we in Hastings County are anxious to help you in any way we can.

 We could not help but notice that your entire contingent of children was made up of boys. Might we suggest you consider bringing girls on future trips? The gentle women of our county frequently complain of the difficulty in finding good housemaids that I trust there would be much work on offer should you decide to include girls.

 I understand you will be leaving our town in the coming days and journeying to Toronto. Before you bid us farewell, I would be happy to show you Marchmont House. We can begin work on any adjustments you believe the property might need as soon as possible.

 God speed you well in your mission.
 Kind regards,
 A.F. Wood, Warden of Hastings County

Annie MacPherson sat back in her hotel chair and raised her eyes to the ceiling. "Thank you, Lord, thank you," she whispered and then stood quickly, raising her voice so it could be heard throughout the hotel. "Ellen, Ellen!"

Her assistant hurried from the hallway where she'd been logging the children's names into her account book.

Annie MacPherson handed her the letter but continued to talk as her assistant read. "Ellen, the Lord has truly answered our prayers. I can't believe how lucky it is that this letter found us in time. Our early departure could have put it behind us and this bountiful offer would be lost. But now, with this house, and the request for girls, we have so many more opportunities."

She stood and began to pace the length of the hotel sitting room. "They don't say how many children the house might occupy, but given that it is simply a staging post, I don't suppose that matters. The children will only be there while matched with families which, as we've seen on this trip, should take only days. We can have children in transit while a newly arrived group are found homes." She paused briefly. "We can have a continual stream of children pass through here."

Ellen looked up from the letter. "This is truly a generous offer."

"We need someone to operate the house. Someone who will put it all in place." Annie stopped pacing and looked at her assistant. "Ellen, I think that should be you. In fact, I think you should stay and get the distribution home organised while I journey home and accompany another group to this Garden of Eden."

Ellen shook her head as she rose from the chair. "But I have never done such a thing. I am a teacher. My talents are limited to stirring children to song and teaching scripture. I have no practical experience of running a residential home."

"Ellen, it will not be a residential home. Simply, a staging post as we move children from London to their Christian homes."

"What about organising large meals and laundry? I have no idea how to put together household tasks on such a grand scale."

"My dear friend, Our Lord has brought us this bounty and we cannot refuse. With this home we shall lift children out of London's streets of filth. We cannot turn such an opportunity down because we don't know how to wash sheets or boil gruel. We must learn."

Annie slipped the letter into her purse, lifted her cloak and hastened to the Belleville County Offices in the centre of town.

Albert Wood's face hovered two inches above the pages of accounts that detailed the financial incomings and outgoings of Hastings County. Short-sighted vision made this monthly scrutiny a job he despised, so Annie MacPherson's stolid figure in the doorway was a welcome reprieve.

She dropped the letter he had sent onto the desk. "I accept! Now, when can I see the property?"

Albert and the county councillors had sat up late the previous evening debating the offer of Marchmont House. It was a fine property that could sell well. But Miss MacPherson and her children offered a solution to their labour shortage, and a distribution centre in Hastings County would be well placed to take the cream of the crop from future shipments of orphans.

"It doesn't need a lot of work, you understand," Albert said as he led the way up the residential street toward the two-story house.

Annie's eyes took in the large garden with tall, shady trees where children could play, but her eyes really grew large when she noticed the width and depth of the house. "This looks like it could easily bed over one hundred – will the running costs also be paid in addition to the rent?"

Albert paused, such costs had not been included in the council debate, but he knew the city elders would hate to lose out on having the distribution centre in their community. They wanted local people to have the first selection of all the children Miss MacPherson brought over. "We can do that, I'm almost sure."

He ushered Annie MacPherson across the wide porch, through the broad doorway and into the lofty hall. Annie sighed with satisfaction at the sight of the wide stairway, the bay windows in the front rooms, the carved wood above each doorway and the vast space that stretched across each room. Marchmont felt like a proper home when compared to the utilitarian blandness at the Home of Industry.

Albert Wood coughed. "There is one delicate matter I do wish to put to you." He paused briefly and then coughed again. "We would like the children who are brought here to be British."

Annie's gaze moved from the high mantle above the front-room fireplace to the warden. "All our children will come from London; they are all British."

"Yes, we know this. But what I am trying to say is, the good people of Hastings County take pride in their link with the homeland, and we do not want children who look foreign, no matter if their birth place is on the steps of the Queen's own palace."

"I see." Annie walked through to the next room. A grand chandelier hung over the centre of the room. She gave it a cursory glance and moved into the hallway.

Albert followed her up the wide staircase. "I do hope you understand that when one is so far from one's homeland, one feels the pressure to draw in more British stock or be drowned out by foreigners."

Annie stopped on the stairs and looked at him firmly. "I understand you are suffering a severe labour shortage and I agree to send you children who are reliable in work and affordable. I agree to send no children whose skin declares any foreign parentage. But I hope the good people of Hastings County understand that all our children must be taught the Protestant Scripture and that comes with strict stipulations – all must attend Protestant Sunday School. Their dispersal assists in the spread of our faith. We will give no child to a family who follow Rome."

Albert held out his hand. "I think we have an agreement."

Annie hurried back to the hotel, forming her plan to get children to Belleville as quickly as possible. Marchmont needed beds, bedding, kitchen utensils and crockery, but otherwise it needed little adjustment to provide temporary accommodation for one hundred children.

At the hotel, Ellen sat in the sitting room with a boy who had been handed over to a local farmer three days before.

Annie looked at him suspiciously. "What's he doing here?"

Ellen led her out to the hotel foyer. "It's a delicate situation," she whispered. "The farmer said he was lazy. Frank says he was put out with the pigs to sleep. He said it was cold and he couldn't sleep from hunger."

Annie gave him another glance. "I'm sure we'll easily find him another home."

She sat down at her desk to write. "Ellen, I will leave you here to prepare Marchmont House – Albert Wood will help. I must hurry back to London. Give me time to arrive there and prepare a

51

hundred more orphans for shipment, and you should expect to receive a new contingent in around two months."

Ellen looked up to the ceiling as if appealing for strength and hurried back to the boy who had been returned to them.

Annie MacPherson returned to the letter she was writing to the Home of Industry:

So keen are the good people of Hastings County to receive our children that they have offered our mission a large, comfortable home to use as a staging post for the dispersal of our children. Of course this means that you in London must begin looking for suitable children. They are keen for strong boys to work on farms and girls suitable for housemaids. In return the children will be sent to Sunday School in our faith and will attend school whenever the workload allows.

I do not need to tell you good people what an opportunity this provides our mission. Nor must I remind you that it also requires a great deal of work to put the plan into action before other missions decide to transfer their own children. Dear Brothers and Sisters, the children to whom we teach the Lord's scripture are lost souls who take up our message like soiled rags take up caustic soda.

The cost of preparing and shipping each child to Canada will be around £12. I trust you can persuade some of our benefactors in the merits of the mission, especially when you compare the cost with the upkeep of an orphan in the Home of Industry. Remember to emphasise that we are rescuing children whose parents would have dragged them down into the haunts of drunkenness and sin from which it would be difficult to reclaim them in later years. We are lifting children from overcrowded streets and taking them to a land where they have a value lacking in their homeland.

I will return to London in three weeks. As previously instructed, I hope you will have one hundred children ready for shipping and I will accompany them immediately on my return (please include none of a dusky skin colour. These people will accept only British stock). I understand I am not giving you much time to have children uniformed and prepared but do your best. The sewing will be too much for the widows group, so I would advise you to engage the Mothers' Union to ensure all uniforms are ready in time. In addition, prepare one of our number, perhaps Constance Petrie would be a good candidate, to bring a third contingent of children. They should be ready to leave the following month. This group should include girls trained in housekeeping for I believe they will find ample opportunities in this fair land.

Happy in the bounty of our Lord,
Annie MacPherson

*

Mary sewed the seam of a heavy grey serge jacket. Next to her a woman in a loose smock stitched a cap, while all around the mothers of the Beehive children gossiped as they sewed.

"The sanitary man closed off Pereira Street yesterday, said it was the cholera and no one's allowed in or out. My sister went out in the morning to work the market and came back to find the whole street barricaded – couldn't get in. She's staying with us, but doesn't know if she'll ever see her family alive again."

"Oh, I'll tell you right now, it's not any cholera. There's no such thing. They just use that as an excuse, don't they? They want to knock Pereira Street down and make room for one of those new railroads. They did the same in Hackney – shut down whole streets and after a few weeks, just when the poor folks trapped inside had starved to death, they carried out their bodies. Then they tore down the buildings and ran the railway through there. Tell her to get her family out."

"But there's policemen – won't let anyone in or out, they say it's to stop the epidemic."

"Epidemic! All lies! Tell her to get her family out or the next time she'll see them it'll be in a wooden box."

The bandages wrapped around Mary's fingers made sewing difficult, but she used a metal thimble to help push the needle through the thick serge. Miss Constance had put a liniment on her sores and told her to keep them covered for good healing. She was a good one, Miss Constance. Mary had her suspicions at first, wondered what she wanted – whether she was one of those smugglers who acted all friendly but then took your children away and you never heard from them again. But she wasn't like that.

53

She'd saved the family from more than starvation, although Tommy still cried to take off his jacket, especially at night. She had done it once and without that weight his little face had grown younger. But Rose had persuaded her to put it back on.

"It's for his own good, Ma. You should've seen the other boy – his back was as straight as ours."

Tommy had cried as she'd refastened the ties, but George persuaded him it was the right thing, and he'd settled down.

A woman with an Irish voice broke the silence. "Did you hear? They found Fanny Pigburn's stays at the Williams' house – shows that it wasn't just that Italian orphan they done in."

"Do they know how Fanny died?"

"Probably the same as the Italian boy – a bit of laudanum in the rum, then the poor kid falls into a heavy sleep – which is just as well because then they don't know anything, do they? They never wake up. All the while their teeth are sold to the dentist, then it's the hair to the wig maker, then the rest of the body makes the rounds of the hospitals for the highest bidder."

"I don't believe it."

"It's true. When they found Fanny Pigburn's stays, they found the Williams' kids playing with the Italian boy's white mice – still in the cage that everyone knew was his."

"Do you think they'll hang?"

"Should do, kids and all – evil, the lot of them."

"It makes you not want to let the young 'uns out of your sight."

Mary's thread knotted. She tugged gently but it was tight and needed cut. It was so long since she'd done any sewing. She'd been a weaver once, her and husband working together while the children played in the small square between the weaver's cottages. That had been a good life. She and Jack thought they'd grow old and comfortable, maybe George taking over while the girls married out. But then the machines came and the hand-worked loom wasn't needed. They lost the house, and Jack had signed up for the ships. That's what his brother did, and the money was always regular – except when you went overboard and missing. Trust Jack!

"My son's going off to Canada with Miss MacPherson. They say she can get him a job on a farm with good pay when he's older and maybe he can even buy his own bit of land."

A woman held up a bodice. "Maybe he'll be wearing one of these jackets. What size is he?"

"That's too small, he's going on for his fifteenth summer."

"Is he nervous?"

"I don't think so. Minister Beckett says it's almost two weeks at sea, then a day or so on the train. I think he sees it as a big adventure."

"Boys do though, don't they? I hear they want to send girls to this Canada place."

"I don't think that's right. Girls need the protection of their home or anything can happen to them out there."

"It's that Miss Constance who's taking girls. She said they need housemaids out there."

"Well, I don't agree with taking girls."

"But Miss Constance is a good 'un. It's not like they're going with just anybody."

Mary found herself nodding.

"Yeah, you have to trust them. I mean, my Sam got help with his leg here – he was almost lame – but now he's running and brings in a pay as big as mine."

"I've heard Miss Annie is the bigwig – pulls all the strings that get them money – and that Minister Beckett, he only thinks he's in charge. It's Miss Annie who really runs things."

A short silence settled until broken by a whisper. "I wonder why all the women who work here are 'Miss'. Do you think any of them have ever had a man?"

A few of the women giggled.

"Sometimes, I wish I'd never had a man, the amount of trouble he gives me. Given the choice between him and Canada – I think I'd choose Canada."

The women fell into a silence.

"Where is Canada anyway?"

"I don't think it's in England."

"So, who's in charge there?"

"I don't know."

"Do they have their own King or is it our Queen?"

The woman whose son was going to Canada shrugged.

Winifred opened the door. "Good, ladies, it's time for meat broth and bun – a reward for all your hard work."

The women followed her to the dining room where a large pot of broth and plates of bread and bun sat at the centre of the table.

"Mothers, please sit where you may," said Winifred as she began to spoon the broth into bowls and pass them around.

She served all thirty women and then broke the bread into almost equal pieces.

"Now, Mothers, we all know that the world outside these walls is an evil place." She paused and gave each woman a searching look. Some watched her as they chewed their bread, while others drank eagerly at their broth, paying little heed.

"But, Mothers, you must know that we can only be saved from the evils that swell around us by taking The Lord into our hearts. For he sent his son Jesus to be our Saviour."

Mary paused to stare at Winifred. She'd heard about this Jesus and his father, but she wasn't really sure what it was all about.

"Mothers, you must know that to be Saved, and for your children to be Saved, you must accept The Lord into your hearts." Winifred held up a heavy Bible. "For only then will the darkness be dispersed and you can behold the Righteousness of His world. Now let us pray."

The women bowed their heads and cupped their hands at their chests. Mary copied them, shutting her eyes tight.

Winifred talked of lightness and dark, evil and good and called on The Lord to help them all. The speech carried on longer than any talk Mary had ever heard. Finally, Winifred called "Amen".

"Amen," replied many of the voices.

Mary opened her eyes and glanced around her. She would like to understand more. For certainly, her own world was lighter since her children began work at the Home of Industry.

*

Constance hurried up Petticoat Lane, her footsteps striking out her sense of mission. She had thought of little other than Canada since Annie MacPherson asked her to accompany children on a future mission. For Constance, it was as though God himself had picked her out. Her brother Mathew might have his work among the heathens of Africa, but now she herself had her very own calling – no need to grow where she was planted. She smiled at the thought of it, even though her mother wasn't happy. She still said taking the children across the ocean was wrong. But Constance believed she would prove that the mission was right. All the children who accompanied her would have the best homes and families. She would see to it.

As she hurried toward the gate of the Bethnal Green workhouse, she noticed a family awaiting admission. At least, Constance thought it was a family until she realised that the man was too old and infirm to be father to the children. The mother, young eyes in a face drawn old in misery, held a baby while three young children hugged her ragged skirt. The elderly man lay on the ground, his cough throwing flecks of blood onto his shirt.

The warden opened the gate and threw a dart of disdain on the small group. But his face turned bright when he saw Constance.

He drew her in and quickly pushed the gate shut, leaving the needy outside. "It's always a good day when we see you here, Miss Petrie. What can we do for you today?"

Constance glanced behind at the poor people left outside the gate. "Mr Marsh, I'd like to talk to some of your orphans and families. I have a proposal that might interest many of them."

Mr Marsh smiled showing three wooden teeth. "Well, it's work time. The men are at their stone breaking, and the women and girls are in the laundry."

Constance forced a smile. She had been on the panel that selected Mr Marsh to run the workhouse. He'd presented himself as a decent Christian who wanted to work for the poor, but recently she'd found it hard to like him. It was nothing she could name, just a feeling at the back of her neck that made it hard to look at his face.

She kept her gaze on the brick wall behind his head. "Mr Marsh, it will only take a few moments, and if you could possibly gather the inmates, you will find that my proposal may benefit you by reducing your numbers."

He threw her a look of suspicion. "I can only call them from work if it's important, Miss Petrie."

Constance nodded. "I can assure you, Mr Marsh, my mission here is important."

He scowled as he turned, and Constance listened to his feet retreat along the cobbled floor. A few minutes later, a clatter of boots grew loud, and Constance saw Mr Marsh leading a throng of workers. With no instruction they shuffled into lines across the courtyard, creating four long rows of figures clad in faded and patched cloth that hung loose on their thin bodies.

Mr Marsh watched until they stood in columns – men at the back, women in the middle and children up front. Tots with heads too large for thin bodies stood in almost perfect alignment. Constance wondered what punishment they'd suffered to learn to stand in this way.

The keys on Mr Marsh's belt rattled as he stepped quickly forward. "Now, don't think this here break is a rest 'cos it just means you'll have to work later to make up for it. Now, this here lady is from the Home of Industry. They do a lot of good things for people who are poorer than you and a lot more grateful. So, listen and show her the Christian respect someone like her deserves."

He smiled at Constance.

She turned away from his wooden teeth, feeling suddenly nervous. "Perhaps we should begin with a prayer." She bowed her head as she recited the Lord's Prayer. A few in the gathering muttered while most stayed mute. But the words spurred Constance, giving her the strength she needed to begin her speech. Annie MacPherson frequently gave such talks to large numbers of wealthy benefactors. All Constance needed to do was persuade some of the poor children that their lives might be better off in Canada.

"I come to you today with an offer of a new life. There is a green land far away, a land of Christians where food and work are plentiful. In fact, the only thing lacking in this bountiful land is labour. Our Church Sister, Annie MacPherson, has found homes and jobs for the one hundred orphaned boys she took there. So successful has been her mission that the Christian families have asked for more children – both boys and girls to take into their homes. These families promise food, clothing, scripture and schooling to all children. Boys could be working on a farm or in a family business. Girls are much needed as housemaids." Constance scanned her eyes among the orphans. In the dim light she could see little of their reaction to her news.

"So, I am here today to gather children for our new mission. Canada is a large and pleasant land with a soil rich and fertile. It is a land that lures many young people who wish to make a fresh start in their lives. But knowing no one and with little guidance, such a move carries risks. We at the Home of Industry are offering to accompany children and promise to carefully scrutinise all families. Older children taking this opportunity are guaranteed an income from age fifteen, an income that will be saved for their future. Orphans with no one to help them in the world are our priority. But I ask the parents among you to seriously think about the future of your children. If you wish them to move through life with hope, then I ask you to offer them to me today and I will take them to the promised land."

Constance knew her mother would disapprove of this last plea, but surely even she would agree that going to Canada offered more hope than staying in the workhouse.

Some faces looked intently at the small thin woman who stood before them, but most gazed forward as though they'd heard nothing.

"Please," Constance said a little louder. But Mr Marsh had moved forward to herd the columns back to work. Constance took a chance. "Please stop and talk to me now. Mr Marsh should not mind and I will answer all your questions."

A small mob of children and adults stepped from their lines, passing Mr Marsh as they did so.

"Could the whole family go?" asked a man with a wife and three children at his side.

"No," Constance said, immediately uncomfortable at turning them down. "But perhaps later, after the children are settled, they can find good work positions for their parents."

"Will my children be able to live together?"

"We try to place siblings in the same home, but this may not always be possible."

"Will my children learn to read and write?"

"Most certainly. All families taking children must agree to schooling."

"What if my children are badly treated? Who will protect them?"

"We will personally approve all families and arrange follow-up visits to ensure each child is well cared for."

"Do we get paid to give you our children?"

"Certainly not! But you do gain the satisfaction of knowing that you gave your child a fresh start in life with a future that they could never hope to achieve in this overcrowded city."

"I would like my boy to go," called out a woman who pushed forward a small child with carrot-red hair.

Constance smiled. "Then I should need his name."

"Harry Twistle," called out the woman quickly, as if she feared Constance might change her mind.

As she hurried from the workhouse, Constance thought about discussing Canada with the mother who waited outside. But another look at the children showed the oldest was barely five and much too young for shipment to Canada.

She sped through Bethnal Green, holding her nose as she passed the paste factory. At Spitalfields she gave the hawkers a sideways glance and clasped her pouch with extra firmness. But even under such threat, she couldn't help but smile. She was truly on a rescue mission, carrying children out of darkness and lifting them up to a green and pleasant land. She began to sing quietly to herself: "There is a better world, they say, and it is oh so bright."

A boy stepped into her path. He held out a floral bowl. "Nice piece of pottery for you, luv."

Constance knew without any scrutiny that it was likely stolen. "Is this what you do for a living?"

His greasy head looked briefly at his friends who each pushed crockery toward all who hurried past. "Sometimes, depends what's on, don't it?"

"Wouldn't you like to do something else? Go somewhere that offers an honest living, a decent bed, regular food?"

"Look, that don't sound like the workhouse to me." He glanced at one of his friends who was making a quick sale to an old woman. Constance saw him consider darting over to try his chances.

"I'm not talking about the workhouse. I'm talking about a foreign land where the people are Christian and have so much work to offer that they are willing to open their homes to boys like you. They will give you a home, feed you, clothe you, even pay you if

60

you're more than fifteen. They offer a healthy life, where you won't have to steal to make a living."

The boy stood upright in exaggerated indignation. "Look 'ere, I didn't steal nothing. These 'ere dishes belonged to my grandmother who passed away not two weeks' since."

Constance folded her arms to wait for another story. The boy stared at her defiantly. Constance took out a pencil and wrote out the address of the Home of Industry. "Look, if you're interested, come and see me. Canada could give you a whole new future. Tell your friends." She hurried on, proud of her initiative at taking the search out to the streets.

Back at the Home of Industry, Winifred held a weeping Lawrence on her lap. She nodded to the notepaper beside her chair. "He had a letter from his father."

Constance picked up the thin parchment and began to read:

My dearest son,

I need to begin this letter by telling you how much I miss you. Not a day goes by that I do not think of you and wish we could be together. Unfortunately, that day may take a few years. Work has been difficult to come by. I have been clerking for an old friend, you may remember him, Mr Wallace, a legal man who sometimes visited us at Prickwillow House. While this position has helped me provide a roof over my head and regular meals, it goes no way toward paying off my debts or helping me save for a new home so we can be together.

However, all is not bleak. A gentleman I have met through Mr Wallace has offered me an opportunity that may make our lives easier in the distant future. This man has offered me a position as manager of his estate in Africa. I will have free board and lodge and therefore will be able to save all my income, which is a great deal more than I earn at present. With this opportunity it should be able to pay my debts in only a few years and provide for our own home some years later.

My dear Lawrence, I know I must be strong, and so must you. The years before us must be passed with great industry so that each day will speed through to the next. I ask this of you, my boy, because I know you're as keen as I to be reunited. Schooling at the Home of Industry is basic, and I know you need a great deal more to obtain any satisfaction. If a family should pass through the home who are keen to house a boy of quick intelligence to add to their household, please take the opportunity to live with them and continue your education. While this letter may distress you, please realise that I will find you when the time is right. I have written to the Home of Industry stressing that while they may transfer guardianship to a suitable family, they are not to allow adoption. You are my son and we shall be together again.

I leave for Africa this coming week but will write often. The warden at the home tells me that the exercises to your dear foot are progressing well. I have a vision of you as a strong young man when I next see you. We shall have great adventures together. Think of this often, my son. These are dark days, but sunshine shall come back into our lives again. I promise.

All my love, Father.

Constance stroked the boy's arm where it circled Winifred's neck. "Do not fret, dear child. Your father does what he must."

She promised herself she would find him the perfect family in Canada.

*

The Trupper room was cleaner than before with the rags folded and the floor swept free of sawdust. Constance sat on the bed, unsure of which words should come first.

Finally, she decided God would guide her. "Mary, you know that the Home of Industry wants the very best for your children?"

Mary looked up quickly, suspicion already in her eyes.

"Well, the Lord has given us a wonderful bounty – a new home in Canada, and families who are keen to give all our children warm homes, good food and learning. So much so that one of our dear Sisters has just taken one hundred boys there and found them good homes ..."

Mary's hands flew up to stop any more words. "Now look, Miss, you've been good to us, but I knew in my guts there had to be a catch." She stood, her body shaking in anger.

62

Constance lifted from the bed so that Mary didn't tower over her. "There is no catch. I will accompany the children on the ship and personally ensure each child is found a good home."

Mary's voice grew loud. "My kids already have a home. And you don't need to worry. We'll go back to the way we used to be. I see your plan now, but you aren't taking my children away. No, no," she shook her head for added emphasis.

"Mary, please, taking your children into the Home of Industry wasn't a plan to send them overseas. We're simply trying to do our best, and Canada is a huge fertile land where there are good Christians who need help with their large farms and homes. All children will be sent to church on Sunday, receive schooling and learn a trade. As they get older, they'll earn a monthly income that will be saved for their future, so that at age eighteen they may buy their own land or start a business. This is the very best mission we've ever come up with, and I would dearly love your children to benefit."

Mary shook her head. "We've been happy with the Beehive. We're earning a living, and they all have full bellies plus they get a little bit of schooling. We don't want any more."

Constance raised her eyes as though beseeching divine help. "Mary, it's a wonderful opportunity. Families are lining up on Liverpool Docks for passage to Canada. George could be ahead of them all. At age eighteen, he'll have three years' wages in his pocket. The girls – Rose would make a wonderful housemaid. Who wouldn't welcome such a girl into their home?"

Mary felt her heart race in her chest as she thought of her children going so far away. She shook as she spoke. "No, no, no. I won't do it. The Beehive's been lovely for the kids, but if you keep pushing on this then we can always go back to working here. We were fine on our own."

Constance stood in front of the curtain that acted as a door. "Please, don't take the children out of the Beehive. They are thriving there. I only brought up Canada because I truly believe that if you love your children you will be happy to let them ..."

"Stop!" Mary held up both hands as if holding back a speeding omnibus, and Constance knew she would listen to no more.

*

63

Down at the Beehive, the children were having an unscheduled break to hear a lecture from Minister Beckett.

"Who among you here has ever dreamt of living in a new land – a place with fresh air, wholesome food and where jobs with good pay are plenty?"

The children looked at each other. Those who'd been at the home a long time expected to hear about Heaven or the Garden of Eden.

"We have a new mission here, Children. Our good Miss MacPherson has been to Canada and found families and jobs for one hundred boys from our streets. They have left the dirt and uncertainty of our streets and now live in clean homes where they work in good jobs, receive Scripture each Sunday and learn their schooling. Every day they breathe fresh air, none of the grey stench we must put up with, and their food is fresh – no watery meat broth, no weevils or sawdust in the bread – just good wholesome food."

At the back of the room, Helen felt her chest grow tight with anger. She'd thought Minister Beckett would talk about salvation, but this was temptation.

Standing tall at the podium, the Home of Industry's Minister grew more animated.

"And children, the true miracle is that this opportunity is not limited to these one hundred boys who bravely accompanied Miss MacPherson across the sea. No, this opportunity is open to all of you. Good Christians in Canada are ready to open their doors and offer you a home in exchange for honest work. You will receive food, clothing, scripture and education. Older children will also receive a wage: $3 a month for those over the age of fifteen. And what is vital to remember about that wage is that it is saved for you, and when are eighteen you will have money in your pocket to begin a good life, buy land, start a business, pay for a good education. The possibilities are endless."

George's eyes grew round with eagerness.

"And it isn't only boys the good families of Canada want to take into their homes. They want girls to train as housemaids, governesses, cooks. The opportunities are limited only by the goodness of The Lord."

Junie sucked her thumb vacantly, while Rose wondered who among the workroom would volunteer. She knew it wouldn't be her. She could never leave her mother.

"Children, think about what I have told you today. Talk about it with your guardians. God sometimes announces his bounty with only a gentle knock on our door and if we do not pay attention it is easy to miss his offerings."

Helen could feel her chest grow full, and she swallowed, forcing back all her anger.

The minister led the children in a short prayer and then left to preach to the class next door.

But the tightness in Helen's chest didn't ease. Four hours later, she didn't drift into a relaxing snooze as she usually did during the evening prayer meeting. Instead she silently played over the speech she would make.

Next to her, Constance sat calmly listening to the voice of Minister Beckett. Helen knew her daughter would not be happy with the fuss she was about to make.

The minister's voice dropped an octave as he neared the end of the prayer, and Helen's heart raced as she prepared her dissent.

"Amen," Minister Beckett called out. "Now, Brothers and Sisters, we can go in peace."

Helen pushed her hand into the air and stood so no one could miss her need to speak.

Minster Beckett paused at the top step of the podium. "I believe our dear Sister has something to say."

Helen's mind fogged momentarily as she thought of all the statements that might pour into her mouth, but she knew she needed to start gently. "Minster Beckett, Brothers and Sisters, I feel there is an issue that needs our careful consideration."

She took a deep breath, pulling at carefully selected words she had practised all afternoon. "We have begun one of the most ambitious ventures we have ever attempted. Namely, taking children from our city here and placing them in faraway homes in Canada. I know I have spoken before against such a policy, but I understand that the mission has the support of the majority in our church."

Constance let out a sigh of relief, and Helen knew such relief would be brief.

"I do, however, believe we need to be responsible in how we recruit children for Canada. I think we must take great care in depicting this land – of which we personally know very little – as a Garden of Eden. We must also be responsible in selecting the children who take this great journey. Children with families should stay with the families who love and care for them – there should be no unwanted split of brother from brother or child from mother."

A murmur rose from the congregation.

Helen paused, her voice croaking slightly. "Therefore, I do believe our mission should not involve tearing families apart and sending children across the ocean like parcels."

Murmurings from the floor grew, and Helen could not tell if she had incited agreement or anger. She felt Constance's glare and kept her gaze firmly on the window above Minister Beckett's head.

He held up his hand, motioning for the congregation to quieten. "My dear Sister, you may sit while we hear from other members of our church. But I must say I agree that children without mother or father should be a priority for our mission to Canada. However, we must not turn a blind eye to those children whose parentage will drag them down into drunkenness and sin. Left in such homes, children learn vice from parents and redemption becomes, as many of us well know, nigh on difficult."

An older man stood and turned to look at Helen before addressing Minister Beckett. "I believe we must keep in mind the larger picture, namely, there are too many people in this city. By some estimates the population in London increases by one million every three years as we take in those from the countryside seeking jobs, those fleeing wars overseas and, all the while, still great numbers of Irish continue to pour in looking for work. It is a pestilence of overcrowding, and we must find a solution. No society can grow healthy in such conditions."

"Yes," called out a younger man, "we must face the reality that many of these children's parents are too debauched to seek work or find redemption. As a result, there are children out there learning only sin. If we can take those children out of the sewers and place them in pure surroundings, they will grow to be healthy in body and spirit."

A woman stood. Helen knew her as an organiser of the Mother's Prayer meetings where she sat alone mixing little with those who might need help. "If we keep the children of debauched parents here, then we all know what happens as the children grow – they take on all the sins of the parents and later imprint them onto their own offspring."

Helen stood again. "I take your wisdom, Brothers and Sisters, but plucking children from parents is not a simple exercise. How do we decide who to pluck? Do we take away children whose father is a drunkard, but whose mother works hard to provide her children with food?"

Minister Beckett held his hand out to speak. "I believe, dear Sister, that your question can be answered by the law. Our mission can take away no child unless the parents sign guardianship over to the mission. As a result, no child shall be plucked from any parent unless permission is legally given."

Helen's voice rose and she feared sounding hysterical. "But don't you see that depicting Canada as a heavenly salvation, then you are luring children away from parents and toward this unknown land?"

Minister Beckett stood back from the podium as if stung. "Sister, you speak as though I were beckoning the children into the depths of hell itself."

"No, not at all," Helen coloured. "I simply see the children's faces grow excited as you speak of Canada and I worry that they might be tempted away from the families who care for them."

A voice from behind called out. "But surely if those so poor that they attend our mission are lured to a better life in Canada by Minister Beckett's speech, then that is a good thing?"

Helen turned, not sure who she was addressing. "It is not a better life if they leave behind families who love them. And how do we know they will face a better life in Canada? There are cruel people throughout the world and the more children we send to Canada, the more likely we are to find host families who are less than Christian."

A sudden movement next to her caught Helen off balance. Constance stood, her hand raised for speech. "I must call all our congregation's attention to the work of Miss MacPherson. She personally guarantees all our children shall go to Christian homes.

Now, I must ask if this congregation would doubt the word of Miss MacPherson?"

Helen stared at her daughter. Her voice weakened. "I do not doubt the word of Miss MacPherson. But I am calling on our congregation to carefully consider their responsibilities in selecting children for this mission. I do not believe we want to see families torn apart with children growing up across distant seas and never seeing their aging parents again." Her eyes grew misty as she thought of her own son, far away in Africa.

Constance knew her mother's thoughts were of Mathew, and she sat down feeling that sometimes her mother was too emotional.

Minister Beckett raised his hand. "Brothers and Sisters, may I recommend that we make true orphans the priority for our Canada homes, and those signed to our care by parents who voluntarily wish their children to seek better lives abroad take secondary positions."

"Amen," sounded throughout the hall.

Constance took her mother's hand and squeezed. Helen looked up, unsure that anything had changed.

*

Beryl lay down on a heap of her mother's clothes. Mild weather had brought out more custom than she'd seen for a while – four, all quick, although the last had needed a bit of help to get started. Beryl had worked with him until he made a remark about her mole, said she had the mark of the devil on her. After that, she'd stood against the wall and let him stiffen all on his own. But he'd come fast, and she'd run off as soon as she had his money.

Four shillings she'd come home with and all of it much needed now her mother wasn't earning.

Next to the small attic window, Ruby played with her doll, stroking its hair with a bald brush and singing a song she'd heard from the hawkers.

Beryl felt a rush of juices run into her drawers. She knew she should sit on the pot and flush out her insides to keep out disease, but a fog of tiredness phased out all except the image of her last client's cravat chugging back and forth in her face.

The door slammed. Beryl heard her mother's fast breath and then felt a slap on her thigh.

"Quick, get our Ruby bathed. I've just found her a gentleman. Two of them wanted her, and I worked them up. After all, it's not every day a pure girl like our Ruby's on offer. The first bid was one pound, then two and, just like that, they kept going up and up until they got to seven. It's more than we ever got for you." Jean knelt down and her face grew flushed as she pulled a chest out from under the bed. "We can live on that kind of money for a long time."

Beryl sat up. "Ma, Ruby's only seven."

Jean pulled out a purple dress that Beryl once wore. "Well, what are we supposed to do? I can't work, remember!"

Beryl shook her head. "I brought home four shillings this morning."

Jean flicked her hand as though at a fly. "That won't keep us in food and gin, never mind rent." She pulled the doll from Ruby's hand and held the old dress against her daughter's small frame. Jean shook her head at its tattered lace.

Ruby reached out and grabbed her doll, holding it behind her back.

Beryl clasped her sister's hand, knocking the doll to the floor and pulling her away. "Ma, you're not doing this."

"Get the bath out. She needs to be clean."

"Ma, we need to think of another way."

Jean turned, her eyes wet with drink. "Well, I don't know any other way."

Beryl tightened her grasp on her sister's hand. It felt so small, like it could be squeezed to nothing. She thought about her own first time, and her fear and how she'd thought about her baby sister so she wouldn't cry while the man pushed and hurt her.

Without thinking of too much more she ran past her mother, out the door, pulling her sister down four flights of stairs. They were still running when they reached Whitechapel. Beryl wasn't sure where they would go, but she knew where she would start. The woman who worked with George and his sisters said she was on Commercial Street. They could help Ruby. Train her as something or maybe she could work at matchboxes with the Truppers. Beryl looked down at her sister who hurried obediently beside her. She released her sister's hand and squatted down to talk.

"Listen to me, Ruby. We're going to have to make some changes. Ma can't work anymore. So we're going to find someone to help us. We're going to visit some people, and they may let you stay with them. And if they do, you've got to be good and do everything they tell you. Do you understand?"

Ruby's large grey eyes looked back at her, and Beryl wished their mother would be more like Mary Trupper and rely on honest work. They could all pitch in together. But Jean had grown too fond of the gin. She'd sold Beryl off to her first man when she was only eight, and he'd been gentle compared to some Beryl had had since.

But Beryl still cried when she thought about the day her mother bathed her, put her in that purple dress and said there was a man who would be very nice to her. She'd picked up her mother's excitement as she was led to a big house. A maid dressed in black took Beryl and gave her another bath. She was put into a soft pink gown and had her hair curled into ribbons. The maid put her in a huge bed and placed a beautiful doll beside her. Beryl had waited there, holding the doll, stroking its hair, pretending it was her baby and holding her like her mother held Ruby. Then the man came in. He didn't say much but he lifted her gown. Beryl had been terrified. She'd tried to remember what her mother had said – think about something nice. Beryl had thought about her baby sister and how she smiled when you talked to her. But it was hard to think of Ruby when it hurt. She kept her promise to her mother and didn't cry out loud, only little tears that he didn't see. She was given a plate of chicken pie afterward and allowed to keep the doll. Her mother was really happy and even gave her three pennies of her own. Beryl had never had her own money before and she'd bought cakes for her and Ruby. She'd even given the doll to Ruby. She hadn't wanted to play with it anymore.

Beryl slowed her pace as they reached the Home of Industry. She stood at the bottom of the steps while Ruby jumped playfully. Beryl suddenly feared they would get no help from the do-gooders and what she would do then?

Ruby paused from play and looked up at her sister, waiting for a next move.

Beryl pulled her sister behind her as she hurried toward the heavy door knocker. "Okay, let's give it a try."

Winifred opened the door and looked cautiously at the two girls before giving them a smile. "Can I help you, young ladies?"

Beryl took a step closer to the door, pulling her sister behind her. "Yes please, Ma'am. I'd like you to help my little sister, take her in like, give her a home."

Winifred opened the door wider and led the girls into the cleanest room Beryl had ever seen. Bright sunshine came in the windows even though the day wasn't sunny. Winifred told them to sit and then left them alone. Beryl felt the softness of the seat beneath them.

Helen came in first. She noted the older girl's bright rags and guessed her trade. Constance recognised Beryl as the Truppers' neighbour.

Beryl sat a little uncomfortably on the soft settee. Juices from her work gushed onto her dress and she feared leaving a stain. She twisted so she rested on one hip. "I must be quick as my ma may have followed us and I promise to be honest so you'll see that we really need help." She pulled Ruby a little closer. "My ma and me work in the trade – you know, with men." She looked earnestly to see that the women understood her meaning. "My ma now has the sanitary man after her, so she can't work. He says she has a disease and has to go for tests. So now she wants to put my little sister out there. She's only five, but my mother says she's found a gentleman who will pay us £7 for the first time. That's a lot of money, and my ma is all set for it. So we ran away and came here because I hoped you could take our Ruby in and protect her. Please say you will. Please promise."

A silence fell over the room, and Beryl feared they'd guessed she'd lied about Ruby's age. Or maybe she'd offended them by talking about her trade.

Constance opened her mouth to talk, but her mother held up her hand so she could speak first. "Winifred, would you mind taking little Ruby for a cup of broth and maybe a biscuit. I'm sure the child's thirsty after all her excitement."

The older woman led Ruby by the hand and closed the door behind them.

"Would you like something also?" Constance asked.

The girl shook her head quickly. She was too impatient to eat or drink.

Helen glanced at her daughter before speaking. "From what I can understand of your story – and I fully understand your worries and appreciate completely why you ran from your family home – your mother is the legal guardian to both you and your sister. And because of this, we can do little to intervene."

Beryl sat forward quickly, forgetting about any juices staining the chair. "But you must. Do you know what I am talking about here? A full grown gentleman using my little sister as he would use a grown woman. Now, do you think that's fair?"

Helen held up her hand. "No, we don't think it's fair, but we have brothers in our church who are lobbying Parliament as we speak to outlaw this very trade." She paused, her voice a little slower. "But we can give you advice and assistance. We can even go and talk to your mother. But what we can't do is take your little sister in as though she were an orphan."

Beryl sat back in the chair wondering what to do next. She'd really believed in these people; after all, they'd helped the Truppers. A silence settled as she wondered where she could take Ruby next. She had four shillings in her pocket and could always earn more. But where would they stay?

Constance stood. "Look, while your sister is here, why don't I walk back to your house with you and try and talk to your mother. We may have some success."

Beryl shook her head. Her mother hated the do-gooders. She said they were interfering with the gin sales.

Helen's voice stayed soft. "Look, your sister can stay here until this crisis is over. Once your mother sees sense, we'll send your sister home. But what we are trying to tell you is that we can't take your sister in as though she had no kin. Do you understand?"

Beryl nodded miserably. She followed Constance out the door but knew the greeting her mother would give them.

*

Jean Brown threw a shoe as soon as they stepped in the door. It grazed Constance's ear, drawing a sliver of blood. Beryl led her outside and down to the street. Constance held her handkerchief to her ear to stem bleeding.

Beryl looked up at the tiny window that was her attic home. "I'm sorry, she's just drunk."

Constance grimaced. "Does your mother drink a lot?"

"Every day!" Beryl turned more earnestly to Constance. "Can you please keep Ruby until I sort this out?"

Constance looked at the girl's soft pink skin, marred only by the mole on her cheek. From her tiny stature and slim chest, she could be no more than eleven, although her small grey eyes knew more than they should. Constance felt that no child should have to struggle against such wickedness, and the thought gave her an idea that neither her mother nor the other governors at the Home of Industry would approve of. But sometimes didn't The Lord himself advocate extreme measures to fight evil. "Can your mother sign her name?" she asked.

Beryl shook her head.

Constance hurried forward, pulling Beryl after her. "I have an idea."

*

Sixty boys, naked except for their short trousers, stood in a snaking queue that travelled around the dining tables and along the kitchen wall. Dr Colpress sat at its head, beckoning each child one by one. He measured their height, scrutinised their skin for lesions, checked their teeth and peered into their eyes.

"How old are you?" he asked, fingering Lawrence's distended foot and pushing apart the toes.

Lawrence flushed, hating scrutiny of his foot. "I'm ten, Sir."

Dr Colpress pressed against Lawrence's foot, gauging the arc of the heel. "Well, the Canadian farmers may not like the look of this, young man."

Constance stood from where she'd been sitting at the doctor's side. "He's well educated – reads and writes better than most adults, even helps some of the other boys with their schooling. Someone will be grateful for his education."

Doctor Colpress let Lawrence's foot drop onto the floor and turned his attention to the boy's height. "You're a bit short for ten, aren't you?"

73

"Cook used to say it was because I didn't like eggs, although I did try and eat them to please her."

The doctor turned Lawrence to the side and scanned his posture. "No hint of any other deformity, and he's well spoken. I dare say you're right, someone will be happy to have him." He added Lawrence's name to the list of those headed for Canada.

The next boy stepped forward, his naked chest sunk down toward a distended belly.

"He hasn't been with us very long," Constance said. "But he'll fatten up."

The doctor ran his fingers over the boy's ribs. "Cough!" he instructed.

A crackled rasp erupted.

"It's more than food this lad needs – sounds like consumption." He shook his head and called the next boy forward.

This one was tall, almost the height of Constance herself. He gave her a wide grin. "Making sure me bits is all right, eh, Doctor?"

Constance recognised him as the boy who'd tried to sell her crockery at the market. "Name?" she asked him.

"Mikey Jones."

"How old are you?" Doctor Colpress asked.

"Before she died me ma says I was ten and that was five winters ago."

The doctor scanned the young man's skinny frame. "Nothing here that hard work won't cure." He wrote the name Mikey Jones on the Canada list.

The dark form of Henry stepped forward, his brown skin a sharp contrast to the pallor around him. But Constance held him back from the doctor's examination. She pointed to Horace, who was next in line, and beckoned him forward. The boy hurried to stand next to his brother.

She shook her head at the doctor. "They shouldn't be here. These boys are not going to Canada."

The doctor scanned their robust frames. "But they both look healthy lads, good and strong for farm work. How old are you, boys?"

"Twelve, Sir," they answered together.

Constance rested her hands on the boys' shoulders and spoke quietly to the doctor, although both boys could hear. "Annie MacPherson said the people of Toronto only want children who look British. She was very specific – no foreign skins."

The doctor shrugged. "Well, it's their loss. They're good, healthy boys."

Next to come forward was a ginger-haired boy with freckles. "I suppose this one will make our Canadian friends happy," the doctor muttered.

Constance ignored him.

At the doorway George watched the boys line up for physical examination. He wished he could go to Canada. All the boys in the Home of Industry were talking about it. You would get all the food you could eat, nice clothes and warm homes. There was even a good pay when you reached fifteen. The orphan, Lawrence, had worked out the total pay – $3 a month from age fifteen until eighteen. At the end of the three years they'd have $108. None of them knew what a dollar was, but if it was anything like a pound they'd be rich.

Lawrence said he'd use the money to pay off his father's debts. Mikey, the new boy, wanted to buy a big house with servants. Henry and Horace said they'd buy their own farm. George decided he would use the money to bring his mother and all his sisters to Canada where they could live in a nice house with a garden. He'd even told his mother what he would do. But she wouldn't hear of it, said it was too far and strangers don't take care of anyone but their own.

A tap on his shoulder made George jump. He turned quickly to see Constance.

"Aren't you supposed to be at work in the Beehive?"

George blushed. "I just wanted to see what was going on."

Constance smiled. "You really want to go to Canada, don't you?"

The boy blushed even more. "Me ma won't even let me talk about it."

"Do you want me to talk to her?"

George's eyes widened. His mother hadn't been happy about the Beehive, but Miss Constance had made a good job of persuading her.

Constance pointed to the line. "Well, get your shirt off. There's no point in talking to your mother unless the doctor gives you the all clear."

George stripped off at the doorway and stood in line. By the time he reached the doctor, the man's shoulders were sagging with weariness.

"Age?" he asked.

"Ten, Sir."

The doctor peered at George's nose then pushed it side to side. "What happened here?"

"A fight, Sir. I lost."

The doctor smiled. "You look fine." He wrote George's name on the Canada list.

*

But the word "Canada" had barely left Constance's mouth before Mary rose from her stool. "I said before – no – now what else do you need to hear?"

Constance stepped back, almost standing on George's toes. "I wouldn't bring it up if ..."

Mary pointed toward the rag that acted as a door. "If you won't drop this, then get out."

"It was just a suggestion," Constance said.

Mary dropped her hand but kept a firm glare on Constance. "Even if it means taking my kids out of your Beehive – there is no way I'm sending any of them off to this Canada."

"But Ma ..." George said.

"Don't 'Ma', me. We don't know where it is, or who you'll be with. Anything could happen there. What would your father think if he came back and found I'd let you go off to strangers?" Mary sat down, took up her paste brush and resumed work as though none of them were there.

Constance and George watched her bandaged fingers push against the rough grain of the sandpaper. Constance noticed a new sore had opened in a fork between Mary's fingers, and a new tactic occurred to her.

"So this is what you want your children to do for the rest of their lives – fold and paste matchboxes! Great future – stooped deformities, sores that won't heal, payment that barely affords a room in a cold attic."

Mary looked up quickly. "Well, if it's not good enough for you – you can leave."

"This is not about me! Is this really the life that you want for your children? Making matchboxes?" Constance pointed. "Do you want George growing older, never earning enough to take a wife. Tommy fighting the deformity this work has already given him. Rose and Mary are pretty and likely to attract men, but who's going to provide for them around here? Junie, well, you've said before, you'd like her to go into service."

Mary scanned the faces of her children.

Constance shook her head. "This is the life you think is good enough. No hope of anything better like a proper trade, plenty of food, regular schooling, a decent salary to save for a new beginning." Constance stared at the children. "Sorry, but your mother doesn't want much for you just so long as she has you here beside her – all poor."

Mary jumped up ready to swat at the words and the mouth they came from. "Who do you think you are? Miss Charitable who's never had her own children but who's high and mighty enough to tell me what to do with mine. You've no idea what you're talking about. You've no idea how a mother feels when a child steps outside the house and faces danger from thieves who'll murder them to steel their teeth and scalp them for their hair. You've no idea how it feels to see them work day and night and still not be able to earn enough for a bone to make broth. You've never heard your children's stomachs groan in hunger. How dare you tell me what I should and shouldn't do to help my children."

Constance felt herself shrink as Mary's dark eyes glared red with anger. Sense told her to back down, retreat from such rage. But another instinct, the one that told her Canada was absolutely the right answer, filled Constance with righteousness.

She straightened her shoulders and lowered her voice: "If the way you live now causes so much grief, then let your children go."

Constance felt Mary's palm burn through her cheek and didn't wait to see what would follow. Her feet took the steps as her heart raced through her ears.

*

Beryl heard the row. She heard Mary Trupper and Miss Constance yell at each other and then listened as the mission woman hurried down the stairs.

With her mother's snoring, she reached under the bed and pulled out the document Miss Constance had given her. She couldn't read what it said, but she knew where to put her mother's thumbprint. Miss Constance had placed an X near the spot.

Jean Brown lay on the bed. Her breath was heavy with gin and her nose flattened from disease: at least that's what she'd heard was a sign of the disease, although Beryl couldn't see why taking dirty pricks in the fanny could cause her mother's nose to fall flat.

She leaned forward and lifted her mother's hand. The heavy breathing slowed. Beryl waited until it settled into a new pace, then she drew the box from her pocket, opened it and pushed her mother's thumb against the ink. Despite her mother's greyish skin, it came away clearly dark. Beryl lifted the document.

In the best interests of my child, I, Jean Brown, hereby pass guardianship of my daughter Ruby Brown to the governors of the Home of Industry, 60 Commercial Street, London.

Beryl pushed her mother's thumb against the X.

Underneath, a second document bore her own name. With a smile, Beryl pushed for a second thumbprint. It was fainter than Ruby's but good enough. Without pausing to wipe her mother's hand free of ink, Beryl escaped to the Home of Industry.

*

Dear Papa,

I hope you receive this letter before you leave for Africa. I tried to write earlier but I cried so much that I was unable find the right words. Miss Winifred, who takes care of us here, eventually took the writing paper away because she said it upset me greatly. I am proud to say I am now calmer and write to wish you well in Africa. I am much interested in what you might find there.

I am not too sure whether the Home of Industry told you, but soon I will be making my own voyage – to Canada. I know a little of the country from my old tutor, Mr Johnstone. It is vast and a great deal unknown. The journey by ship will take two weeks. How long is the journey to Africa? Please write soon with all your news. Miss Constance says if you write to the Home of Industry in London, all letters will be forwarded to the Canadian family who offer me a home, so I shall still hear from you.

I must confess, I was not happy about travelling to Canada and seeking a new family. But Miss Constance promises that it will be temporary while I await news from you. She also promises to find me a family who value books and learning. She said I should be a great asset to such a family, so I am growing a little excited. In fact, many of the children here are excited about Canada, and now I feel I should hate to be left behind. We watched Miss MacPherson leave for Liverpool yesterday with one hundred boys. Some of them cried, but most waved happily as they climbed aboard the omnibus that was to take them to St. Pancras.

I shall leave with Miss Constance at the end of the month. Many of the boys here are already planning what they will do with the money they will have earned by age eighteen. I hope I shall be with you by the time I reach such an age. But if not, Father, I should have enough money to help you with your debts – $108.

Many of the boys expect to work on farms, so they are learning about farm animals. Unfortunately, the Home of Industry possesses no farm creatures so they are showing us pictorials instead. However, some of the boys do not understand scale and I heard one boy yesterday argue that a hen is bigger than a cow because that's what he saw in Miss Constance's drawing. Father, I am sure you will agree that this boy is in for a big surprise.

I will finish now as this is my only sheaf of paper, but I hope to hear from you soon. Maybe your ship is delayed and you can see me before I leave for Canada. I love you and think of you every day. Please remember me always.

As Lawrence signed his name Constance leaned over his shoulder and read the letter. "You have handsome penmanship," she said.

He looked up smiling at the praise while his eyes clearly watered from thoughts of his father.

Constance rested her hand lightly on his shoulder. "And you are very brave. Your father will be proud of your strength when he reads this letter."

Lawrence looked away, sudden doubt pulling at his emotions.

Other boys in the class stayed crouched over their notepaper. Some bit the ends of their pencils while others chewed their fingers and worried over what word to put next.

"Miss!" Mikey Jones put up his hand. He was now accompanied by a friend, Sam Pike. The two of them had signed up for Canada although neither of them paid any attention in class.

"What else will I tell me sister?"

Constance walked to the space between Mikey and Sam's desks. "Well, Mikey, what have you written?"

Mikey held up his letter. "Sally, I am off to a place called Canada. Don't ask me where it is as I don't know but I have heard the food and work is good there."

"Mikey, for very little schooling, that is a very good letter."

"Miss, a man in the penitentiary taught us."

Constance stared at him, her heart fluttering at the sudden news. "You were in a penitentiary? What for? Why didn't you tell us?"

Mikey shrugged. "You never asked so I didn't think you wanted to know."

Constance felt herself turn pale. She was sure Canadian farmers didn't want young criminals.

"It was thieving, Miss. But we did our time. And we learned some writing from one of the wardens, didn't we, mate?" Mikey pushed Sam's shoulder affectionately.

Constance slowed her breathing. The boys had been corrected. They'd been punished and now it was only decent to offer them a new beginning. And what better place to start than a completely new environment far from temptation, where a living could be earned honestly?

"Miss, what's it like on a boat?" Sam asked.

Constance thought quickly for an answer. "Sam, I believe it is just like being in a coach except you are on water. I have heard tell that there can be some sideways motion."

Sam raised his hand again. "But Miss, I've heard that the movement makes you ill. For days, you can vomit until there's nothing left to come out, Miss."

Noises of disgust came from several boys.

Constance feared losing some of their enthusiasm, but then a knock on the classroom door brought Winifred into the room. Constance sighed with relief.

"A visitor," Winifred said. "She says it's important."

Constance left Winifred in charge of the classroom of boys and hurried to the reception hall where Mary Trupper sat in a visitor's chair. Out of the attic apartment, she looked small and grubby, although her hands were wrapped in fresh bandages.

She rose when she saw Constance. "Miss, I've come here because ..." she paused, stuttering over the next word, and Constance feared she was removing her children from the Beehive.

Mary took a breath, almost coughing before speaking quickly: "I've been thinking about this Canada. I'm sorry I struck you but you can't go telling people what to do with their children." She stared at Constance, making sure her words were understood.

Constance nodded and indicated a seat.

Mary sat but her words came out fast: "No matter that, I've been thinking and maybe you're right – although I'm not giving you all my kids, mind. Just George, cos he's desperate to go. And Junie because I think she would do better if she trained to be a housemaid. She needs things to think about or her mind just wanders and matchbox making just makes her drift off so she doesn't do well."

Constance leapt to her feet ready to give all the reassurance she could think of. But Mary spoke quickly:

"Of course, George says he will write every month because his letters are bound to get better when he gets over there and goes to school more regular. And, he says, with Rose and the girls getting lessons here then they'll be able to read and write back so we'll be in constant touch. And he promises to take care of Junie and that they'll stay together."

She paused for a moment. "If I'm honest with myself, I trust you, after all we're doing so much better than we used to."

Constance restrained the urge to hug Mary. Instead, she took the woman's bandaged hand in her own. "I'm so pleased you've changed your mind. You won't regret this."

Mary swallowed her breath causing a large knot of anxiety to knit in her stomach.

*

Constance held up an oblong pot with a lid. "A salmon kettle," she announced to the girls who sat before her.

She placed it down on the table, her arms shaking a little at its weight, and lifted a pot that was square. "A turbot kettle," she said.

The next dish she took up was taller and narrower. "Now, this kettle here is very useful as it can be used for any kind of fish."

The girls stared at the dishes with a mixture of fear and worry. Most of them only had one pot at home. Beryl wondered what salmon and turbot looked like that they needed their own dishes. She glanced at her sister. Ruby held Junie's hand. Despite being neighbours for years, the girls had barely seen each other. But since joining the housekeeping classes at the Home of Industry they'd become tight friends, sitting together, whispering and giggling as they shared Junie's rag doll. Beryl felt guilty about leaving Ruby's doll at home, but she wasn't going back for it now.

Constance held up a large pot she called a milk pan. "Those of you who go to town families may not need to use this. But for the girls in the country, it will be your closest companion."

She placed the pan on the table and held up a drawing of a cow. Beryl thought it look like a plump horse. "This is where we get milk, cream and butter. And, as most of you know, butter comes from cream which comes from milk." Constance walked over to a small wooden barrel that sat in its own stand. "Every single day, no matter how many other chores you have, you must skim your cream until it thickens. And, when the cream is suitably thick, it should be warmed slowly – near a coal fire is fine – before it is poured into your butter churner." She patted the wooden barrel.

Beryl's mother loved butter, and guilt pricked Beryl's conscience. If she could just know her mother was fine, she would relax more easily into the classes, maybe even look forward to her new life in Canada. But she couldn't help but wonder if her mother was out looking for them or had she gone back to work? Was she worried about them or was she too drunk to raise a fuss? Or maybe the Sanitary Man had found her.

The empty butter barrel made a knocking sound as Constance turned the handle. "You need to churn for the time it takes for a candle to burn the length of your little finger. It's hard work, but slowly butter will form."

Constance grew a little breathless from turning the barrel. She paused and stood upright: "If it doesn't come together, put in a little bit of warm water to loosen it up and keep churning."

In the next classroom, a gentleman farmer, a friend of Minister Beckett, was teaching the boys the signs of a healthy cow.

"Look into its eyes," Robert Pascal said as he peered at them through a monocle. "The eyes should be bright – no spots. Next check its back for straightness and watch it walk. Any sign of limping and tell the blaggard who's selling it that you want better for your money."

Mikey and Sam laughed. Others, unsure of showing disrespect, stayed silent.

"The most important part of the cow to examine are the teats!" Mr Pascal stood a little straighter and pointed a forefinger at the drawing on the board. "They should be firm and full, no hard knobbles."

"Yeah, not like some of the old whores outside the penny theatres," Mikey whispered, too loudly.

Mr Pascal turned to the voice. "Yes, you are right, young man. They shouldn't be anything like the sagging dugs you see on the women of our streets. You know, you can always spot an old cow who's been milked for too long because her teats will hang lower and swing as she moves. Young cow udders sit closer to the body."

George couldn't picture a cow's teats. All he could visualise were whores' breasts – like Beryl's mothers.

Mr Pascal held up his forefinger again. The boys knew that he was about to make an important point. "Now, to milk a cow, use the fingers of your hand – no thumbs." He held up his own hand with the fingers curled and the thumb upright. "And you must squeeze gently on the udder and teat all at the same time, pulling slightly downward. Let me see all of you hold up your hands and pretend to milk a cow."

The boys curled up their fists as if to squeeze on a pretend udder. Sam and Mikey laughed as they talked of girls whose breasts they would rather work. George couldn't keep his thumb out of the action. Lawrence held his upright and out of the way until he had the motion perfectly.

"Great form!" Mr Pascal called to them. "Those Canadian farmers should be proud to have all of you."

*

Upstairs, Helen checked each child's record, noting especially that guardian permission slips had been thumb-marked or signed.

Lawrence's father had sent a letter forfeiting all rights to his son. Helen put it to the back of Lawrence's file as though hiding it from the boy himself. He still believed his father would come for him, even travel to Canada to get him. But the man was a gambler who had already lost the money he'd earned to pay back his original debts. Helen shook her head at the loss of it all.

Sam Pike and Mikey Jones had declared themselves orphans, and Helen had no reason to doubt their honesty. They clearly had learned life on the streets and now they saw fresh opportunity overseas, who could deny them the chance to succeed there.

But Helen was puzzled by the files of Beryl and Ruby Brown. A mother keen to sell her youngest child into prostitution rarely agrees to give the child away. She examined Jean Brown's thumbprints but saw nothing suspicious.

Thumbprints from Mary Trupper were more smudged, but Helen had seen the woman make her mark, tears tracking her grey face as she did so. "I do believe you when you say it's the best thing," she had said to Constance.

Helen prayed her daughter had the wisdom to recognise good parents from bad in Canada. While she had been exposed to evil and degradation through the Home of Industry, far more than most girls of her age, she had been protected from those who were openly deceitful.

The parents who came through the Home of Industry were easy to gauge; they'd either succumbed to weakness or been buckled through bad fortune. Judgements of them were easy. In a foreign land with a shortage of labour, those seeking extra hands for hard work might believe their own words when they promised to provide a home worthy of their own offspring. But farm work is hard and food can run short even in lands rich in good earth.

Helen's heart felt heavy as she gazed at the children's names before her. Finally, footsteps made her look up, although she recognised the fast pace that belonged to her daughter.

Constance threw herself into the small armchair. "Mother, I must confess, until that class I did not know my salmon kettle from my milk pan."

Helen rubbed her face as though trying to wipe away doubts about the project. "Constance, we must be clear in what we are doing here. If learning about pots is too complex, maybe we should concentrate on more basic instruction such as washing laundry and bed-making."

Constance shook her head. "Annie MacPherson said the women in Canada want housemaids, not scullery maids. She said they can find local women to do the really dirty jobs. They really want housemaids as good as those in England, and we can train our girls. I know they'll be good."

Helen sighed then leaned forward across the desk so that her hands almost reached the other side. "Constance, you know I have grave doubts about this venture. But my voice is a minority and I accept that this business is going ahead."

"It's not a business," Constance said quickly. "It's a vital opportunity to take children out of our city squalor and let them grow in a land ..."

"Yes, yes, I've heard all that," Helen said quickly. "But, I need you to promise me certain things. It is a huge responsibility you are undertaking – all the hopes and dreams of those children and their families is being carried by you."

Constance nodded, her mother's gravity causing her to pause.

"I need you to promise me that you will visit each home before sending a child there. You must question all the family, and if you have any doubt whatsoever that our children might not receive good care, then you must dismiss that family from any application. Do you understand?"

Constance nodded.

Helen stood, feeling more confident in her advice. "You must ensure that siblings stay together. These children have already lost their homeland, some have left parents behind. I want you to promise me you will find homes that will take siblings and rear them together. I also need you to emphasise to these foster families that the children will be visited and the homes checked for good care. They must not neglect the children we give them."

"Mother, I understand the responsibility I carry on this trip."

Helen turned to stare at her daughter. "I hope you do. They are not parcels we are delivering. These are innocent children who have received little in life. We must protect them."

"Mother, trust me. I will care for the children as though they were my own." She stood and looked at the files on her mother's desk. "Now, what paperwork is still to be done?"

Helen sighed. "Don't dismiss what I say, Constance. Only a mother knows the wealth of the cargo you carry."

"I am not dismissing your concerns, Mother. But I am asking you to have faith in me. I understand the importance of my mission. My brother Mathew may have carried Bibles to Africa, but I truly understand that my treasure is far greater."

Niggling doubts played in Helen's chest and would not go away.

*

Winifred sat with a stack of cards at her desk. The boys pushed forward as she handed them out:

I hereby promise to abstain from the use of all Intoxicating Liquors, including beer, gin and cider, and refrain from all profanity.

"What does it mean?" George asked the boy behind him.

The small red-haired boy shrugged. "My ma said I was to do everything that they asked me, so if they want me to stick ma thumb on it then that's what I'll do."

"It means," said Lawrence, "that you promise not to drink alcoholic spirits or to swear."

George let Winifred blacken his thumb and push it heavily beside what he recognised as his name. She gave George the card, and he held it against his chest.

"I will never drink anyway," said the red-haired boy. "My da drank so much he fell into the river and put us in the workhouse. Me ma made me promise never to take it up." He let Winifred push his thumb next to his name, Harry Twistle.

Lawrence held his hands behind his back. "Please, Miss Winifred, must we use my thumbprint? I am well able to sign my name."

Winifred handed him the pen and smiled as he wrote a carefully stylised *Lawrence Charles Anthony Masterton*.

"That's a grand name," she told him.

"My mother named me after both grandfathers," he said.

Over in the girls' line, Beryl held out her thumb before Constance could ask for it.

"What are we doing?" Ruby asked.

"We're promising not to drink gin or swear," Beryl said.

Ruby pointed her finger at her sister. "You've drank gin, I've seen you. You were all silly and it scared me."

Beryl pulled Ruby to her. "Well, don't worry it won't happen ever again."

Constance pushed Beryl's thumb against her name.

"Do I have to do it too?" asked Ruby.

Constance took the small girl's hand. "Well, we don't want you falling into evil ways while you're in Canada, do we?"

"But you said Canada didn't have any bad things."

Constance smiled. "There is bad everywhere, even in Canada. Temptation can lure even the most virtuous among us, Ruby, and we must be on our guard at all times. We are all soldiers for The Lord."

Ruby gave Junie a puzzled look as she let her thumb be blackened and pushed against the paper. She stood back and watched as Junie did the same.

With the Temperance Pledges signed, Constance led the children to the dining room. Instead of meals, the tables were laid out with clothing, bags and stacks of books.

"Children! We need you to line up in ranking of height, with the smallest at the front," Constance called out.

With boys at the right, and girls at the left, the children took several minutes to find their places. A dark-haired girl stood between Junie and Ruby.

"I'm Hannah," she said.

Junie gave her a quick glance, searching her features for Ruby's prettiness. She turned quickly away and smiled over her shoulder at Ruby. "Would you like to hold little Victoria?" she asked her friend.

Ruby nodded, and Junie quickly passed her the rag doll.

Constance called the smallest girl forward. She looked about five and still wore the striped dress from the workhouse. Her eyes grew wide as Constance held up a corduroy dress, measuring it against her.

It was a little big, and Constance tutted at a button that hung by a long thread. "Our Mothers Union need better supervision. Some have been lax in their sewing," she called out to Winifred, who was busy holding up a blue serge jacket against a small boy.

After two hours each child was matched with a jacket or cape, corduroy suit or dress, strong boots, red scarf and a cap or bonnet.

"This is your travelling outfit," Constance told the children. "You may try it on now, but it must not be worn before next Friday when we leave for Liverpool Docks."

Noise rose like smoke from a fire as the children hurried to try on their new clothes. The boots had been donated by a church member, and many of the children struggled to move as the stiff leather clamped their ankles and restricted their toes. Lawrence gave up trying to push his bad foot into the new boot.

"Please, Miss Winifred, do I have to take these?"

Winifred shook her head. "Do your own boots still fit?"

Lawrence held his brown leather boots up for display. "They're a little worn but very comfortable, Miss."

"Then, I'm sure they'll do."

Constance helped the tiny workhouse girl into her dark blue dress. She pulled the ties into a tight bow so the dress fitted around her small waist. "Dora, it's a little big, but I think you'll grow into it very quickly."

The small girl looked down at herself and grinned, showing two rows of rotting teeth.

Beryl helped Ruby and Junie with their dresses. The girls held hands, happy to be wearing the same outfit. "I wish we had a dress like this for Victoria," Ruby said.

Constance let the children enjoy their new clothes for a few more minutes and then clapped her hands. "Now, we must all fold our clothes neatly, and place them on a table near your name – I trust you will all recognise your name by now. Any problems, then ask myself or Miss Winifred. Now do this quickly as we have one more important item to give you."

Boosted by the prospect of another surprise, the children moved fast, many finding their own name while Dora and Junie needed help from Beryl.

Constance held up a brown canvas bag with a long shoulder strap. "Children, this will be your travelling sack. You will all receive one of these and in it you will have …" She placed the bag on the table and pulled out a white towel which was rolled around a tin bowl, a mug, a knife, fork, spoon, pocket knife and a Bible.

"Also in this bag," Constance announced, "you should carry your Temperance Pledge, for many families will want to know that you are clean-living children. And you may take one small item from home." This was Helen's idea, although Constance wasn't sure that Annie MacPherson would approve.

George immediately knew that Junie would bring her doll. He would like to have a pictorial image of his mother, but that was something they didn't have. Instead, he would have to carry her in his mind.

Lawrence decided he would take a copy of his favourite book, *Robinson Crusoe*.

Beryl shook her head. She and Ruby had nothing from home. They would have a completely new start.

*

Mary lay on the bed, hiding her sobs in a pillow. Lying beside her, Tommy's tears ran freely, and he wished his mother would hug him. He turned, rubbing his face into Rose's dress, but his sister cried her own quiet tears, her hands holding onto Maggie, as they watched their mother's shoulders tremble in suppressed sobs.

Across town, George tried not to cry as he boarded the train. But the loud rumble of the engine, the whistles, the vast station in the evening darkness and, most of all, the image of his mother's face as he'd left the Home of Industry, all crept up his chest and into his throat like a lump of wadding and made him sob despite all his efforts to be strong.

He could still feel his mother's arms as they'd wrapped him tight, his skin tingled as if it still felt her touch. George pulled a rag from his pocket to wipe his tears, but then a blow to the shoulders made him turn.

He saw Mikey, his arm ready to give another slap. "Don't wail like a baby – maybe in Canada, you'll get a new nose as well as a new life."

Junie looked up at George as if surprised to see him there. She held her rag doll as if she were out for a daily jaunt. There had been no tears when she'd left their mother, and George wondered if she even knew where they were going.

George led her quickly to an empty pair of seats and spoke quietly. "Junie, we'll come back and get Ma and the others. When we're grown and done well, we'll come back." Tears coursed forward again as he saw his mother's wide eyes as she'd tried to give him last-minute instructions to take care, watch Junie, all the things he expected her to say, but no words had come.

Thinking about it again, George wanted to bawl like a baby, but he had to be strong for Junie. He took a deep breath and looked out the window at a large steam engine on the next track.

Across the aisle, Beryl stroked Ruby's hair. The younger sister had been sick during the omnibus ride, and Beryl worried that she might throw up during the whole journey.

Ruby's pale face looked up at her sister. "How long until we get there?"

Beryl smiled. "A lot of days – too many to count." She smoothed a wisp of curl away from her sister's face. "Miss Constance is with us, so I'm sure we'll all be fine."

Lawrence peered anxiously out the window, watching the crowds that pushed in all directions, peering for the sight of a small man with deep, dark hair like his own. A man wearing a dark blue overcoat and a tall hat faded with wear. Maybe, somehow, his father hadn't left for Africa, but had paid off his debts and was now on his way to the station to get him so they could be together for always.

Lawrence's eyes hurt from staring at all the men he saw in dark coats and tall hats. His heart raced when he thought he saw his father's long nose and dark eyes, but then the man hurried closer, and Lawrence saw that the chin was all wrong and the build too frail.

"Who you looking for?" asked the boy beside him.

Lawrence turned, seeing the boy's red hair through watery eyes. "My father, I thought he might appear."

The boy gave Lawrence's arm a gentle shove. "Maybe he's busy with something."

Lawrence nodded, thinking of his father working hard to pay back debts so they could be together.

The red-haired boy's breath was sour. "I cried when I left me ma at the workhouse. But she said I've to grow strong and work hard so we can be together. She made me promise to be good and do everything I'm told. She said this is the best opportunity we could ever have." He looked down at his blue serge trousers. "She cried when she saw me in this uniform, said it made her heart sore with pride. Soon she had me all blubbing and then got annoyed because I wiped me nose on me sleeve." He smiled at the memory. "She said, 'Harry, be sure to keep your manners because people always respect manners whether you're nine or forty-nine.'"

Lawrence looked at the boy who was smaller than him. "If you're nine, then you're smaller than me."

Harry nodded. "I suppose I am. Me ma worries that someone might bully me, but I can take care of myself."

"And I'll help," said Lawrence. "Given that I am a bit bigger."

Harry smiled.

"Look!" Constance's voice startled them. She pointed toward a group of men in black carrying brass instruments. "It's the church band."

As the band hurried forward, Constance saw her mother and Minister Beckett leading the way. "Children, the church band have come to play us off." She moved quickly through the carriage aisle and stepped down onto the platform. "What a lovely surprise."

The band grouped into a semi-circle in front of the train windows. The children pushed against the windows to watch. The tuba began, and then the trumpet and they launched into "There Is a Better World, They Say".

Helen pulled her daughter to her. "Please, take care."

Constance nodded. "Mother, of course I will."

"Think always of your precious cargo."

Constance looked up at the train carriage where children crowded each window, all wearing the jackets, capes, caps and bonnets that had been carefully sewn for them.

"I understand, Mother."

Helen shook her head. "No, you don't. You've never been a mother and you can never know the responsibility that's now on your head. All I can say is go by your instincts. If you don't feel good about a family or situation, pass them by. Don't leave a child where you think there's the remote possibility that they might be ill-treated."

"Mother, these are my children now, and I will be sure they go to good homes." Constance leaned over to give her mother a final hug.

Helen looked into her daughter's eyes. "The other thing to remember out there is that there's a shortage of women to make good wives. Keep your eyes open. I may get grandchildren out of you yet."

Constance smiled playfully. "Mother, I'm going to be much too busy for any of that."

Down the platform, the conductor blew his whistle and Constance quickly boarded the steps. The train vibrated beneath her feet then slowly began to move. Constance hurried into the children's carriage, hearing the band play more heartily behind her. Some children cheered and waved, but others wept quietly. Constance scanned their heads, happy at the prospect of their adventure.

"Let us sing!" She called out, beginning a stirring verse of "Jesus, Bid Me Shine". Most of the children raised their voices and sang their way through the dark tunnels that led the group out of London and into the green fields of Finsbury.

*

It was late when Constance passed through the railway carriage to check on the children. She smiled when she saw Lawrence and Harry snuggled together in sleep. They were both alone and would make good companions. In the next row Junie dozed against George's shoulder while he stared out of the window watching the dark countryside pass before him.

Beryl slept with Ruby folded across her lap, the two sisters breathing in unison. Hannah, who liked to stay close to Junie and Ruby, lay cuddling Dora, the smallest girl.

Sam threw three fours on the dice, but Mikey looked up to see Constance headed their way. He scrambled fast and shoved the coloured cubes under his thigh and pretended to sleep. He didn't understand why she was so against dice. It wasn't really gambling, as they had no money to make bets. They just liked to see if their number came up.

Up in the baggage netting were canvas bags marked with each child's name. George had puzzled over what to bring from home. Eventually he packed his father's old shirt, the one his ma let him wear when he sold newspapers on cold nights. It still didn't fit, but his ma said he would grow into it. Junie had her rag doll and a matchbox. Rose had given it to her so she'd always remember home.

Constance sat back in the last row of seats and dozed until her head jolted forward in sleep. She decided to sit upright and read her scripture, but the day had been so hectic that the rhythm of the train easily lulled her back to sleep. A smile played around her lips as she felt the excitement of Canada where good, clean families waited anxiously for her children. Annie MacPherson said it was green and fertile and you could travel the country roads for a whole day and see only two or three people. She'd also said the air was so fresh it filled the soul with the breath of Jesus.

A whistle drew many awake as the train pulled into Liverpool Docks. Through the window, the dawn sunshine lit through a heavy fog.

"Is this Canada?" asked Ruby.

Beryl gripped her sister's hand. "Not for another two weeks. Remember, we've to take a boat."

George pointed to a large steamship with men carrying barrels and crates on board. "Is that ours?"

No one answered, not even Constance. She climbed down the train steps to seek help on where they should go. The children watched from the window as she approached an elderly man in a uniform. He was probably a captain, said Mikey. The man pointed behind him, and the children watched Miss Constance hurry toward a plump man who directed her into a small wooden office where she disappeared.

"I'm hungry," Junie said to no one in particular.

George pulled a small chunk of bread from his pocket and pulled it into two parts. He passed one to Junie, but a fast hand intercepted it.

"Hey, Beak Nose has food," Mikey said as he swiped the second piece of bread from George's hand and passed it to Sam.

Junie looked at her brother and began to cry.

George pulled her into a hug. "It's okay. Miss Constance will be back soon, and she'll see we have something to eat."

The children watched eagerly for their guardian to emerge.

"I need a piss," Sam said.

"I'm thirsty," came a voice from the back.

Inside the wooden office, Constance sipped a refreshing cup of tea while the shipping clerk copied all one hundred names of her children onto his register.

Constance watched him, wishing he would write a little faster.

The clerk's crisp white cuffs were wrapped in a handkerchief to protect them from inky pages. "Miss, we've already had your sister missionary here with two lots of street kids. Now you're taking a bunch. This should make the streets of London a lot safer. Maybe you can start to clear them out of Liverpool soon. The city's awash with the little thieves."

Constance sat a little taller. "My children are not thieves. They are simply in need of good Christian homes."

He looked up at her from beneath his brows. "I beg to differ. I believe a good hiding would do many of them the world of good, teach them to respect other people's property."

Constance knew there was no point in prompting an argument. She sipped the last of her tea. "Our sister church in

Liverpool are meant to meet us here with food and refreshment for the children. Do you have any idea where I might find them?"

"Over at the ticket hall, Miss. They can't come any closer, but you can talk to them through the fence."

"What about the food and refreshments we need?"

"They'll pass them through the fence, Miss." He handed her papers allowing her to board the *S.S. Sardinian.* "You must be aboard by 8 o'clock for a noon sailing."

Constance stepped out into the cool fog and looked around for the ticket office. A grubby man, dark and dried up from the sun, directed her to a path between warehouses. She hurried back to the train and ordered the children to disembark with their bags.

"In twos please, and stay together! Follow me closely, we don't want anyone to get lost and end up on the wrong ship."

Beryl took Ruby's hand firmly in her own. George held on to Junie so tight she squirmed for him to let go.

They followed the other children through damp air that smelled of old fish. George's stomach growled.

"Hey, Beaky, half your food's for me!" Mikey's voice came from behind.

"And I'll have half your sister's," Sam said.

George hurried ahead to put distance between them. He could see Constance's bonnet as she led them between warehouses and out to the ticket office. A brass band broke into a tune, startling Junie and sending a flock of birds into the sky.

Constance stopped and the children gathered around her. George's stomach gnawed at his chest, and he moistened his mouth before swallowing. The band moved into a slower tune, and George wondered how many more songs they had to suffer.

At the centre of the group, Constance's eyes grew moist as she gazed at all the little ones she was saving. Finally, a trumpet let out the last sound, and a woman in a large bonnet stepped forward and began ladling broth into bowls. She handed these over the fence to Constance who handed them out to each child. George saw Junie served, then took his and led his sister to the far side of the group, looking over his shoulder to see Mikey and Sam weren't following. He drank the broth quickly even though it burned his mouth and throat. "Hurry, Junie, before those boys take it away."

Junie sipped. "It's hot," she said. George blew on it for her.

Constance came around with a basket of bread to dip in the soup and noticed George's empty bowl.

"Why, George, there is more."

He followed her through the throng of children and watched over his shoulder as Constance passed his bowl over the fence and received it full. Mikey walked forward, his eyes tight on George.

"There's seconds!" George told him quickly. "Miss Constance will help you." He hurried back to Junie, relieved to drink his second bowl without fear.

*

The gangplank trembled under Beryl's feet, threatening to throw her off balance. She felt Ruby's small weight on the plank behind her, but then as more children joined them, their heavier tread sent out vibrations and Beryl felt sure they would fall. She gripped the rope balustrade tight with both hands while two canvas bags weighed down her shoulders. "Ruby, hang onto my skirt!"

Beneath them the water swirled between the ship and the dock. Beryl felt the pull of Ruby's hands on her skirt as she stepped forward and onto the deck. When both girls were safely aboard the *S.S. Sardinian*, she let out a sigh of relief even though its wood flooring felt strangely fragile.

Around them, small boats sheathed in dirty tarp hung over the deck while four tall masts towered above them. Doorways within the floor stood open and dark, tanned men stopped work to watch the children's arrival.

As Beryl felt the men's stares, her thighs clenched tight. She gripped Ruby's hand and hurried after Mikey and Sam – who trailed George and Junie – as they pursued the trail of children behind Miss Constance. At a narrow passageway they funnelled through a doorway that led down dark stairs to the sleeping compartments.

Constance stood in the narrow passage watching as each child tumbled down. "Girls to the right! Boys to the left!"

George slipped back and pushed Junie's hand into Beryl's. "Take care of her in there, will you?"

Beryl didn't want any more responsibility, but she knew that George didn't have a choice. He had to sleep separate from his sister. Beryl led Ruby and Junie through a small doorway. Hannah and little Dora kept tight behind.

A dim light came from two portholes. Columns of beds, three high, spanned the room with a long narrow table at the centre. On each bed lay a rolled up straw mattress and a blanket square. A large bucket stood in the corner. Beryl wondered if it was for drinking water, washing or body sewage.

"Don't worry," Constance called out as she scrutinised her own bed roll for stains and dirt. "We won't be spending much time down here. We'll use it for sleeping and keeping our bags, but during daylight hours, we'll be up on deck making the most of the fresh air."

She put her own large bag on the bed. "Now, choose a place to sleep, leave your bag neatly on top and file quietly out onto the deck. I'll meet you there after I talk to the boys."

Beryl led Ruby and Junie between beds, shuffling sideways because there was so little room. They made their way to the corner where she felt they would have more privacy. On the floor lay wisps of cotton that must have fallen from a crate on the previous voyage. Beryl put their three bags on a tier of beds and sat down. The skin on her neck felt rough and sore from the rub of her serge collar. She inspected the girls. Junie's neck was so thin that the collar barely touched her skin, but Ruby's neck had grown red with abrasion. She unbuttoned her sister's top button then unfastened her own.

"It's cold," Ruby told her.

"It's just to give your skin a rest. You don't want sores on your neck, do you?"

Ruby shook her head and smiled at Junie. The two girls clasped hands. Junie held up her grey rag that still shared the vague outline of a doll. Beryl gave a sigh of relief, feeling that Junie might be a help rather than a drain.

"Can we play?" Ruby asked.

Beryl shook her head. "Not yet, let's go up on deck. Miss Constance wants to talk to us."

The girls followed the others up the stairs, all blinking as they reached daylight. A passing sailor winked at Ruby. Beryl pulled her sister toward her and fixed him with a glare.

"It's alright, Miss, I have a daughter about her age at home." He hurried on and disappeared into a hold.

Miss Constance clapped her hands for attention. "Now, children, the captain has said we can have a special part of the deck just for ourselves. I think it's somewhere down here." She led her flock through a narrow passageway between the bridge and a lifeboat. "He said it is to the rear of the ship, near lifeboat number thirteen." Constance felt the reputation of this inauspicious number, but she was happy to see the area was spacious enough and the boats offered shelter from the wind that blew off the sea.

She bid the children sit in a circle. "Now, children, the captain says we must depart in less than two hours to catch the tide, and I think it beholden on us to sing a song that calls on the blessing of our Lord to see us on our way. Don't you think?"

Several heads nodded, and Constance tapped her foot three times as an introductory beat.

Beryl's head dropped onto her chest. She hated singing. She didn't know the words and her voice couldn't make the high and low notes like the others. Ruby, who'd learned the words and tunes easily, always giggled when she tried. So she opened and shut her mouth mutely while listening as Ruby and Junie sang the words:

"What a friend we have in Jesus,
All our sins and griefs to bear ..."

Constance eyes brimmed with tears as the children reached the end of the song. Stirred with emotion, she clapped her hands. One hundred hopeful faces gazed up awaiting her next instruction. She would not let these children down, she promised herself. They had faith, and she would see them to the Promised Land.

"Now, children, we are on a quest for a new life, a better life. You have all been very brave so far. But I must ask you to stay good and orderly. Everyone, including Our Lord above, will be watching you for good behaviour. I know you are good children. Our Lord knows you are good children. Now, we need to show the rest of the passengers on this ship that you are good children."

Sam farted, sending a wave of foul air downwind. Mikey clamped his hand to his mouth and giggled.

"We will be living in cramped conditions for the next two weeks, and we must be tolerant of each other. Now, I am going to give you instructions and I ask that you follow them absolutely, do you understand?"

Rows of heads nodded.

"The toilets are to the rear of the ship, down two flights of stairs. Step carefully going down, we don't want any accidents." Constance hadn't seen the toilets yet, but the captain had told her the location and warned her about the steps. "Our food will be delivered to our berthing rooms, but we must serve ourselves. To avoid fighting, I will serve you. I will start in the girls' berth then move to the boys. You are all responsible for washing your own bowls and spoons. A bucket of water will be provided in each cabin for this. Another bucket of water will be available each morning for washing. You must all wash your faces each day. Do you understand?"

Heads nodded.

"We are going to a new land for a new life, and we must all look our best."

Noise like the heavy tread of a thousand feet and deep bellowing groans made Constance turn. Two sailors led cows and pigs up the gangplank.

A few of the children let out frightened squeals.

Mikey pointed. "Miss, what are they?"

Constance smiled. "Why, Mikey, I thought you might recognise them from Mr Pascal's lessons. The taller one is a cow, while the other is our friend, the pig."

Mikey sank back in wonder. "I thought they were smaller – like birds."

Lawrence giggled, and Sam sent him a warning glare.

"No, Mikey, cows and pigs can be bigger than us." Constance watched as two sailors led more cows onto the boat. "I hope you remember that we need the cows for milk as well as their meat."

Mikey nodded vaguely, trying to reconcile the drawings Mr Pascal had shown him with the vast beasts that had just passed by. He leaned over to Sam. "Did you see those dugs?"

The boys laughed out loud. Constance decided it was time for another hymn. "Children let us sing. Let us raise our voices to God and ask for his guidance through our journey."

She tapped her foot to signal the intro to "With Mercy and With Judgement", but the sound of another song came through the air. Constance turned in the direction of the notes. Within moments, a young woman emerged from the gap between the bridge and lifeboats. Her lace bonnet and ribbon-edged crinoline looked out of place against the faded and patched lifeboats. Behind her followed a line of girls in descending height all dressed in identical hats, cloaks, dresses and boots. They sang, "When Israel's tribes were parched with thirst", like their hearts and hopes depended on it. Constance and her children watched as they slowly filed onto the rear of the deck and sat at the opposite corner.

The young woman and Constance stared at each other for several moments. Constance wanted to ask the fashionable woman what she was doing. The Home of Industry was supposed to be the only charity taking children to Canada. Annie MacPherson and Minister Beckett were sure of this. Constance swallowed, realising she needed to do something. But as Constance opened her mouth to call out a greeting, the woman turned her back to sing with her flock.

Constance looked at her own children. They could hardly sing a different song. The children stared, awaiting her instruction.

"Children, why don't we talk about Jesus?"

Behind her the large group of girls raised their voices in "What a Friend We Have in Jesus" while Constance told her children about Moses fleeing Egypt and the search for the promised land.

*

As the *S.S. Sardinian* lurched from its moorings, Ruby looked up at her sister and tugged on her dress. "Will we be rich in Canada?"

Beryl smiled. "I think so."

The fog had lifted, and George felt dizzy as he gazed at the expanse of space that lay ahead. He had never dreamed that the world was so big. He turned to watch Liverpool's dense docks shrink from view and felt his mother, sisters and brother grow already distant. He wondered what they were doing at this moment, no doubt at work and thinking of him and Junie. Tears, salted his lips and, as he rubbed them dry with his sleeve, the gruff serge scraped at his skin.

Then a push made him stumble against Beryl and Ruby.

Mikey grinned down into George's face. "Yah! Beak Boy is crying! Must be missing his ma."

George turned angrily. "It's the wind." He stepped toward the older boy, his jaw set for a fight.

Mikey lunged forward so his head clearly towered over George. "Yeah, like we're all crying."

"Boys, stop that right now," Constance called out as she moved between them. "Mikey, you stay to the right of our group. George, you stay to the left. Only when the two of you can get along will you be allowed to mix freely."

George moved away pulling Junie with him. Beryl and Ruby followed with Hannah and Dora behind.

Junie gripped her brother's hand tight. "I don't like them boys, George. They scare me."

"Shhh, Junie. I'll take care of you."

Mikey and Sam strode in the opposite direction throwing threatening glances behind them.

Lawrence and Harry stood against the railings watching the waves.

"There are fish as big as men in this water," Lawrence said.

Harry thought of the fish he'd seen at the market before he went to the workhouse. "Fish are small things – no bigger than your arm."

Lawrence nodded. "But out here there are fish too big for the nets. I've read that some of them are as big as this ship. They're called whales."

Harry grinned. "You're a good one for stories, Lawrence. If we see a fish as big as a man then I'll have you write a letter to me ma telling her, because she would never believe me if I said it."

The two boys stared into the water watching for large fish. A punch on the back, the first aimed at Lawrence the second at Harry, made them both turn quickly.

Mikey leered at them. "What you two doing – planning to swim back to your mas?"

Lawrence shook his head. The pain from the punch ached. "We're watching for big fish."

Sam laughed loudly. "Big fish – What? Like Jonah?" He turned to Mikey, grinning. "They think those church stories are real. This pair are ready to be locked up in Bedlam." He gave Lawrence another punch on the arm, then looked down at the child's deformed foot. "And look what he has to drag around with him."

Mikey gave Lawrence's foot a kick, making the small boy groan as he dropped to the deck. Mikey raised his leg ready for another kick when Harry grabbed Mikey's foot, almost toppling the bigger boy.

"Hey," Sam grabbed Harry from behind, trying to pull him off. But Harry held fast, giving Lawrence time to scramble to his feet.

"Stop!" yelled Constance.

Across the deck, the fashionable young woman and her girls paused in their singing to watch. Constance blushed, knowing she had to keep the children under better control.

"Right, children, I believe it's time to lift our spirits in song. Let's raise our voice for 'With Mercy and With Judgement'." She tapped her foot three times as an introduction.

Mikey and Sam glared at Harry as they mouthed the words to the hymn.

The children's voices sounded weak as the wind carried their sound off the port deck. Constance swung her arms, stirring the children to sing more heartily. The other woman's group of girls had sung well, and Constance wanted to show that her children were even better. She smiled as the wind dropped and the children's voices hung in the air. Her own voice grew propelling the children louder.

I'll bless the hand that guided
I'll bless the hand that planned
When throned where glory dwelleth
In Immanuel's Land

But the words faded as a heavy tune came from the other side of the deck. Constance glanced quickly over her shoulder to see the other woman and her girls raising their voices to drown out the Home of Industry singers.

Constance turned back to her own children and sang louder, exaggerating her arm movements so that the children would be stirred to greater voice.

For a few bars, the Home of Industry children, with Beryl only miming, could be heard above the other group. But the girls from the opposing mission were older and better disciplined. They followed their leader, raising their voice in decibel and octave so that "A Green Place Faraway" could be heard well above "With Mercy and With Judgement."

Constance's voice dropped as she wondered what to do. She couldn't meekly halt the song before its end, but nor could she continue to have her children drowned out.

The dinner gong peeled from the galley door, preventing any decision.

"Quick, children, we must be in our cabins when the meals are delivered." Constance steered her children along the deck and watched them file down the stairs and into the boy and girl cabins. Two sailors carried large pots of stew and placed them on the tables. Constance served the boys first because she figured they would be less patient and perhaps even tempted to serve themselves.

"Miss, can we have seconds if there's any left?" Mikey asked as he received his bowl.

Constance rolled her eyes. "Let's see how we do," she said and hurried next door to the girls' cabin.

Mikey swayed a little with the movement of the ship. "Hey, Beak Boy, you better eat slowly, cos if there's no seconds I want yours."

George took his time eating, but not because of Mikey's threat. His stomach felt stormy. That was the best word he could put to it. He felt like his guts could erupt and rain its contents across the table.

"That's right, Beak Boy, go slow," Mikey told him.

George felt a sweat break out on his brow and placed his head on the table beside his bowl.

Beside him Lawrence retched. "I need to go," he called out and ran to the toilets down the hall.

Mikey laughed then reached across and pulled Lawrence's bowl to him.

Harry glared but then turned pale and took after his friend.

Sam pulled George's bowl toward him. George didn't move. If he stayed still and kept his eyes shut, he could cope, he told himself.

He heard Mikey, Sam and the others slurp and swallow. Inside his head, George sang a hymn to drown out their noise. It was "Jesus Bids Us Shine", his favourite hymn because it was bright and hopeful.

A spoon dropped onto the table. "Shit!" said Mikey as he ran across the floor and out the room. George allowed himself a small smile and began to sing again inside his head.

*

In the girls' room, Ruby led the first run to the bathroom. Beryl followed, holding her sister's head while she retched up all an empty stomach contained. When she was sure nothing more could possibly come forth, and her little sister was plagued only by dry heaves, Beryl carried her to the bunk and laid a cold cloth on her brow.

"Close your eyes and think of nothing," Beryl said. On the middle bunk Junie clasped her faded doll.

"Do you feel alright?" Beryl asked Junie.

The girl thought for a moment then nodded.

At the table, Constance felt nausea of her own as she saw one young girl vomit into her stew. She needed distraction or she would join the children in illness. She also felt agitated by the other missionary. They couldn't go singing against each other. They had to talk, agree a plan, and perhaps even work together.

Constance left her stew and found the captain while he was at his own lunch. "Sir, do you mind if I ask the name of the other missionary – the one who is accompanied by a party of young girls?"

The ruddy cheeks of the captain stretched tight in a grin. "Ah, she's not your usual missionary is that one. Made the crossing before, although I don't believe she belongs with a regular church. The children are from the port town, I believe," he said. "Aye, she's unusual is that one. Maria Rye operates on her own."

Constance recognised the name from the papers. Maria Rye was frequently mentioned in the society papers. Constance followed the captain's directions to Miss Rye's berth. A girl dressed in a simple blue serge dress answered her knock.

Constance stood straight. "May I speak to Miss Rye, please?"

The girl, who looked about fourteen, glanced quickly behind her before speaking. "I'm sorry, Miss Rye is taking her rest at this time. Who shall I say called?"

Constance paused at the formality before giving her name. "It seems that she and I are on a similar mission, and I thought perhaps we could talk about our work and maybe share ideas." Constance leaned forward toward the girl. "I am assuming you are all orphans."

The girl took a step back. "Miss Rye instructs us not to discuss our background with anyone."

"Then please tell Miss Rye I would like to make her acquaintance. I can be found, with my children, on the rear deck."

Later that day, Maria Rye appeared on deck with a smaller group of girls. They took their position near lifeboats eleven and twelve but made no movement toward the Home of Industry group.

While her own children drew Bible stories on their slates, Constance watched as Maria Rye lectured her girls. The wind carried her voice out to sea, so the words could not be heard. But Constance noted Miss Rye's rich bonnet and the lace that decorated the sleeve of her fashionable gown.

She looked down at her own shapeless dress, feeling undermined by its rough simplicity. Her mother always said appearance mattered, but Constance had shaken her head at this. Hard work in God's service, easing the burdens of others, protecting the vulnerable; these were true measurements of worth.

She asked the children to finish their drawing and join her in singing her favourite hymn, "There Is a Better World, They Say". Its stirring stanzas always filled her with strength and vigour. She tapped her foot and the children raised their voices in song. They were at half strength as many of the children lay in their bunks too ill to climb the stairs, but those that remained sang heartily, pushing out the words as if to make up for their ailing friends.

Lawrence had been one of the first to fall ill, but he'd recovered quickly and now stood with his small chest pushed out as he sang God's praises. Beside him Harry's mouth moved to its own rhythm, as though he were making up his own words. Constance smiled, one day she would teach him the real words.

Nearby, George sang less vigorously, his mouth sliding through some of the longer lines as though he didn't really understand. Constance knew she needed to go through the words of the hymn with him, explain its meaning so he could enjoy its sentiments.

As they moved into the third verse, Constance closed her eyes, enjoying the sound of the children lifting their voices to the sky. But another sound came, jarring with different notes and words. Constance looked behind and glared at her rival. Maria Rye didn't turn. She kept her back to the Home of Industry mission as she led her girls in song. The erect poise of her stature made Constance feel that this woman enjoyed her disturbing behaviour.

But this time, she wouldn't win, Constance decided as she increased the strength of her own voice and pushed her clenched fist into the air for the children to follow. They guessed the game and entered it fully. Even Beryl, who barely enunciated a sound until now, let her voice erupt with a spoken yell simply to drown out the girls across the deck. They reached the final chorus unable to hear the rival singers and they grinned as they sang.

"There is a better world, they say,
Oh, so bright!
Where we can find the Lord
And he will help us everyday,
And never let us fall."

With the final words, they let out a cheer. Constance turned to look at her rival whose girls sang quietly, as though they'd never attempted to drown out the other song.

Constance felt sudden guilt. She bid her group sit down. She needed to sit herself as her stomach grew giddy, and a sweat she'd never felt before erupted across her brow.

"Children, I think I need to be excused. Lawrence would you please talk to the others about …" She couldn't think of anything except finding a toilet. Her legs shook as she tried to run across the deck. Behind her, she could feel the eyes of Maria Rye. Constance slowed a little, determined to walk with dignity.

*

Her bunk felt airless and sweaty. Constance heard Hannah and Dora play chase while other girls giggled and the boys next door thudded up and down the stairs in a game that seemed to involve jumping. She needed to direct them in play and learning, or they would grow bored and disruptive. But she couldn't lift her arm, let alone her neck and head.

She'd spent the night lying on the toilet floor until one of the girls, she thought it might be Beryl, had helped her to bed. Now all she could do was lie in a sweat and listen while the children did as they wished.

HOOOOoonk

This new sound put the room of girls into silence.

Constance lay on her bunk welcoming the momentary silence.

"Miss, what was that?" a young voice asked.

"Miss, does it mean we're going to crash and drown?"

Several girls screamed in horror.

Constance tried to shake her head but nothing happened.

"Miss, are we going to be alright?"

HOOOOoonk

Silence.

"Miss, do we need to run to the lifeboats?"

Girls screamed again until a knock on the door brought silence.

A small voice called from outside. "Miss Constance, it is Lawrence here. I thought you may be curious about the sound emitting from the ship. We are surrounded by fog, and the captain must sound the horn every three minutes so that other ships stay clear of our passage."

Constance smiled in gratitude at the small boy's wisdom. "Thank you, Lawrence," she said weakly.

The girls reverted to their giggles, the excitement of the foghorn sending their tone upwards.

HOOOOoonk

Constance rolled over. The damp bedroll beneath her smelled like it was fermenting. The sweaty clothes in which she lay clung to her skin. She wanted her mother. Helen would peel the dress and petticoats off, bathe her in tepid water, lift clean water to her lips and help her out of bed and into the fresh air where she would no doubt feel better. Constance began to cry.

HOOOOoonk

She heard the girls giggle again and knew it wasn't Bible stories that caused the amusement. Outside, the sound of boys shouting and running up and down the stairs made her cringe. She felt too tired for all their activity. Why couldn't they just stay still and quiet? Again, she wished her mother were there.

Constance wiped her face with the skirt of her dress scratching herself with dried vomit. The sight of it made her want to cry even more.

As tears coursed her cheeks, a knock came to the door. One of the orphans opened it, and then crept to Constance's bedside. "Miss, it's that other woman – the one with all them girls."

HOOOOoonk

Constance tried to wipe her face on the smelly bedroll while lifting her head to greet her guest. The woman's small, sharp face was before her. Constance shut her mouth so she wouldn't breathe foul air onto her neat clothes.

"Your children must be controlled. For four days they have been out on deck running and chasing each other as if this were a playground. Their noise is so great many passengers have complained to the captain. He, in turn, has asked me to take control during your illness, and I am here to tell you I have no such inclinations."

Constance let her head fall back onto her pillow in exhaustion.
HOOOOoonk

Finally, with Maria Rye glaring down at her, Constance found words. "I need help. We need not work against each other."

The woman stood upright. "For over one year now, I have been carrying girls across to Canada and settling them into good homes. During that time, not one of my children has displayed the poor behaviour that is taking place among your children. Now, I suggest you strengthen your back bone, climb out of that stinking bed and take control of your responsibilities."

Constance felt a cool breeze as the woman turned, almost running out of the room.

HOOOOoonk

Constance's first instinct was to cry even more, but she knew Maria Rye was right. She needed to be stronger.

"Please," Constance called on two older girls who sat gossiping on a bunk. "Bring me a basin of clean water and help me change my clothes."

*

Up on deck, Lawrence and Harry stood scouting the waves for large fish. The leeward wind pushed at their backs, forcing them against the rails.

"What colour are the big fish?" Harry asked.

Lawrence shrugged. "Lot's of colours. Whales can be white, or black or with bits of black and white together."

Harry whistled. "Are they the biggest fish?"

Lawrence nodded. "I've only seen them in books, and they're much bigger than sharks."

Harry stood straighter and pointed to a dark colour amidst the white foam. "What's that?"

Lawrence held onto the railing and peered forward into the spray. "I can't see anything."

Harry pointed. "Right there!"

Lawrence saw a dim shape. He peered further, leaning a little over the railing. "I think that might be it."

Harry leaned forward, staring hard at the dark seam in the sea. "It must be a great big fish – I didn't believe you, but you were right – it's a great big fish." He thrust forward, pitching his head over the rail. "I can't believe it's …"

A huge wave hit the deck. Lawrence felt the cold chill flood his body and gasped. His hair, jacket, trousers and everything through to his underwear were drenched. He let out a laugh, and looked at Harry. But Harry wasn't there.

"Harry," he yelled, dropping down to look under the lifeboats.

With no sign of his friend, he ran looking in all directions for sight of Harry's red hair.

"Harry!"

He stopped and peered over the deck but saw nothing other than white foam waves, not even the dark shape that had excited them.

"Harry," he yelled as loud as he could.

"Hey!" a harsh voice came from behind. "Quit your yelling!"

Lawrence turned to see a sailor. "It's my friend Harry, he's not here. He was there next to me at the rails when a big wave came and now he's gone." He pointed toward the sea, even though he didn't want to believe that Harry was really down there.

The sailor peered overboard, and then hollered to the crew.

Lawrence sank to his knees as he heard the rush of activity around him. He gazed hard at everything under the lifeboats, trying to see or hear Harry. Tears tracked down his cheeks and chin until he felt Miss Constance lift him to standing.

"They're looking for him, Lawrence. Two men have set off in a lifeboat, and God will guide them in their search."

Lawrence shook his head. He'd read a great many sea-faring stories.

*

Constance held Lawrence through the night. As drowsiness finally conquered his sobs and he fell into a sleep, she let herself cry. Harry had been her responsibility. She'd promised his mother she'd take good care of him but now he lay at the bottom of the ocean.

She knew she'd failed by letting the children play on deck alone. She'd known there were dangers, the Captain had told her. But the illness had made her lax. This wouldn't happen again. Annie MacPherson had never allowed one of her charges to be washed overboard.

Constance's own sobs grew heavier as she wondered what they would say back at the Home of Industry. Her mother would never forgive her. But the journey had been harder than anything she had ever done, and the children were not always on their best behaviour.

With the grey dawn she knew she had to take a firmer charge of the children. They would be reaching shore in a few days, and Annie MacPherson had told her to ensure the children arrived free of lice. Constance decided they should clean their cabins, clothes and their bodies.

She lay Lawrence down on his bunk, and hurried to the storage trunk where she opened a large jar of vinegar and hurried into the girls' cabin.

The sharp smell of vinegar tugged Beryl awake as she thought of the douche she'd used to wash out her insides after customers. She opened her eyes to see Miss Constance with a bucket.

"Beryl, I'd like you and the older girls to swab out our cabin. The Captain said we'll reach land soon, and we must leave the place clean."

The young girl pushed gently out of bed, taking care not to waken Ruby who had climbed into her bunk during the night. She took the mop and bucket but looked around at the floor which was littered with canvas sacks, jackets and even bonnets. "Where should I start?"

Constance seemed to suddenly notice the heaps of belongings and shook her head in confusion. "I'm not sure. Maybe it would be best to wait until all the children are called on deck for Scripture."

Beryl nodded as she eyed her warm bunk. She wanted to climb back in and snuggle up to her sister.

"Why don't you help me with other preparations? We must see that all the children are scrubbed and deloused before we go ashore. Miss MacPherson said no one should arrive with vermin."

Beryl scratched at her head and underarms then reached for her clothes.

Up on deck, the air was damp and cold.

Constance pulled her cloak tight and walked quickly. "The captain said we could use the bath used by the crew. Right after breakfast, we should start with the girls."

"Miss, can I return to bed till then?" Beryl asked.

Constance nodded reluctantly. She wanted to start the transformation of her children now.

When, eventually, the breakfast bell rang, she fed her troops quickly, keen to begin their cleansing. Beryl was still at her porridge when Constance nodded for her assistance. The girl followed Constance down steps, deeper into the ship's belly. They paused, both peering right and left, seeking direction before following the smell of carbolic. At the entrance to a small room they stopped. Maria Rye stood at the door, her girls in line for bathing.

Constance stepped back. "I am sorry. I thought the captain said we could have use of the bathing room."

Maria Rye peered from beneath her lashes. Beryl noticed the ribbons that criss-crossed her skirt and couldn't help but compare it to Constance's faded dress.

Finally, the chic woman answered. "We shall be a while yet."

Constance's voice croaked before growing strong. "When might you be done?"

The other woman turned away. "I shall send word when the bathtub is free."

Beryl gazed at the three girls in the tub. Their naked bodies were thin and pale and the biggest child was badly bruised. Beryl had received some beatings from clients, but her body had never been so badly marked.

As they hurried back to the deck she whispered to Constance, "Have they been beaten?"

Constance raised her eyes. "They are workhouse girls to be sure, and from Liverpool according to the Captain."

Beryl thought about the girl's white skin, pock-marked with bruises that were both old and new. "Do they really beat people in the workhouse?"

"While those hired to run workhouses frequently promise benevolence, the power of their position frequently turns them malevolent."

Beryl wasn't too sure what that meant, but she took it to mean that beatings were common.

When word came that the bathing room was clear. Constance hurried ahead to run the water and add the vinegar, while Beryl led a line of girls toward the small room near the crews' quarters. As they neared the damp steam, two sailors stepped out of a cabin.

One whistled at the sight of the young girls. His eyes lit up bright as he looked down at Beryl. "You're a precious little thing, aren't you?"

Beryl froze, behind her she felt Ruby's chest against her back.

A young thin voice called out from behind him. "Get away with you or I'll call the Captain."

The man turned to see one of Maria Rye's girls standing there. He paused, giving Beryl and the other girls a long look, and then hurried onto the deck.

Maria Rye's girl smiled at Beryl, and then hurried back into the changing room.

Beryl bid the girls follow her. The stench of vinegar and steam in the bathing room made their eyes sting. Junie and Ruby stripped quickly with Beryl pulling at their clothes.

Ruby allowed herself to be led in by her sister, but Junie, still clutching her rag doll, held back. "Come, Junie, it makes your skin feel all queer."

Junie stepped gingerly in, but then hurried back out. "It's too hot – it'll burn."

"No, you'll get used to it," Beryl pulled on Junie's hand, directing her back into the water. The two girls splashed tentatively.

"It smells funny," Ruby said.

Beryl thought she'd better get them moving so the others could bathe. She quickly dipped herself under the water, and then pitched Ruby and Junie under, wiping both their faces free of water as soon as they surfaced. Dead lice and fleas floated on the scum. Beryl pulled the two girls out and waved Hannah and Dora to hurry forward.

She pulled Ruby and Junie into the dressing area. The Maria Rye girl who had shouted at the sailors was there tying up her boots. She was about the same age as Beryl, and about as dark haired as Beryl was fair.

She watched as Beryl hurried to dress herself while assisting the younger girls and ushering Hannah and Dora out to get dressed. "Let me," she said and knelt to tie Junie's laces. She smiled, staring into Beryl's face. "Are they your sisters?"

Beryl nodded toward Ruby. "She is, but I'm watching Junie for a friend; he's with the boys group." Self-consciously she kept her head turned to conceal her mole.

"You are bound for Canada?" asked the dark-haired girl.

Beryl nodded.

The girl smiled. "It is a wonderful place. I am sure you will all love it there."

Beryl turned quickly, forgetting about her mole. "Have you been there?"

The girl shook her head. "No, but I've read about it."

"Are you a workhouse girl?"

The girl finished tying the final bow on Junie's boots. "No, I'm from a church orphanage." She looked up and smiled. "But I've read *Anne of Green Gables*, a most wonderful story which tells of a beautiful land and kind people who give warm homes to good orphans."

Constance's voice came from behind them. "Hurry on, you girls, we have more children who need to be dried and dressed."

The dark-haired girl stood. "My name is Meg. Maybe we will be placed on nearby farms and can visit each other."

Beryl smiled, no longer worried about her mole. "I hope so," she said as she watched Meg hurry to catch up with her group.

*

Lawrence sat huddled on the deck as the other children looked out to sea. Tears fell as he thought of Harry somewhere out there, swimming, floating, clinging unconscious like Robinson Crusoe, waiting for rescue, or being chased and eaten by the big fish they'd seen.

He began to cry again, great hurtling sobs. "I should have taken better care of him," he cried.

Constance pulled him to standing. "Children, I think we should all say a prayer for our little brother, Harry, who now sits with God in Heaven."

Lawrence tried to think of Harry next to God's throne, but he couldn't picture his small friend amid the clouds, only deep in the grey waters fighting for his life.

Constance patted his shoulder. "And, I think it would be best if Harry's best friend, Lawrence, read the prayer."

Lawrence stared at her, his voice ready to break out into a sob. "I can't, Miss."

"You can, Lawrence, because you are doing it for Harry. You knew him best among all of us, so who better to lead the prayer."

Lawrence shut his eyes. "Our dear Fath ..." Lawrence's lips trembled. "We ask you to care for Harry." He let out a deep breath, feeling suddenly calmer. "You will know him from the other boys who arrived with you yesterday because he has bright red hair and a happy face. He is a wonderful boy and a great friend with a curious mind and the best friend a boy like me could ever have. He never laughed at my foot like some children do. In fact, he tried to protect me from some of the names and bullying. But really, God, I should have taken better care of him. He is small for nine, you see, and I said when we first stepped out on this journey that I would take care of him. I am sorry, I failed ..."

A deep sob pulled away the other words, and Constance hugged Lawrence to her as she finished the prayer.

At the end a silence settled over the children.

George wondered if Harry had a mother.

Beryl looked down into the water as if expecting to see the Harry's red hair among the waves. As she raised her eyes, she saw a shape in the distance, rising out from the sea.

"Land!" called out a sailor.

Everyone peered silently into the mist.

Then George pointed. "Yes, see, through the fog, an outline."

"You mongrel, that's another ship," called out Mikey.

"It's not – look above the handrail, to the left of the knotted rope – look and you'll see it."

"Nahh – your beak's playing with your eyesight. There's nothing there."

After a few moments, Lawrence called out. "It is land. See."

Constance smiled, glad to hear his voice.

Slowly, the vague shapes grew more defined against the sky. The white fog cleared, revealing land to the west, hillsides dark with trees. Constance and her children watched in silence.

"It doesn't look like home," George said.

"I don't hear no bawling or trains," Mikey said.

Ruby stretched tall. "I can smell something sweet – like sugar."

Constance nodded. "It's the promised land – just like I told you."

A passing sailor paused in his work. "That's Nova Scotia – Canada."

The children let out a cheer, and Constance felt tears creep forward. She dabbed quickly at them quickly. A small hand slipped onto her wrist. Junie's face, still roughened red after the Carbolic soap, looked up at her. "Don't worry, Miss Considerance, our George will take care of you."

Constance gushed between sob and laughter as she took Junie's hand in her own. "No, I will take very good care of George – and you."

George thought of his mother and sisters and wondered when he'd see them again. It felt like such a long time since he'd left home that already he wanted to return. He promised he would work hard, save all his pay and bring his mother and sisters to this new land. But he had four long years before him until he could earn a salary. Suddenly his family felt so far away.

Tears crept from his eyelids. He blinked them back and pulled on his sister's hand. "We have to work hard here, Junie. Take all the opportunity we can so we can see ma again."

Junie looked up, blinking like she was suddenly to see her family before her eyes. "How long will it be?"

George shook his head. "The more we work, the faster it will be."

She was silent for a few moments, and George wondered how much she understood.

The ship passed heavily wooded hillsides with little evidence of man or beast. Everyone watched from the deck, no movement as the ship carried them forward.

Finally, Junie broke the silence. "It looks lonely," she said, pulling on George's hand. "You will stay with me, won't you, George?"

George nodded.

The children saw a sparse town. Constance said it might be Quebec, although one of the sailors shook his head and muttered, "Prince Edward Island."

Mikey thought he could see a market visible through a broad street. Deep in his bones, he knew there was a living to be made here.

The ship moved up-river as the hills flattened out, showing a land as vast as the ocean. A few homes could be seen, all set far from each other. Some of the children lost interest in the scenery, but Beryl kept watch, wondering about the life that lay ahead, wondering how her friend Meg would visit her.

As the next settlement approached, the Captain rang a loud bell. The crew ran to untie ropes. Constance could see buildings all neat with trim wood and paint. She smiled and thought of the Promised Land until the ship bumped against its mooring, throwing her off balance.

With a few unintelligible calls from the sailors, a heavy gangplank was thrown against the deck. The children moved forward ready to run ashore and feel the earth heavy under their feet.

But they were blocked by the sailors who stood in line as the other passengers disembarked. With most gone, Constance worried what she should do next. Annie MacPherson said someone would meet her but she couldn't remember if she were to wait on the boat or move ashore.

Constance dropped to her knees. "Children, let us pray!"

Beryl followed, pulling Ruby and Junie with her. The other children copied.

Our dear Lord...

George prayed silently that he should start work quickly so he could get these long years over with and see his mother again.

Amen

Constance rose to see the two men in top coats and tall hats smile at her as they climbed aboard.

The portliest man held out his hand. "Mr Bernard at your service. I understand you have some orphans for us."

Constance glanced protectively at the children who had gathered on either side of her. "I bring some of our finest children, all eager to begin a new life in Canada."

The two men smiled down at the line of children. The portly gentleman nudged his companion. "Well, Murray, I will take care of this group if you see to Miss Rye's little tribe."

Constance and the children followed the gentleman. Beryl hesitated as she stepped onto the gangplank. But it felt sturdier than before and, as she stepped on the muddy earth, she let out an audible sigh at the sudden weight in her legs.

But on land, Lawrence tripped, his club foot felt heavier and seemed to collide with the earth at every step. Behind him Mikey and Sam laughed. "Little Stumpy won't cop much work out here."

Lawrence lifted his foot a little higher and found he stumbled less, but by the time he reached the immigration shed he was tired and sweating.

As Constance and Mr Bernard talked, two elderly farmers, their faces burned red from the sun, pointed to Lawrence. "He's no good that one, can't walk in a straight line without breaking out into a sweat."

The other nodded. "But there are a few bigger lads worth picking."

"Most of the girls look too young for hard work," said a woman in a large bonnet. "I need someone with a good arm for scrubbing."

Beryl stared at her.

"And that one looks like she'd give some cheek," said the woman.

"But look at her hands. They're plenty rough, a few good feeds to build up her strength and she might be just what you need," said her companion.

Ahead in the line, Constance clapped her hands for attention.

"Children, we will stay tonight at an orphanage nearby. They have beds at the ready. Tomorrow, Mr Bernard has arranged for a few of you to find homes here in this fair town, while the rest of us travel by train to Belleville."

George felt his knees grow week and his face flushed as he realised he should have listened to his mother when she spoke out against Canada. It was all too big, too far away and he realised he didn't want to go and live with strangers.

Junie pulled on his hand. "Are we going to have a new home tomorrow?"

George breathed hard to keep back tears. "I don't know."

Beryl grabbed his arm. "It's okay," she said. "I talked to one of the girls from the other group. She's read about this place and said it's wonderful."

George stared ahead, wondering how he could even begin to believe her.

*

Dear Miss Bilbrough

My husband and I would like to give a home to one of your poor orphans. We run a farm out north of Belleville and my husband is always saying he could do with spare hands. We are good churchgoers except when the harvest time comes around and the work won't allow us spare time. We have four children, all under 5, so there isn't much hope of them helping for a while. Our Minister promises to send you a letter telling of our good natures. We would like a boy, strong in body and quiet in nature. That would be God's answer to our prayers.

Your faithful servant
Mrs Harold Winters

Ellen put the letter in the centre of the table, feeling Mrs Winters cared more for a helping hand than she did for helping poor orphans. She wished Annie were there to help discern those offering love and care and those with other motivations. But Annie had gone to investigate another home they'd been offered west of Toronto.

The next letter was on crumpled paper with writing marred by splashes of ink.

Miss Bilbrough

We would like to have one of your boys. 14 would be a good age. Our Minister says we are good people and you can contact him to ask about our character. Please send one as soon as you can.

Robert Marsh

Ellen placed this letter in the rejected pile and picked up an envelope so crisp it could have come from the Queen herself. She opened it gingerly, fearing tearing at the expensive parchment.

Dear Miss Bilbrough,

Our hearts were touched when we read of the poor orphans in our homeland being raised in lives of sin and depravity. After much consideration, we would like to offer a home to one of your poorest children.

We promise to feed the child well and ensure a full education that would include Protestant Scripture at the very finest church in our town.

We are comfortable though not rich. However, our spirits are good and we try always to follow the ways of Our Lord. A letter testifying to our characters is enclosed.

We do hope you will find it in your hearts to let us help you in your mission.

Sincerely,
Mr and Mrs Clarence Simmons

Ellen opened a small letter enclosed in the envelope.

To whom it may concern:

I am pleased to be able to testify to the Christian characters of Mr and Mrs Simmons. I have no doubts whatsoever that any child given to them would be raised in a kind and generous Christian home. Indeed, any orphan taken by them would be the most fortunate of children.

Kind Regards,
Reverend Keith Peters.

Ellen placed the letter closest to her and hoped she would find more letters like this.

The next letter came in an envelope that smelled of wood smoke.

Dear Miss Bilbrough,

We are a poor family who work hard and trust in the word of the Lord. Our children are many and, praise the Lord, all boys. They are a handful, but we believe our dear lads will be our virtuous bounty in old age.

After reading your announcement in the newspaper, my wife would very much like to bring a girl into our home. I believe she would like to have a young woman who can share in womanly things that, the Lord help me, but I just can't understand.

Our preacher promises to send a letter testifying about our character and I hope you will see fit to award us the girl my wife wishes she could have.

Humbly, your servant,
Bill Grouver

Ellen placed this promising plea atop the beautiful letter that came from the Simmons and continued to read:

Miss Ellen
Please send us a child to help with the milking and farm work. We are getting older and our boys have gone out west ...

Miss Bilbrough,
We would like to have three of your children, big ones, boys and girls, for the work on our farm. We don't have no Minister out this way as our nearest neighbour is a two-day ride, but my wife says our home is better than any orphanage and we only beat when it's deserved ...

Missie Ellen,
I am a woman running a farm alone and would appreciate the company of a strong child to take over some of the tasks. Presently I am up before dawn and not in bed until after dark and find I am growing weary working alone. A strong child could take some of my burden ...

Ellen dropped the letter and shook her head. She couldn't decide on any of these people.

*

George lay on his back, peering through the window at the night sky. Tears flowed past his temples and into his hair, leaving two damp patches behind his ears. Outside it wasn't the same moon they had at home. It was larger, whiter and with bigger markings. He wished his mother could see this moon. He pictured his mother lying next to Tommy, Rose and Maggie – all four of them asleep together in the attic bed. A sob rose through his chest, and he pulled his wool blanket tight across his lips so no-one would hear.

Nearby, someone else wept so hard that it threatened to rise into a full-grown wail.

"Lawrence," George whispered.

On the next bed Lawrence lay still.

George sat up and peered through the darkness. "Lawrence, please stop weeping. You know the others will tease you."

The weeping stopped, and Lawrence's small chest let out a low snore.

George lay back down to stare at the moon and think of his mother asleep with her arm wrapped around Tommy.

Nearby, Sam held his breath in an effort to quell his sobs. He shut his eyes, seeing nothing other than his grandfather's face with his eye almost knotted shut, the pock-marked cheeks and the mouth caved in around swollen gums. The old man had raised him after his mother died from fever. He'd been a tot, but his grandfather had taught him to earn a living. They'd gone pick-pocketing in church until word spread about the old man and his tiny urchin. When times were really rough his grandfather had run a three-card stand, with Sam barely five but buttoning the crowd to make bets.

But even that was too much for his grandfather nowadays. All he could do was beg. Tears soaked Sam's cheeks as he wondered if his grandfather earned enough to eat. The old man hadn't wanted him to go to Canada. "You don't need to be off to strangers," he had said. "There's plenty new tricks to learn here."

Now Sam wondered if his grandfather was right.

"Pssst, Sam!" The voice from the next bed was Mikey's. "Do you think we'll do okay here?"

Sam held his breath, afraid talking might give away his tears.

Mikey tossed onto his back. "Oh, I hate it that everyone's asleep. I don't like it here. I want to go home."

He could think of nothing other than his brothers and sisters. He hadn't even told them he was going to Canada. It had all been Sam's idea, but he didn't think Canada was this far. Maggie and the others wouldn't have worried when he didn't come home for a week, they'd have thought he was busy on some heist, but now they'd be checking the prisons and the morgue.

Next door in the girls' room, Meg lay in a thickly starched nightgown that Maria Rye had issued. The starch made Meg itch, but Miss Rye said they had to learn how it felt to be a lady if they were to take good care of one.

After one long scratch around the collar, Junie nudged Beryl in the ribs. "Has she got fleas?"

"No!" Beryl whispered. The two small girls had left their beds and climbed into Beryl's for comfort. Ruby lay close to sleep, her head tucked into her sister's neck, while Junie curled around Ruby's back.

Meg's voice whispered through the dark. "It must be nice to have a sister."

Beryl nodded, a small smile on her face as she stroked Ruby's hair.

"I had a sister once – not a real sister with blood and everything. It was in a foster home. Amy was her name. She was older and used to teach me sewing, and we would read together everything we could. She did most of it, letting me sound out words until I could read whole pages. I really missed her when I went back to the home."

"Why did you go back?" Beryl whispered.

"I don't know. I just woke up one day and was told I was going back to the orphanage. Then I was taken in by a spinster, but she wanted to put me on the game. Kept bringing gentlemen to see me and they would all whisper stuff about money."

Ruby stirred, raising her head a little. "Ma wanted to put me with a gentleman."

"Shhh!" said Beryl, patting Ruby's head back down for sleep. "So what happened then?"

"Well, I knew enough, I'd heard the girls at the orphanage talk. So I ran away. That's when the governors decided to send me to Canada with Miss Rye."

A silence settled over the large dorm until Junie's thin voice rang loud. "What's a gentleman want with small girls?"

Meg giggled, and Beryl let out a long sigh. "We'll talk about it later, Junie. Go to sleep."

The room faced west and had none of the moonlight that lit up the boys' dorm.

"Were you on the game?" Meg whispered.

Beryl nodded lightly, her head making a small stirring noise against the pillow.

"A lot of the girls at the orphanage were. Some of them had diseases," said Meg.

Beryl shut her eyes tight; she didn't want to think about all that. Those pawing men, and her ma shouting about money. She liked the way Miss Constance took care of them, seeing to food and beds, and in return asking only for good behaviour and a few songs. If the people in Canada were like her, then they had nothing to worry about.

"Are you taking the train to this place called Belleville? Miss Constance said its name means beautiful town."

Meg shrugged. "I don't know. Miss Rye hasn't told us."

"I'm sure you are going. It's where they check out all the new families – make sure they're good enough for us."

"It's probably like the orphanage where Anne lived before she was sent to Green Gables."

"What's Green Gables?"

"It's the name of a house. It was in a book I read about an orphan girl in Canada. She had bright red hair and was taken in by a brother and sister who have a farm. At first the sister doesn't want her and tells her brother to send her back to the orphanage. But, even though Anne does some terrible things – that are really very funny – they grow to love her and decide to keep her for their own."

The two girls lay in the dark for a few moments thinking about the orphan Anne landing in a good home.

"And is everyone in the story nice like the brother and sister?"

"A few, some of them are cold at first, but by the end of the story they all love Anne." Meg paused as she remembered parts of the story. "You should have read about the place. Green Gables was painted white and surrounded by apple trees. Anne fell in love with it as soon as she saw it."

Beryl smiled. If they were going to homes like Green Gables, then they would all be fine.

*

After breakfast Maria Rye and Constance stood at opposing corners of the room. They hadn't talked since Constance had been ill in bed.

Maria Rye pointed to the door. Her girls rose quietly and filed toward it.

Meg tapped Beryl's shoulder and waved as she moved away. Beryl smiled. "See you on the train," she mouthed.

Constance clapped her hands and bid her children rise. They filed out to a large hall where the children were guided into two long lines of boys and girls. Beryl stood with Ruby and Junie on either side. Lawrence stayed close to George.

From the podium, Mr Bernard, who had met them at the boat, coughed. "Children, you have been selected for homes in this beautiful country, and many of the good people right here in this town are excited to see you arrive. I'm going to bring some of them in here this morning and let them choose who they would like to take home."

George felt the blood drain from his face. This was too soon. He didn't want to go home with anyone.

"Now, my advice to you, good children, is to stand up straight, smile – but be careful not to show any of those bad teeth. No one wants to think they're taking home a bill for any dentist."

Beryl thought about her mole and pulled her hair forward to cover her cheek. She held tight to Ruby and Junie.

"Now, be ready, good children, for your new families might be right outside that door."

Mr Bernard pointed to a clerk who freed a latch that let in a group of men and women. Some were well dressed in frock coats and smart cloaks, but others looked dried up and dusty.

Beryl watched as they walked in groups of two through the rows of children. Everyone, except George, stood straight with their mouths shut in a tight smile.

"I'd like this one," called out a man with a bald, shiny head who held Mikey's shoulder.

Mikey's eyes grew wide.

"If I could have this girl," said a woman gripping a tall girl who looked like she was about to cry.

George felt a heavy hand on his shoulder and turned to see an elderly man, with a back as bent as Tommy's.

"I'd like me this one!" he called out.

George pulled back, his heart racing as he looked first at Junie and then at Constance. "No, Miss, please tell him he can't have me. I promised I would go with Junie. You told my ma I would, and I can't break my promise. I need to stay with Junie. I said I would take care of my sister."

Junie pulled away from Beryl and ran to her brother, taking his hand and pulling him away from the old man. George gripped her tight, feeling his heart race at the thought of losing his sister.

The man peered at Junie over his spectacles and shook his head. "I don't want no small girl – and that one's very small. She'll be no good to us." He looked up at Constance as though expecting to barter.

Constance shook her head. "No, we promised to keep siblings together where possible. But we have other children who are alone and would be happy to live in your home."

The old man turned, catching sight of Sam. "He looks like he might be healthy," he said.

Constance nodded. "All of our children are blessed in God's eyes."

He scrutinised Sam, peering into his eyes and squeezing his arms and shoulders. "Are you strong?"

Sam nodded, taking care not to show his blackened teeth.

"Well, I guess he looks better than that one." The man pointed to George. "His nose is straight for a start."

From the podium, Mr Bernard clapped his hands. "Ladies and gentlemen, if you have made your selection, could we ask you to take your child outside to the clerk's desk where we can register the details."

Sam kept his gaze on the ground, remembering his grandfather. He didn't like the old man. Mikey grinned, relieved that he and Sam would be in the same town.

George let out a huge sigh as he watched Sam and Mikey leave the hall. It was relief to know they would no longer bully him. But his heart still raced. It all felt too fast. One moment, Sam and Mikey were calling him names, picking on him, making him miserable; then they were gone, off to new homes, and he would never see them again.

Junie tugged at his arm. "Why did that man want to take you away?"

George looked down at her tiny face, reddened and peeling. Her ears stuck out from her dark, lank hair, and she gripped her ragged doll like it was a talisman. He suddenly wondered who would want them. He could work, would work, putting in all his efforts to save, buy his own farm and bring his mother, Tommy and sisters out to Canada. But what could Junie do? His mother wanted her to be trained as a housemaid, but Junie looked too young for any type of work.

"You will stay with me, won't you, George?"

George glanced up at Constance, who was helping a boy fasten his coat. "Miss Constance promised we would be kept together, Junie."

His sister let go of his hand and ran happily back to join Ruby.

*

Beryl pushed her head out of the tiny train window and looked for Miss Rye and her line of girls. Feeling a cold wind on her face, she retreated back into the carriage, but seconds later she looked out again, hoping to see a row of smart girls on the platform.

"What are you doing?" George asked.

"She's looking for her friend Meg," Ruby said.

George looked puzzled.

Ruby sat forward. "You know, one of the girls with that other woman."

Junie's eyes drooped in tiredness. George pulled her rag doll out from his bag. "What makes you think those girls will be going with us?"

Beryl turned quickly from the window. "Because we talked about it. She said we'd find beautiful homes in Canada and she would come and visit me and Ruby."

"How does she know all that?" George asked, placing the doll next to Junie's face so its smell would help her sleep.

"Because she's read about it. She said Canada's a wonderful place and told me a story about an orphan who arrives at a beautiful white house surrounded by apple trees and everyone there falls in love with her."

"Anne of Green Gables!" said Lawrence.

They all looked at him. He'd barely spoken since they'd left the ship.

Lawrence wriggled to sit up. "It's the story of an orphan taken home by a farmer. But the farmer's sister doesn't want her. She wants a boy to help out with the hard jobs. But Anne tries to win the sister over –dyes her red hair because she thinks no one likes it." Red hair made him think of Harry, and he gazed at the empty seat beside him.

"Is this story true?" George asked.

Lawrence shook head. "No, it's all made up."

The train whistle blew and the children felt the engine tug slightly back, then forward. Beryl peered further out the window. A few people waved to the train, but there was no sign of Miss Rye and her girls.

She sighed and sat down, sinking back into her seat. "I wonder who we'll end up with. I didn't like the look of those people who turned up this morning."

George shook his head, thinking of the stooped old man who'd wanted to take him.

The train moved slowly, passing large warehouses that could have been in London except they were clean and made of wood.

Beryl pointed to two brightly painted houses that sat side by side – one painted yellow with its neighbour a pale lemon. "How many families do you think live in those?"

Ruby stared out the window. "I think they look like fairy castles."

Junie, whose eyes had been shut, sat up quickly to look. "Where? Did it have fairies outside?"

George smiled. "There was no castle. It was just a house – go back to sleep."

Junie lay back for a moment and then sat upright. "Where are we going?"

Beryl shrugged.

George patted his sister's head. "We're going to another big house where we'll stay a while before going off with a family who want us."

"Who are they?" Junie asked.

George shook his head. "I don't know yet."

"Will they be nice people?"

George nodded. "Miss Constance wouldn't let us go with anyone who wasn't nice."

Junie lay back with her eyes closed, and the others watched the vast Canadian countryside stretch by.

Lawrence looked up slowly. "How do we know we'll go with someone nice?"

George looked at Beryl.

"Because Miss Constance said we would." Beryl spoke emphatically.

"But suppose she's wrong. What if someone tells lies and we end up with someone cruel." Lawrence thought of the serialised stories of *Oliver Twist* and *David Copperfield* his father had read him.

"That's not going to happen," said George as his stomach churned at the thought that Lawrence might be right. "Miss Constance will see we go with good people."

He looked up to see Miss Constance coming along the carriage aisle with a bucket of berries, a gift from Mikey's new family. As she distributed a handful to each child, George put up his hand.

"Miss Constance, you said we're all going to stay with good families, but how do you know the families are good?"

Constance smiled at the anxious faces before her, and sat down, edging as much space as she could next to Beryl and Ruby.

"All the families who take you good children will be Christian families. And we will know they are Christian families because we ask them to provide a letter from their preacher. Without this letter no family will be considered good enough to receive any of you."

The children waited for more.

Constance wondered what else she could say to give them faith. "You know Miss MacPherson has planned this very well. The children she has brought here are all happy in their new Christian homes."

"The families who took Sam and Mikey, were they Christian?" George asked as he remembered the stooped man and his pinched fingers.

Constance nodded. "They most certainly were, and you can be sure Sam and Mikey are both counting their blessings as we speak."

"What if we don't like our new families?" asked Lawrence.

Constance gave him a large smile. "But I'm sure you will like them. After all, we would not let you go off with anyone if we didn't think they were good people."

But Lawrence thought of David Copperfield and the brother and sister who treated him cruelly and the detestable Uriah Heep. "How can you be so sure they are nice? Supposing they just don't like us?"

Constance laughed. "Lawrence, how could anyone not like you? And besides, Miss MacPherson has set a wonderful procedure in place. You will all be visited in your new homes by the local minister, and he will make sure you are happy and treated well."

She looked at the faces around her, hoping she had stilled their anxieties.

"But suppose," Lawrence said. "Just suppose, we don't like our family."

Constance reached out and patted his shoulder. "Lawrence, if you are not happy in your home, then you can write to Miss Bilbrough, and she will have you brought back immediately."

Lawrence looked up, his face a little brighter. "We can really do that?"

"Absolutely," Constance turned and spread her gaze around the tight circle. "You all can."

The children smiled at each other, except Beryl who had her own question.

"Miss Constance, what has happened to the other girls, the ones who were travelling with Miss Rye?"

Constance shrugged and lifted her bucket of berries. She gave a handful to Lawrence and George. "I believe those children have been found homes in Quebec."

She held out a handful of berries to Beryl, but the girl didn't notice. Instead she shook her head. "But what about my friend, we thought we would see each other on the train. We promised to visit each other at our new homes."

Constance shook her head. "This is a large country, Beryl. I'm sure you will make new friends."

But Beryl shook her head, waving away Constance's handful of berries.

*

The train journey lasted four days. The children grew tired of dozing or sitting still. As he watched the vast countryside pass by, George felt his old home pull further and further away. Junie grew fractious, wanting to play chase with Ruby, Hannah and Dora even though George told her repeatedly that there was no room for chase between the bags that littered the floor. Beryl tried to amuse the girls with quieter play, but Ruby grew easily bored and, on the second day, announced that she wanted her ma.

"You can't," said Beryl. "She's too far away."

She began to cry. "I miss her."

Junie's own eyes watered as she called out for her ma and for Rose, Maggie and Tommy.

Hannah and Dora began to cry too although they didn't have a ma, brothers or sisters.

"Stop!" cried out Beryl.

George looked around for Constance.

"Let's sing!" Beryl surprised herself with the suggestion.

"Sing what?" asked Ruby. "You can't sing."

Beryl smiled. "Oh, yes I can."

Up and down the City Road, in an' out the Eagle,

That's the way the money goes, pop goes the weasel

The girls laughed as Beryl's voice warbled.

Constance came through from the next carriage and smiled to see the children happy.

*

By the time the train pulled into Belleville Station, night had fallen. The large group bundled out onto the platform with Constance looking for Ellen Bilbrough or a messenger seeking one woman accompanied by ninety children. She watched anxiously as a few men walked toward them, all staring at the young woman guarding a mob of tired children. Constance followed them with her eyes as they greeted others who'd climbed from the train.

As the train pulled out, Constance hailed a station porter. "Excuse me, sir, but I wonder if you might know the way to Marchmont House. It is late and we were expecting to be met by one of our church members."

The tall porter gave the line of children a long stare. "Some of them are a bit young, aren't they?"

Constance looked at her charges and smiled. "They are all good children and eager for a new life."

The man nodded slowly. "Well, I'm sorry no one came out here to greet you, but I think that perhaps no one knew of your arrival." He lifted his lamp. "If you let me light this and lock up a few things here, then I'll be happy to show you the way."

Constance's sigh was audible, and the children stood a little straighter as they held tight to their canvas satchels. The night air was cold after the heat of the train. Junie snuggled close to her brother, as he unfastened his jacket and pulled it tight around her shoulders so they could share in each other's warmth. The stillness in the air kept the children quiet, as though they were afraid to disturb the space that surrounded them.

Soon, the railway porter appeared with his lamp. The children followed him two by two through the streets of Belleville, the shuffle of their feet against the cobbles the only sound. George listened, trying to hear a noise from taverns, singing or arguments that might turn physical, but there was nothing.

He turned around to look at Beryl. "Where is everyone?" he mouthed.

She shrugged, relieved that there were no street whores plying a trade and no gin stalls – just a silence that felt like peace.

The railway porter rang the bell of Marchmont House twice. Behind him, Constance wondered if he'd brought them to the right place. This large two-story home, with its walk-around porch and huge garden could only belong to a rich family.

"I'm sure Miss Bilbrough just didn't know to expect you," the porter said.

Constance looked up quickly. "Miss Bilbrough lives here?"

The porter laughed. "Well, how else is she going to take care of all those orphans you've brought us?"

Constance shook her head, finding it hard to reconcile the Ellen Bilbrough she knew from crowded London with the grand home before her.

The door opened and Constance stepped back in relief at seeing her church sister.

The tall Miss Bilbrough smiled in surprise at the faces lit by the pale moonlight. "The letter I received told me to expect you tomorrow." She clapped her hands as though stirring herself to action. "Children, I am so sorry I wasn't there at the station to receive you." She rested her gaze momentarily on Ruby then let her eyes skip to Junie.

"But, no matter, I am happy to see you all." She stood aside to let them enter.

The children stood still, all except Lawrence who limped up the steps as if such grand homes were his regular domain. Beryl held her breath, expecting to see his way barred and his bent frame redirected to the servants' entry. Instead, Miss Bilbrough smiled and patted his head as he stepped through the doorway.

The rest of the children surged forward, and Constance held up her hand as children three and four abreast hurried through the wide door. "Stop! We must be orderly!" she called out.

Ellen shook her head. "They've been restrained for long enough in the train, let them explore their surroundings."

As the children hurried from room to room shouting about its space and fine walls and claiming beds as their own, Ellen ran downstairs to the kitchen where the cook had spent days preparing food for the new arrivals. Not all of it was ready, but Ellen pulled out trays of bread, ham and jelly.

"Call the children to the dining room," she told Constance.

Constance glanced right, left and then behind her. She still clutched her suitcase. "Where is the dining room?"

Ellen pointed. "Behind the day room – you can't miss it – turn right at the stairs, then left."

Constance hurried upstairs, garnering children to follow her direction.

The dining room might once have held grand balls. Constance didn't know how much floor space a ball might need, but she was sure there was space to dance here. "Mother would love this room," she whispered to herself as she admired the floral wallpaper and heavy damask drapes.

The children dropped their voices as though in church and moved slowly to find a place at one of the two long tables.

"This is a rich man's house," whispered George.

Lawrence nodded as he felt the rich texture of the wallpaper. He felt faintly at ease, even though he wished Harry were with him.

Ellen hurried in carrying a huge tray of bread. "There's ham on its way, and Constance would you bring up the jugs of milk from the pantry." She hurriedly placed the food on the nearest table. "Now, children, you'll have to be patient with me. I wasn't expecting you until tomorrow evening, but you know I'm happy to see you, it'll just take me a little longer to get you all served."

George smiled. He felt very welcome and was more than happy to wait for his food.

*

"You have two letters," Winifred whispered to Helen as the two women hurried upstairs. "I left them on your desk – one has a Canadian stamp, the other has come from Africa."

Helen hurried, pushing through the mass of children as they surged downstairs toward the dinner hall. One child, an older orphan tried to stop her and ask about a spelling word, but Helen only patted the child's head as she sped along the hallway to her small office.

The letters sat side by side: Constance's hasty scrawl next to Mathew's careful print. But which to open first? She did want to know how Constance had fared. One hundred children wrenched from their homeland to be deposited among strangers was no simple mission. But Mathew, how long had it been? She slit open his envelope and fed her eyes on his bold black writing.

Dear Mother,

I must apologise for the delay in writing. I could explain it away by saying I have not had time for the days are too short. But, in truth, I must say I have been simply too tired. Work here carries Roger and I through many miles of bush and, when we arrive in a

134

*village, the initial thrust of persuading the chief to let us stay,
finding beds, food and simply beginning in the spread of Our
Lord's word finds me exhausted. I must also admit there are times
when I hold back from writing because thoughts of home could
send me crazy with longing. Simple thoughts of London with its
busy streets gives me a yearning that threatens to tear my chest
apart. So, I do what you would wish, Mother, and I simply try not
to think of home with you and Constance in the cosy chaos that I so
well remember.*

*But before you fear for my condition, I must tell you that this
has been a good week. Two weeks ago, we arrived in a small
village in a remote district north of Lake Kariba. At first we feared
the chief was already against us as he refused to meet with our
guide, saying he was resting. Three days later, with us taking all
our rest in a torn tent, finding ourselves bitten by mosquitos, and
eating up our own supplies, we were still told that he was resting.
Roger, being more temperamental than I, pushed our guide for
more information. Finally, we were told the chief had fever. Our
Christian ways are wonderful, Mother, for with this information we
were able to bring forth our medicines, and the chief was feeling
much better after only a few hours. With such an introduction, the
chief and his aides treated us with a wonderful feast, providing us
our own hut with grass mattresses and, of course, permission to
talk to the people about our Good Lord.*

*So, Mother, I am feeling well. I miss you so much I dare not
write of it. But our mission is faring well. I will send this letter with
a trader heading to the coast. By the time you receive it, we should
be heading south toward Salisbury. Please write soon, that I may
receive words from home when I arrive there.*

I think of you always,
Your loving son,
Mathew

Helen held the page to her cheek, feeling the tracks of her
son's ink against her face. She inhaled, hoping to catch a smell of
his. But after a few moments, tears erupted and Helen pulled the
parchment from her cheek, fearing tears might wash away her son's
words. She wept quietly. Her boy was not happy on this far-flung
mission, and he should have stayed home. Spreading word of Our

Lord was not a task that came easy to him. Such a quiet boy didn't like to vent his feelings on others. That was more the way of Constance, whose strong conviction strived to conquer even the most sceptical of audiences. Mathew preferred his privacy, holding his thoughts to his chest. His mission to Africa had surprised Helen. Her son had kept a polite distance when Minister Beckett had talked of the mission. Now, she wondered if Constance had ushered her brother toward Africa because she herself couldn't go.

Helen glanced at her daughter's letter and slit it open slowly.

My Dear Mother,

You will be pleased to hear we have arrived in Canada safely. The journey on board the ship was long and made difficult by the loss of Harry Twistle. He is the boy from the East End Workhouse. His mother may still be there and, Mother, I ask that you please visit her and relate the story of her son's demise. He was with another boy, our dear Lawrence, and they were watching from the deck for sight of large fish when a strong wave washed over the boat and swept poor Harry out to sea. I feel strongly that he didn't suffer. But, Mother, you must contact his mother and relay the information as well as you can.

Helen thrust the letter onto her desk and sat back in frustration as she wondered how she could tell a mother that Constance had lost her child at sea. She fingered her son's envelope trying to remember the boy called Harry, but the children had been rounded up so quickly that she had no clear recollection of a boy from the East End Workhouse.

She picked up her daughter's letter, holding it further from her face than before.

The children have all been very well behaved. We had some problems on board the ship, but they did not come from our dear boys and girls. A woman boarded with a large group of orphan girls all heading for Canada. You may recognise the name – Maria Rye – she is occasionally mentioned in the newspapers as a friend of Lord Salisbury. Anyway, I do not believe her to be a firm Christian as she frequently taunted me by bidding her children to sing louder than ours. Of course, this only spurred our efforts, so our voices were rarely drowned out. You will be proud, Mother, to know that I did attempt to engage Miss Rye in conversation so we could share experiences, but she is a very cold fish. In fact, on examination of her, I am surprised that she is involved in the care of orphans. Her clothes are expensively fashionable, which seems greatly at odds with someone who attempts to do good for those less fortunate.

The good news, Mother, is that we housed ten children as soon as we arrived in Halifax. Just as Annie MacPherson promised, Mr Bernard met us at the port having arranged accommodation at a local orphanage for us. The very next morning he had a host of prospective families waiting to select children from my care. Of course, I told him they could only have ten. He was hugely disappointed, as there were the people who had gathered hoping to take home an addition to their family. But we saw our first group taken off to good Christian homes and I must admit to having a tear in my eye as I waved them off.

Mother, you must tell the mothers that their children are happy in this fair land. We could not hope for a better setting for any venture. Ellen has hundreds of letters offering homes to our dear orphans. Mother, I know you had great doubts about this venture, but I can assure you that if you could see little Lawrence run in the sun as he chases the fair Ruby; and George as he grows pink from sunlight, you would be as firm as I in your conviction that Canada is the answer to all our prayers.

I will write soon.

Please think of us and pray always for our dear children.

Constance.

Helen folded the letter, gathered it together with the pages from her son, and placed them in a drawer.

*

George pulled his feet from the cold water, hopping from one foot to the other until he reached the shore. "My feet are frozen."

Beryl giggled. "It can't be that bad."

"It is! I swear." George looked around quickly to see if Miss Constance had heard him, but she was busy talking with the Miss Ellen – the two women slicing bread and cheese in preparation for the picnic.

When Miss Ellen announced the trip to the lakeside, George had thought that this was where they might meet their new families, and his stomach had tightened with nerves. But instead, that good woman had brought them to play at the waterside, spreading out blankets so they could enjoy the sun and promising them an outdoor luncheon with fresh lemonade. George had never tasted lemonade until he'd arrived in Marchmont. Its dire tang had pulled his cheeks inward, making Junie laugh and he'd shaken his head, vowing never to take another sip. But over the last week, he'd taken small tastes that had grown into glassfuls.

Beryl moved tentatively to the water's edge. Drawn by her movement, Ruby and Junie followed, running backward as a gentle wave ushered to meet them. The girls giggled, and Beryl stepped into a wave so that the cold lapped around her legs and she curled her face up to the sky in playful shock.

"Let's go in," squealed Ruby, as she pulled Junie forward. The girls tiptoed until the water stroked their toes and they ran back in wails of joy.

"Lawrence!" George called out to the younger boy.

Lawrence lay under a tree reading his copy of *Robinson Crusoe*.

"Lawrence, come down and play – it's fun!"

The younger boy didn't take his eyes from the page as he shook his head. He didn't want to see the others at play. As he glanced under his eyelids at George, all wet feet and red toes, Lawrence knew he could never let the other children see his bad foot all bare. He didn't want them to stare in horror, like he was some kind of monster.

Harry had seen his foot, and Lawrence had watched his friend's mouth grow long.

"How did it happen?" his friend had asked.

Lawrence didn't know. His father had never told him.

He felt a droplet of water land on his bare arm and looked up to see Ruby standing over him.

"Come and play. It'll be more fun with you."

Lawrence shook his head. "I'm reading."

"Please!" Ruby bent down onto her knees and pushed her face toward his so that all he could see were her playful grey eyes.

"I don't want to," he said, looking quickly away.

"Please!" Thick curls fell onto her face and she pushed them back so she could gaze more intently at her friend.

Lawrence kicked his foot so that it left the ground ever so briefly. Ruby flickered with recognition.

"No one will look. Besides, we just want to have fun."

Lawrence shook his head, his eyes back on the page.

Ruby stood and held out her hand. "It isn't the same with you up here reading."

Lawrence looked down at the water's edge where Beryl and George held Junie's hand as they ran in and out of the water, squealing as each small wave followed them.

"Do you promise no one will stare?"

Ruby held her hands to her chest in prayer. "I promise."

She smiled as Lawrence sat up and untied the laces to his boots.

George gazed for a few moments as Lawrence limped to the waterside. He watched the thickened instep, wondering what filled it so full and gazed at the curled up toes fearing they might reach out and grab him. Beryl nudged him, pulling his attention back toward play. She had seen such a foot on a client, a quiet man who had been one of her more gentle customers.

As Lawrence stood staring down at his own bare feet, Ruby and Junie took his hands and pulled him to the water's edge. He squealed as the cold clamped around his skin and joined the others in hurrying back to shore, all letting out huge screams of delight.

Constance looked up from the bowl of cherries she was portioning out and watched them at play. "This truly is the Garden of Eden."

Ellen stood from the blankets she was spreading out over the soft grass. "It is a fair land during the summer, but I promise you that the winters are harsh. Annie and I landed here in springtime and the wind and frost were still stronger than any I ever saw in London."

Constance shrugged. "Winter is always unpredictable. In London, last winter was cold, whereas the one before brought hardly any snow."

Ellen shook her head. "There is little here to stop the wind as it crosses this vast land. Farmers say the snow can drown houses so they have to run a rope between their front door and their barns or they would lose their way."

Constance smiled. "I am sure the people are good storytellers. There is little else for entertainment."

"No, I believe them when they say the cold and snow bring death to those not prepared. In fact, autumn here is the busiest time as everyone prepares for winter. I myself have been told to stock up on such vast provisions that only the Queen herself could ever store so much in London. They say we should receive no children between October and March because the weather is too harsh for travel."

Constance held a handful of cherries over a bowl. This was August and she knew Annie MacPherson had planned three more trips each with one hundred children before Christmas.

"Surely, the ships still ply the seas, and the trains still find their path along their tracks? We should be well positioned to bring many more children. Miss MacPherson certainly believes so."

Ellen left a long pause before she spoke. "We must believe in the people who know these parts and call for caution on travel during the winter months. We must give way to their wisdom."

Constance turned and smiled. "Ellen, dear, it is faith that must carry us forward. Any delay in lifting children from the depraved streets of our squalid city means exposing them to the vices that clamber for their very souls. Every boatload of children we bring to this fair land is a boatload of children saved."

She pointed to George, Beryl, Lawrence, Ruby and Junie playing at the water's edge. "Look at these children laughing with joy when they might have stayed in their homeland locked in poverty and vice. That oldest girl is but eleven years of age; yet her mother had already pulled her down into the world of prostitution and was preparing the little sister for such a life. George and Junie I found in a dirty attic working on matchstick boxes every hour of their waking lives." She paused to catch a brief breath. "We cannot forget any of this because of a winter's frost. We must be brave, dear Ellen. We must have faith that the way forward will not be easy, and we must battle all that nature throws in our way."

Ellen sighed. She had already written to Annie MacPherson, advising that shipments of children be halted over winter and hoped her letter would be received more sympathetically.

*

Lawrence didn't particularly like the porridge served in Marchmont, but it was bad manners to complain. As he scooped up the sodden grits at the bottom of his bowl, George tapped his shoulder.

"It's today – I bet you."

Lawrence looked blank.

George gave a sideways nod toward the top of the table. "I heard Miss Ellen talking with a man in the hallway. She told him that prospect-ta-tative families would be here this afternoon. I think that means the people who want us to live with them."

Lawrence looked down into his bowl, a deep frown etched across his brow. He didn't want to move again. Leaving his own home had been bad, then living with his father's friend, Mrs Peterson, had been difficult, especially after he wet the bed and he'd been made to sleep on the floor. Lawrence's face still flushed red when he thought about it. He didn't know how it had happened. He'd never wet the bed in his own home. But Miss Winifred had been good and given him a waxed sheet and, here, Miss Ellen had waxed sheets on all the beds. He hadn't wet the bed here, but what if he disgraced himself at the next house?

"How do you think it all happens?" George asked.

Lawrence, the flush of disgrace still on his cheeks, looked puzzled.

"You know – how do these new people decide who they take? Do they get to poke at us again the way they did in that last town?"

Lawrence shook his head. "No, I think that was unusual. I imagine they talk to us – ask questions about our favourite hobbies and what we like to read – after all they have to know where our schooling should begin."

George frowned, realising that his schooling would be back at the beginning. All those letters Miss Constance had taught him at the Home of Industry were completely forgotten.

Constance stood at the entrance to the dining room and clapped her hands. "Dear children, I must tell you that the day you have been awaiting has arrived. Good Christian families from around this generous town of Belleville are travelling here at this moment, so they can choose one of you to raise in their home."

Her gaze travelled the room as she took each small face in turn, proud that she had delivered them from vice and depravity. She clapped her hands once more. "Now, children, you must do some work for yourselves. The people who travel here today all want to take home a good and happy child. Therefore, we ask that you smile and show yourself to be good-natured."

A boy's hand shot up. He was the tallest among them, and George had kept his distance fearing he may be like Sam and Mikey.

Constance nodded toward him. "Yes, Charley, what do you have to say?"

The boy smiled, showing a row of broken brown teeth. "Miss Constance, the man in the last town told us not to show our teeth when we smiled, but I find that very hard so can we show them here?"

Constance grinned, showing her own long, slim incisors. "Of course you may. These good people must want you for who you are and not for a good set of molars."

She looked around for more questions then continued: "But I do ask that you be on your best behaviour. Now, boys, I suggest you stand tall and don't slouch. Girls, you should look gentle and I advise you not look at anyone unless they speak to you."

Beryl drew her thighs together, clenching them tightly. She hated any kind of scrutiny.

"Now, Miss Ellen is upstairs and will supervise the bathrooms. You must file upstairs – the boys to the right, girls to the left – where Miss Ellen will guide you toward a bath. It shouldn't take long. You must comb your hair well after bathing and put on the clean shirt or blouse from your bag. I want to see all of you down here looking very smart."

As a buzz of noise rose from the breakfast tables, George realised he didn't have a clean shirt. He'd missed putting clothes in the laundry because he'd been at the toilet when Miss Constance had asked for dirty clothes. Now both his shirts were as grimy as any he had at home.

He stood in line behind Lawrence. Thoughts of the visitors sent a direct signal to his bowel.

"Please," he asked Miss Constance as she hurried past. "Can I visit the lavatory?"

She rolled her eyes ever so quickly. "If you must, George, but hurry."

The others giggled as he sprinted out the back door to the latrines.

Further up the stairs and closer to the bathrooms, Beryl held Ruby and Junie's hands. Between them, the two smaller girls stroked and patted Junie's rag doll.

"Now, girls, remember we have to look our best. Let's practise smiling," Beryl said.

Ruby spread her plump mouth, showing dimpled cheeks and shiny, pale grey eyes.

Junie's thin smile lengthened her already long chin and showed teeth speckled brown. Beryl looked from Junie's sparse dark hair and ruffled her own sister's thick curls. "Now remember not to talk until someone talks to you first."

*

The children stood in nine rows at the centre of Marchmont's garden. The boys stood upright, slouching occasionally then thrusting out their chests when they remembered that someone might be watching. None spoke as the queue of strangers grew.

At the gate, Constance greeted each new arrival with a smile and called on the Lord to bless this day. She talked with one man and a pretty woman for a long time. George liked the look of them, and felt deep flutters in his bowel as he hoped they might choose him and Junie.

Ellen gave each visitor a more searching look, peering into their eyes as if seeking the devil himself. After giving their names, the prospective families stood in line alongside the hedge. They watched the children, talking quietly among themselves.

Beryl felt the stares of an older couple and blushed. A middle-aged man, his face worn from the sun, also gave her long looks and Beryl clenched her thighs so tight that Ruby whispered, "Do you need to go to the lavatory?"

Beryl shook her head and stood straighter, reminding herself that all these people wanted was help with their homes and farms. And in return, they would provide board and schooling. Whoring wasn't a part of it.

Constance led the handsome couple toward the children and the other adults sped forward. A tall farmer in a dusty jacket pulled at the tall boy who'd asked about hiding his rotten teeth. Several women stopped in front of Beryl.

"Do you know how to bake?" asked an elderly woman in a large bonnet.

Beryl shook her head. "No, ma'am."

The woman hurried on.

"She looks good for training," said a tall, thin woman to her short, fat companion.

The two women stood back to give Beryl their full assessment.

"Not too starved," said one.

"Not too small either," said the other.

"I think she'll do."

Beryl looked up quickly. "I'm sorry, Ma'ams," Beryl nodded toward Ruby, "but I have to stay with my little sister. We can't be separated."

The two women turned their scrutiny on Ruby for only a moment. "I'm sorry," said the plump one, "but we don't need any youngsters. All we need is a housemaid." The two women moved on to another girl.

"I didn't like them," said Ruby.

"Me neither, but we can't be choosey."

A thin woman, tanned by the sun and wearing a faded dress stopped in front of Beryl. "How old are you?"

"Eleven, ma'am," Beryl looked up only briefly.

"Are you a good cook?"

Beryl remembered that her ma didn't think so. "I don't know, Ma'am. It depends on what you like."

"Can folks eat what you cook?" the woman said a little impatiently.

Beryl nodded. "I suppose so."

"What's your name?"

"Beryl, Ma'am."

The woman held out her hand. "Well, Beryl, you've got yourself a new home."

Beryl shook her head. "But, Ma'am, what about my little sister? If you take me you've got to take her, too? She's young and I have to take care of her."

The woman looked at Ruby and shook her head. "I don't think so. My John would say no to another mouth to feed."

Beryl shook her head still more. "Then, I'm sorry, Ma'am, but I can't go with you."

The handsome couple, still accompanied by Constance, stopped in front of Ruby.

"Why, she is beautiful," said the woman, her own hair mimicking Ruby's curls.

"What's your name, child?" asked the man. Beryl noticed his clothes were crisp with barely a crease.

Ruby smiled, showing her dimples in full glory. "Ruby, Sir."

"And how old are you?"

Ruby looked at her older sister before answering. "Seven, Ma'am."

"How adorable," said the woman as she dropped onto her knees so she was on the same level as Ruby. "Tell me, how do you like to spend your time?"

Ruby glanced again at Beryl before answering. "I like to play, Ma'am, with my doll. I left my own dolly, her name was Sarah, in my old house; but my friend Junie lets me play with her doll. We share her." She held up Victoria.

The woman grinned at the sight of the dirty, faded rag doll and then gazed at Ruby, staring into her face, before reaching out and stroking, gently, at Ruby's curls. She glanced up at her husband before speaking. "Dear Ruby, I think I would like you to come and live with us. How would you feel about that?"

Ruby looked up at Beryl and tears came into her eyes. She held up her hands to cover her face.

The woman reached out and held Ruby's shoulder. "Whatever is wrong, dear child?"

Ruby shook her head from side to side. Through sobs, they could eventually hear, "I want to stay with Beryl."

The woman turned her face to the sister. "Are you Beryl?"

"Yes, Ma'am."

The woman stood. "Now I understand." She knelt down again and spoke gently to Ruby. "Please don't cry, child. We won't make you do anything you don't want to."

She stood, took her husband's arm and walked away without a glance at any other child.

Nearby, George was having his arm muscles squeezed by a farmer in a dusty jacket. His face, lined and brown from the outdoors, peered at George. "You look like you know how to work. How old are you?"

"Eleven, Sir."

The man shook his head. "I was really looking for an older boy." He glanced around, noticing the bigger boys were being led to the desk for registration. "I guess you'll have to do."

"Sir, I have a sister, and I promised my ma we'd stay together."

The man dug at the ground with the toe of his boot and let out a long sigh. "Which one is she?"

George pointed to Junie.

"She's a bit young."

"She's seven, Sir."

The man looked up at the sky as though contemplating the weather. "What's your name?"

"George."

"Well, George, you'd better take hold of your sister because you're both coming with me."

George felt the ground move. He didn't know this man from any other.

"Well, come on if you're coming," the man called out.

George's heart raced as he spun around and slipped Junie's hand from Beryl's. "We have to go now," he said, his face flushed red with fear.

"Where?" Beryl and Junie asked together.

George nodded his head toward the man, who stood talking with Constance.

"But I don't know him," Junie said.

"We have to go. He's giving us a home with food and schooling." He tugged at Junie's hand, keen suddenly to get moving and have it all over with.

Beryl watched him pull Junie toward the registration desk. "Good luck," she called out, but the words didn't seem enough. "Write to us – here at the house – I'll find the letters. Let us know you're both well." Tears came as she realised that George couldn't write any better than she could read.

Junie stared back at them. Her mouth opened and closed as though she wanted to cry out but the words were stuck.

Miss Constance waved as they followed the man in the dusty jacket down the path.

Beryl wiped her eyes on her sleeve and then smoothed at the tears that marred Ruby's cheeks. A woman standing before them moved on.

Suddenly, Junie's voice yelled out from the distance. "I've left Victoria!"

Ruby watched the gate, expecting to see Junie run through and claim her dear Victoria.

Instead, she heard a deeper voice, a man's voice, roar louder. "Shut up and get moving!"

*

Helen hurried through the market. It was the day of the bird fair, and hawkers held out cages of small birds in every colour.

A young man thrust a coop in front of her face. Inside a tiny yellow bird sat shivering. "Talk to you, this one will," he barked.

Helen glared at him until he pulled the creature away. She hurried on and passed a man selling pigeons from a large basket while nearby a woman held a tray of pigeon pies.

A tall man stepped into Helen's path and unfurled a blanket to reveal a small dog with long matted hair. The creature's eyes stayed cast down as though it held no hope of rescue in this world. Helen guessed it was a pampered pet stolen from the west end.

She shook her head. "Show some mercy to the poor creature."

He stepped aside and Helen hurried on. With each step she hammered out her anger at Constance for what she was forcing her to do. Winifred had offered to go in her place, and Helen had been tempted. But it was her job. Her daughter had persuaded the poor woman to part with her son and now her daughter had lost the poor child to the sea. She reached the workhouse gate before she was sure what she would say. "I'm sorry, Ma'am, but your son is with the Lord." This didn't seem to have any recompense to a woman who had lost her child.

Mr Marsh opened the gate. "Mrs Petrie, what good work brings you to our door this blessed day?"

Helen gave the man a cursory stare before stepping forward. "I'm here with bad news. I need to speak to one of your women, Mrs Twistle."

"Ah, she's a rough one, that. Not for the likes of gracious company like yours." Mr Marsh gave Helen what she judged as a leering stare.

"I think I can judge my own company, Mr Marsh. Now, if you would please call the poor woman to your office where I trust you will grant us the privacy we need?"

Mr Marsh called out to a woman scrubbing stone steps. "Lizzy, get Twistle up here." He gave Helen another leering smile. "Please, Mrs Petrie, take my very own seat."

He led her into a small room and saw Helen's nose twitch at the stale smell of smoke and the slightly sweet tang of gin. He coughed as though the smell was distasteful. "A bottle was broke here a few weeks since – it was an inmate smuggled it in, and I broke it to show him it was bad – can't get rid of the smell though – haunts me."

Helen rolled her eyes at his story.

He pulled some parchments from his desk. "Sit 'ere in my seat – it's the best in the house."

Helen noticed the dark stained cushion and looked around for somewhere else, but there was no other seat in the room. "Actually, might I use another place – somewhere that might allow Mrs

Twistle to be seated alongside me? I bring her poor news of her son, and she's likely to be upset when she hears it."

Mr Marsh still held onto his precious chair. "Oh, don't you worry about Twistle. She's not like you and me – not much could knock her off her feet."

"Mr Marsh, might we have the use of a classroom or some such place that might be unoccupied at this time?"

He thought for a few moments, knowing he couldn't show her the classroom as it was full of shirts the inmates had made that would be sold at the market for a keen profit. He stood straight like a bolt had struck his spine. "What about the kitchen? Mrs Marsh is out right now, and it's nice and warm down there." He didn't say that Mrs Marsh had left him after she'd found him with a ten-year-old girl whose parents were inmates.

Helen followed him down to the kitchen, her eyes catching sight of two large rats scurrying from a bake tray.

"We can't do anything about them. No matter what kind of trap we set and how many we catch, they keep coming back."

Helen gave a barely perceived nod as she noted the grime across the stove, the fireplace heaped in old ashes and the large holes in the wall that could have let in dogs never mind rats.

Mr Marsh retreated back up the stairs. "I'll send Twistle down to you, Mrs Petrie."

Helen scuffed her toe along the floor, digging up a thick layer of grease and dirt. Short, fast feet from the stairs made her look up. Her heart raced as she wondered, yet again, how she would tell this poor woman about her son's demise.

The red-haired woman hurried forward. "Sir says you have news of my Harry. Is he well? Does he have a good home?"

Helen shook her head at the "Sir". "Please, Mrs Twistle, take a seat." She wondered again where to begin. That the boy was with the Lord echoed through her thoughts, but she knew the poor woman needed more than that.

"Mrs Twistle, my daughter took one hundred children on the voyage to Canada. It was an ambitious mission, but she is a keen missionary and is thoroughly convinced it is the correct path to take."

Mrs Twistle's face stretched long as she puzzled to make sense of Helen's words.

Helen knew she had to speak more clearly. "Mrs Twistle, there was an accident on board the ship and unfortunately little Harry was washed overboard and lost at sea."

The woman gazed at Helen like she was waiting for something else to replace the news she'd just heard – a laugh, a note that it was all untrue. "Are you sure it was my Harry?"

Helen nodded. "I'm afraid so. My daughter writes that it all happened very fast – she doesn't believe he suffered."

Mrs Twistle stared unblinking as if waiting for more.

"He was on deck with another boy, Lawrence, a Home of Industry orphan that he'd made friends with. They were looking out for big fish. But I suppose the waves are big and strong out on the ocean and, unfortunately, the deck was flooded with Harry carried out to sea."

A small gulping sob caused the woman to finally look away from Helen. Another sob followed until Mrs Twistle's chest was heaving with cries. Helen gathered her into a hug, but the woman pushed her away.

"Please, Harry is now with the Lord. He will have no more suffering, Mrs Twistle." Helen whispered the words, knowing she herself would need far more than this. She pulled the woman to her again, but Mrs Twistle's wiry arms pushed her away.

The deep sobs gave way to angry shouts. "Harry, my Harry – at least I kept him safe – but your lot – killed him. Why? Why Harry?"

Tears sprang to Helen's eyes as she tried to appease the woman. "Please, Mrs Twistle, maybe we should pray."

"Pray! What for? My Harry's gone – what good's a bloody prayer." She pushed Helen against the kitchen table. "My only boy and he's gone and you want to give me a bloody prayer. You bastards – you liars – you …"

She lifted her hand to strike Helen, but Mr Marsh was there, holding the woman back and dragging her toward the stairs. Helen watched Mr Marsh pull Mrs Twistle backward and then her head struck the door jam, but the woman didn't cry out. Instead she kept up her curses which faded only as she was hauled further and further away.

Helen let out her own sobs and felt ready to fire Constance with her own curses. She'd promised to take care of the children –

pledged that she knew the responsibility she carried. And now she'd lost a child and brought more misery to a woman who had so little in the world.

Helen hurried up the steps, passed Mr Marsh's stagnant office and heard the gates of the workhouse hammer shut behind her.

Her feet hit the rough cobbles and spattered through the damp mud with speedy steps, but the pained face of Mrs Twistle wouldn't go away.

A short stepped into her path, an open bag of lace collars on his arm. Helen pushed him aside before he could utter a word. She hurried down White's Row and onto Bell's Lane, pounding out anger at her daughter for being so blind, her annoyance at Annie MacPherson for leading the way and her fury at the mission for following. She would speak out at the next meeting. She would tell them about the loss of Harry Twistle and describe his mother's agony – left behind in the workhouse with no hope or comfort – living under Mr Marsh's authority. That was another thing Helen would bring up. Mr Marsh was not just lazy and inept – he was cruel, she was sure of it.

A sudden pat to her shoulder made Helen turn. The thin, drawn woman before her looked like many others, but Helen knew she had seen the tight-set mouth before. She stared into the face looking for clues.

"You're Miss Constance's mother, aren't you? You came with her to our house, helped get my kids into your industry home."

Helen smiled, still unsure who the woman was.

"Your daughter's taken two of mine to Canada – our George and Junie – any news from them yet?"

Helen coloured, and Mary caught the glimmer of bad news. "My kids are alright – they haven't had anything bad happen – have they?"

Helen shook her head quickly. "No, no, your children have reached Canada. My daughter sent me a letter of their safe arrival."

Mary grinned. "You know, I wasn't keen on the idea of Canada – I'm still not sure about it, but I trust that daughter of yours. She's a real jewel is that one. You must be proud of her."

Helen gave a thin smile. "She's well intentioned."

"She was good news to our family. With the kids earning at the industry house and me working at home, I can pay the rent and afford meat for broth." Mary held up a thin sack she carried. "I couldn't have bought this when we was all working at home – without that daughter of yours I think we'd have been lining up at the workhouse door."

Helen's anger eased at hearing her daughter appreciated. "I will send you news of your children when I hear how they are."

Mary's hands fell to her chest. "You would? Oh please – tell my daughter Rose as soon as you hear anything. She works in that big house of yours – Rose Trupper is her name, you'll find her working on matchboxes. She's a good girl and will bring me any news you tell her."

Helen memorised the name. She would write to tell Constance that she must send news of the Trupper children.

*

Outside Marchmont gates, Junie sobbed about leaving Victoria while George watched the dark-haired man and tried to gauge his mood. His face looked harsh, and the muscles and bones too fixed to ever smile.

George whispered quietly into Junie's ear. "Please try and quiet down. We'll get your doll when we see Ruby again."

But Junie cried louder and pulled her brother back toward Marchmont House.

George felt his cheeks grow red with desperation. "Miss Constance will send it to you," he said, even though he knew this was unlikely.

The dark-haired man glared at Junie. "Get in the cart and stop wailing like a scalped calf or I'll be forced to show my hand."

Junie caught his tone, and instinct quietened her wail to small sobs. George looked back at the house, wondering if Miss Constance had heard the threat. But no one emerged from Marchmont gates.

"Get in!" the man commanded again.

George lifted Junie onto the wooden seat, pitched both their canvas bags onto the floor and climbed in after her. The man leapt in on the opposite side and, with a flick to the reins, the cart shuddered forward. The movement made Junie cling to George's arm. He tried to lift his shoulder and wrap his arm around her, but the cart jolted so much he feared falling off. He wanted to turn around and see Marchmont House again, but the speed and motion of the cart kept him fixed forward.

The dark-haired man also kept his gaze ahead, not turning to look as they moved out to the wide countryside where homes grew sparse.

George looked out at the land, wondering what work he would find. He thought about his lessons, how to recognise a good cow from a bad, how to know a good milker? Were the teats supposed to be long or short? He couldn't remember.

Junie kept her grip tight on his arm, so that he felt his wrist grow numb. He thought about freeing himself, pulling away from Junie's tense clasp, but the cart shook so much as it passed over the rough ground.

They turned off the well-worn track and moved uphill. The dark-haired man pointed silently toward a low mound.

George peered through the dimming light, eventually seeing a house built into the slope with a small entrance roofed over like a porch. He wondered if this was where they kept the animals, but as they grew close, a woman carrying a small child came out and watched their approach.

She stared at Junie and, as the cart grew close, she called out to the man. "I thought you was only bringing a boy?"

The man's voice sounded light, like he was making a joke but there was no grin. "It was two for one – special deal!"

He jumped from the cart, looked at George and nodded toward the woman. "Mrs Severn, do what she tells you."

The woman scrutinised him, then cast her eyes onto Junie. "Are they good workers?"

He shrugged. "I guess we'll find out." He pulled their canvas bags from the cart. "You'd best climb down."

George jumped onto the ground, throwing a cloud of dust into the air. He lifted Junie, her body felt stiff and heavy.

The man pointed to his wife. "She'll show you around."

George and Junie followed Mrs Severn through the porch and into a dark cavernous room with mud walls. Poles and branches provided support. A small stove sat at the back of the room, its glow casting a small beckoning light.

"It's not rich, but it's warm in winter," the woman said as she put the small child onto a rug on the earthen floor.

She led George and Junie back outside and around the earthen mound to a smaller hole in the hillside. It had no door, just a wooden gate. Inside, George saw a straw mattress with a dusty blanket.

"You'll sleep here. I was only expecting one of you, so you'll have to share the blanket." Mrs Severn's voice was dry. "You'll eat with us."

She turned and scrutinised Junie like she was taking her measurements. "Can you sew?" she asked.

Junie looked up at George and waited for him to answer.

George shook his head. "We made matchboxes at home."

"Well, I don't suppose she can cook then?"

George shook his head.

The woman stood a little straighter. "Well, she can learn to peel potatoes. Follow me!"

They followed Mrs Severn to a sack of potatoes. The woman pulled a rusty knife from her apron. "Here, use this."

Both children stared at her.

Mrs Severn shook as she raised her voice. "I want eight of them potatoes peeled and put in that pot. It ain't nothing difficult, and if you wants any feeding then get to work."

George reached for the knife, but the woman pulled it away before it was in his grasp. "This is her work. She can work the house with me," she yelled. "You go and see what he has for you."

Junie's wide eyes watched George step backward. She gazed at him as he spoke slowly:

"Take the knife, Junie, and peel the skin off the potatoes then put them in the pot. I'll be back to see you, I promise." George's heart raced with the urge to flee, dragging his little sister behind him.

He walked slowly to where he'd seen cows. They were much bigger than the ones that had boarded the ship in England. Mr Severn was hammering a loose slat onto a fence that held even bigger cows with faces larger than anything George had ever seen.

Mr Severn pointed to the smaller beasts. "You ever milked before, boy?"

George shook his head.

"Well, now you'll learn."

He picked up a bucket and put it at George's feet. "This here bucket will become your friend, because your new job will be taking care of the cows. Do you understand, boy?"

"My name is George."

Mr Severn glared, and George's knees trembled as he felt the man calculate a move.

After several long moments Mr Severn's head pushed forward as he spoke. "Well, boy, out here I work hard and there's going to be a lot of times when I just don't have time to remember any name, so how about you just get used to being called boy."

George swallowed the lump that had plugged up his throat, and Mr Severn grabbed a bucket. "Follow me, boy."

George hurried, his legs shaking as he grew breathless on the gentle slope. The cows followed. George looked back at them warily and then sped forward so that he walked alongside Mr Severn.

"What do you want me to do with the cows?" he asked.

Mr Severn kept his eyes focused on a small barn ahead. "Everything." He walked faster and George had to run to keep up.

Inside the barn the cows lined up like the children in the Home of Industry at mealtimes. Mr Severn hurriedly placed the bucket under the first cow. He pulled at the teats causing milk to squirt in an almost continuous flow. As the outpouring slowed to a drip, Mr Severn pushed the cow forward and the next one moved into place.

"You do it!"

George let out a long breath and fell to his knees. He curled his hands around the two front teats and squeezed.

The cow mooed.

"Get your goddam thumbs out of the way!"

George released his hands, and then curled his fingers around the teats, holding his thumbs stiffly out like they were unwanted body parts.

"Further up!" The voice grew angrier.

George couldn't stop shaking as his fingers curled into the udders. A small stream of milk flowed into the bucket. George felt his sweat grow cold. He curled his fingers again and again, forcing milk out into the bowl. It didn't flow the way it did with Mr

Severn, but a weak flow hit the bucket and it didn't draw anger. George squeezed until the flow dried up, then Mr Severn pushed the cow forward and the next one moved into place. George's hand grew stiff with spasm, but he continued to curl his fingers around the teat and draw milk into the bucket. After the fourth cow the bucket was close to full.

"Take that down to Mrs Severn and then bring it back. There's still more cows to do."

George hurried, taking care not to spill from the heavy pail. As he approached the porch door, he saw Junie stooped over the basin. She looked up as she heard him approach.

"Look, George, I done one."

George peered in the basin to see one small peeled potato alongside peelings as thick as a bread slice.

"Junie, you need to do it better than that. Let me show you." George knelt down. The knife was blunt and, at first, he could only take chunks out of the peel, but soon he could sliver off thin strips.

Junie's tongue thrust from her mouth as she watched.

"See, like this, otherwise you're throwing away what we can eat." George stood up and lifted his bucket of milk but stayed to watch Junie as she chipped into the next potato, taking away a thick layer of peel.

George put down the milk pail and knelt, holding her hands in his so she would feel what to do. "Thin slivers, like this!"

Junie smiled up at him and lifted the thin sliver of peel.

"Please, Junie, do your best." He gave her tight hug and hurried into the dark room with the pail of milk.

"Get that outside and put it next to the churner," Mrs Severn yelled. George hurried outside, not knowing where to find the churner.

Mrs Severn had followed him. "Over there!" she shouted, pointing toward a barrel on a small frame in the shed.

George paused.

Mrs Severn pushed the hair back from her face. "What now?"

George's voice sounded louder than he would have liked. "Mr Severn said to bring the pail back."

Mrs Severn let out a heavy sigh. "You!" she called out making Junie jump. "Come with me."

When Junie paused, Mrs Severn hurried to the potato basin and shook her head when she saw Junie's work. George held out the milk pail. Mrs Severn grabbed it from his hand and poured it into the butter barrel.

"Now, turn this handle and keep turning it and don't stop until I come and tell you to. Do you understand?"

Junie stared at Mrs Severn. George wasn't sure if his sister understood the instruction.

"Junie, please just turn the handle. That's all you have to do. If one arm gets tired, then use the other one. Do you understand?"

Junie nodded and began to do as she was told.

"Now stay there," George told her as he hurried back to help Mr Severn finish the milking.

*

It was dark when they were called to eat. The mud walls of the Severns' house gave off a damp smell that made George think of their attic in winter.

He and Junie ate in silence, plates of mashed potato and bread before them. George watched as Mr Severn's neck chucked forward with every swallow. He barely chewed each mouthful but swallowed his bread and potatoes in whole chunks.

His wife took little fast chews and followed each mouthful with a sip of water. George reached for his own cup of water. The bread and potato were dry, catching in his throat for lack of moisture.

Junie spooned her potato onto her bread, mashing them together.

Mr Severn pointed his spoon at Junie's plate. "If you ain't gonna eat that then pass it here."

"She'll eat it," George said. "I think she's just a bit tired – her arms after turning all that cream. Let me help her."

He spooned a softened mound into Junie's mouth and nodded, bidding her eat.

She closed her lips, and then swallowed.

"Take a drink now, Junie."

His sister did as she was told, and George fed her another spoonful.

Mrs Severn let out a heavy sigh. "If she's gonna need fed every day, then she ain't gonna be much good to us."

Her husband nodded. "Yeah, today was a quiet day – you kids spent half of it sitting on that cart watching the scenery go by. Tomorrow's a whole working day."

George nodded. His arms and legs ached after carrying milk pails, wooden slats and earthen bales up and down the farm hill. With the dry meal over, he was happy to be sent out to the earthen room at the back of the mound.

The two children lay on the straw mattress. Junie put her head close to George's chest, her thumb deep into her mouth, and fell asleep within minutes. George had wanted to talk to her about Ma, Rose, Maggie and Tommy, but Junie hadn't even said a goodnight prayer like Miss Constance had taught them.

George lay, feeling Junie's gentle breath beside him, and watched the night sky through the slats on the gate. A dark cloud cast a silhouette across the half moon.

"What do you think, God?" George whispered. "Is this the Garden of Eden?"

*

The men and women of the church sat up straight, and held more tightly to their Bibles as the solid frame of Annie MacPherson stepped up to the podium and looked down upon the congregation. Her plump, heavy face with the dark hair perfectly parted gave her the look of a stern tutor who took no nonsense from her charges.

"My dear friends, a great deal has occurred since I last addressed you for I have taken many of our street children to the promised land and they have been met by the Lord."

"Amen!" called out several male voices.

"So well have they been received that we have calls for a great many more children." Miss MacPherson held up one hand. "Let me read from some of the correspondence I have received."

She unfurled several sheets of parchment.

"This letter is typical of those I find waiting for me when we arrive in a town: *'I am a harness maker and have a good business. I will treat a boy as one of my own family and am willing to abide by your rules and agreements. My only wish is that you should fit me up with a boy who can keep my account books and write my letters.'"*

That letter was placed face down on the podium. Miss MacPherson's eyes scanned the next. "This is from a boy I placed on the first mission – a boy of sixteen who had run away from home and was living on the streets: *'I am very comfortable and do not think it a hard winter. Tell all the boys that this is a good place for all good boys that will work and try to make a living. I have got a good place and intend to stay here. I have a kind master that always gives me good advice. We have prayer every day and pray that you may be successful in bringing many more boys from a state of starvation to where they may have plenty to eat and wear. I hope you will remember me in your prayers and if you pass Quebec then I should like to see you very much. The master says he would like another boy if you bring more. I hope to hear from you soon, yours truly, Peter Thomas.'"*

Mrs MacPherson waved this letter in the air. "This comes from a boy who would surely have faced sin and depravation in the streets that surround us."

She rested the letter down. "My friends, I cannot tell you how much benefit we bring by taking the unwanted children to Canada. They are greeted with such welcome that I – who has seen such dire sorrow in this city – sometimes feel driven to tears."

Helen wriggled in her seat so that the woman beside her gave a scowl. Finally, she let out a deep breath and thrust her hand high in the air.

But Miss MacPherson's eyes were aimed at the wealthy businessmen who sat in the front pew. "Each journey I take to this promised land takes me deeper and deeper into its farmlands, showing that the need for more children, far from being fulfilled, is only likely to grow."

"Miss MacPherson!" Helen called out.

Annie MacPherson's eyes scanned the congregation until she saw Helen's hand waving in the air. "You have something to say, Mrs Petrie?"

Helen stood, her heart raced as she wondered where she should begin. "My daughter, Constance Petrie, has taken a group of children to Canada and writes with some bad news that should not be ignored." Helen paused, quickly wishing to rephrase her words so that Constance did not sound neglectful in losing a child. "A journey so far is not without its perils and one such child has already been lost overboard. I appreciate, Miss MacPherson, the happy testimonials you have read us, but nothing can compare to the horror of telling a woman in the workhouse that her only child has been lost at sea. Indeed, I can still hear the mother's tears of misery and would hate to bring more bad news to those who give us their most precious offspring."

Annie MacPherson shook her head. "I am sorry for the poor woman, and for the poor boy whose soul now lies with Him in Heaven. But, we cannot let such news keep us from the higher mission. We are offering a new life to children who would face only sorrow, sin and starvation in these streets. The risks are small to those who go – the young boy who died at sea might have died in these very streets for the Lord calls us all when it is our time."

Helen raised her hand to speak even though she was already standing. "But surely we should at least watch how our children are received over a length of time, ensure their journey is truly safe and the children are not used as slaves or scapegoats before we ship even more to this unknown territory."

Annie MacPherson's shoulders shook, sending her chin into a quiver. "If we delay or postpone, all my work will be undone. At this moment, I am receiving new offers of distribution homes all over eastern Canada – all this while other charities are planning to take their own troubled masses to this promised land. We cannot be left behind. We cannot slow the mission or make any delay. Those contacts I have made are so keen for new workers that they will quickly turn to those new missions who are keen to take our place."

"Amen!" called out many voices.

Annie MacPherson held up her hand. "And, I have more. I was planning to delay this announcement until the details were more firmly fixed, but I have been approached by one of the owners of a shipyard in Liverpool and asked to begin a mission in that poor dark city, so that their young ruffians with no hope can be lifted to a land that is fair in opportunity."

Helen looked around at the congregation. All eyes were set upon Annie MacPherson as she smiled down at them.

Helen squeezed out of the pew and hurried toward the door. Winifred pushed through the governors and patrons to run after her.

At the door to the Home of Industry she finally caught up, grabbing Helen's arm before she fled through the doorway. "Miss Helen, I think that what you said was right ... but I just couldn't speak up. I have my job here, and I don't want anyone to think I don't agree with what we're doing. I don't want to lose this place. I can't go back out there ..."

Helen gave her a tight smile. "I understand." She hurried out the door and down the steps, almost colliding with Mary Trupper who stood wrapped in a dark cloak.

"Ma'am, I've been waiting for you."

Helen sighed. She wanted to get away from the mission and all the talk of Canada and retreat to her peaceful home where she could be alone. "Mrs Trupper, I haven't heard any more news from my daughter. I'm not sure how your children are at the moment."

Mary shook her head. "It's not that – at least it's not my kids I came here about – it's my neighbour."

Helen pointed behind her. "Then I'm the wrong person to talk to. I'm not sending any children to Canada – the people you need to talk to are all in there."

"No, no, my neighbour's kids are already in Canada – it's just," Mary shook her head. "I'm not sure she knows about it."

Helen stared at Mary, peering at her small, pinched face as though she was unsure what she might hear next. "What do you mean – you're not sure she knows about it?"

Mary stepped back, feeling that she herself had done something wrong. "Well, I saw her two girls going off on the omnibus with my George and Junie and I just thought that their mother must know about it – well, we had to give our permission, didn't we? I gave your daughter my finger print – it was a funny thing, because I wondered how you would know my finger from anyone else's, but I did it anyway."

"But you say this woman doesn't know where her daughters are?"

Mary shook her head. "I've told her they're in Canada but she doesn't believe me – maybe she doesn't remember making her

161

finger print – she drinks, works the streets if you get what I mean. Anyway, the poor woman seems to be going even further downhill, crying all the time about her girls like she don't know where they are. So, I wondered if you would go and see her, talk to her like, it might make her feel better to know that they're in good hands."

Helen remembered two girls coming to the Home of Industry. "Did one of the girls – the oldest one – have a mole on her cheek?"

Mary nodded.

"What were their names?"

"Brown – Beryl and Ruby – pretty girls, even though the oldest had that big mark. But their mother made them work the streets – especially the oldest. I used to feel sorry for her. I wouldn't do that to my Rose, no matter how hungry we were."

Helen shook her head, wondering how far her daughter would go to rescue children. She remembered the girls quite clearly now – the story about the mother running an auction for the youngest girl's virginity. But the girls did go to Canada. Helen remembered seeing them in preparation classes. She hoped her daughter hadn't done anything stupid – like forged their mother's fingerprint.

Mary Trupper's voice interrupted Helen's thoughts. "So would you come and see Jean Brown? Talk to her – I'm sure she doesn't remember sending her girls off to Canada – must have done it while she was drunk. But she's crying all the time. When she goes out she brings all kinds of men up our stairs – and I don't have any door – just that thin curtain for protection – I heard one bloke give her a thumping this morning. I was scared for her, but I was also scared I might be next."

Helen looked up into the dark night sky, thinking of the calm drink in her quiet sitting room. But she needed to see Jean Brown – maybe a few questions might make her remember something about sending her girls to Canada.

She stayed close to Mary as they hurried through the dark alleyways. A heavy smell of dung followed them all the way, and it wasn't until they reached the steps of the Truppers' building that Helen realised it clung to her own boot.

"Damn!" Helen stooped to scrape at the foul mud.

Mary shook her head. "Don't worry about it – there's plenty more of that when you go up here."

162

But Helen scraped her foot against the lowest step, smearing the dung to a corner, and then hurried up the stairs.

Mary stood at Jean Brown's open door. Helen peered over Mary's shoulder and saw a woman asleep on the floor, her dress untied showing huge sores that dipped down into her bodice to cover her breasts. The clingy aroma of gin gave the room a sweet, overpowering smell.

Helen held her breath as she stepped forward. "Will we waken her?"

Mary shrugged. "I'm not sure if we can. She wasn't like this when I came to get you – she was drunk, like, but then she usually is."

They pulled the comatose woman up onto the bed and sat her up against the bag of rags that acted as pillows.

"Jean!" Mary patted her face to waken her. "I've brought you someone who knows where your daughters are?"

The woman grunted, and her eyes flickered briefly to life.

"Jean! She can tell you what happened to Beryl and Ruby."

Hearing the names of the girls prodded Jean's eyes open. "Ruby – Beryl." But then she fell back into a deep snooze.

Helen sighed. "There's no good talking to her tonight. I'll come back in the morning, perhaps she'll be sober then."

Mary rolled her eyes. "Make it early, before she's out earning a quick penny for more gin."

Helen hurried back through the streets of Spitalfields. The chill in the air made her long for the warm hearth of her kitchen where she could relax with a cold supper and a warm brandy.

*

In the early morning Winifred was still in her dressing robe when Helen knocked at the House of Industry. She stared at Helen as if she were crazed to arrive so early.

"I just have some things to do," Helen told her as she hurried upstairs and began searching through the record drawers for Beryl and Ruby Brown's consent forms.

It took only minutes to find them, and Helen felt some relief when she saw the thumbprints were large, totally different from

Constance's thin fingers. She hurried out through the heavy oak doors of the home while Winifred was still dressing.

Her fast pace took a few wrong turns in the alleyways of Spitalfields, and it was only when she saw the dung scraped on the lowest step of a tall slum that she knew she'd reached the right doorway.

She hurried up the steep stairs, passing a tired-looking woman going down. The woman gave Helen no glance of curiosity but moved as though in sleep. Helen thought about stopping her, asking if she were ill, but she knew there was little she could do.

The door to the Brown room was closed. Helen knocked lightly. Mary Trupper stepped out from behind her curtain, followed by Rose, Maggie and Tommy.

"I don't think she's gone out," Mary said. "I don't sleep that hard. I think I would have heard her."

Helen knocked a little louder.

A small groan from inside was followed by a bottle falling onto the wood floor. Helen and Mary looked at each other as they heard the sounds of Jean Brown scuttle across the floor.

"Who's there?" called out a dry voice.

Helen's eyes moved from Mary to the wood of the door. "I'm from the Home of Industry."

She heard a heavy sigh. "Damn do-gooders, missionaries – I don't need no damned help from the likes of you. Go away!"

Helen stepped closer to the door so that her mouth almost touched the wood. "I have news of your daughters."

The door fell open so fast that Helen almost tipped forward onto the floor.

Jean Brown stood taller than Mary ever remembered. "Where are my girls? If you've got them you'd best get them back because you've no right taking them away from me."

Helen stepped back. "I don't have your girls – at least not now. But you did give them to us – you said we could send them to Canada."

Jean Brown stepped forward as though she'd been assaulted. "I did not – you've stole them – taken them." She turned to Mary as though seeking a witness. "They've stolen my girls – my own flesh and blood – how dare they!"

Helen shook her head and held up her hands as though to ward off any blows.

"You did! You must have. They were here, and now they're gone. What did you do with them?" Jean Brown pushed her face into Helen's.

Helen glanced toward Mary Trupper, hoping she would come to her aid if Jean Brown turned brutal. "Look, I brought the forms here in my bag – maybe we can sit down and check the thumbprints."

The thwarted mother shook her head. "I didn't give away my daughters – I know I'd remember – there's a lot the gin does, but I know I'd never do that. You stole them, must have, I'll have the law on you!"

Helen stepped back so that her feet were at the top of the stairs. She opened her bag and pulled out the two contracts. Her heart raced at the thought of what might happen if Jean Brown's thumbs looked different from those on the contracts. She held up the papers. "Can we look at your thumbs, please?"

Jean Brown stuck out both her hands so that they could all be examined. "There's nothing on those papers that came from me."

Helen examined Jean Brown's right thumb and compared it to the papers. The rounded swirl looked like most thumbprints, but the one on the paper had a small scar at its edge.

"Let me see the other thumb," Helen said.

Jean Brown thrust her other thumb defiantly into Helen's face. Helen peered at it, almost smiling when she saw a small scar at its side. "It's the same – the print on this paper is the same as yours – see the small scar?" She held out the paper to Mary.

Mary stepped forward to examine the paper and Jean Brown's thumb. She nodded her head. "Look's about right to me."

Jean Brown grabbed at the top contract, the one that was Ruby's. "That's not me – I just know it isn't. I didn't sign my girls away – I wouldn't do that." She stared at the fingerprint and looked again at her own thumb. "I know I didn't do this." Tears came to her eyes.

Mary put her arm on Jean's shoulder. "Maybe you just don't remember. You know, maybe it was the gin."

"No, no, no – I just didn't." Jean rubbed her face with her hands as though trying to rub at some memory. She looked quickly at Helen. "Where are they anyway?"

Helen's voice came out hoarse. "Canada."

Jean copied her croak. "Canada?"

As Helen wondered whether she wanted a geographical explanation, Mary interrupted. "It's where my George and Junie went. They'll get a better chance at life there – a good job, with decent pay and a nice home. Miss Constance promised us and she took them there herself to make sure it all works out well."

Helen thought of poor Harry Twistle and coloured. "They were keen to go."

Jean shook her head. "Canada!" she muttered before looking up. "Can I go and get them back?"

Helen shook her head. "It's a long way – two weeks by boat. My daughter promises to look after them. She'll be back by the end of the month, and I'll send her to you. She can give you their news."

But Jean was shaking her head as though she hadn't heard a word. "Canada!" she said again, and then a deep sob shook her chest and she began to wail.

*

Beryl lay in bed listening to Ruby sleep. The small breaths she exhaled made a low whistle, like a lonely train in the night. Another girl on the far side of the dorm snored. Her deep snorts filled the gap between Ruby's high-pitched exhalations. Beryl turned so her back was to the rest of the girls. She stared at the dim outline of flowers on the bedroom wallpaper. In the daytime, a trail of maroon roses etched the wall fabric providing a floral fence around the fourteen beds. But at night, the blooms became tiny vicious devils ready to bring evil on the sleeping girls. Beryl peered at one devil, at the horns that she knew were daytime petals. She stared, feeling that with the blink of one eye, the devil would grow out from that wall and …

She shut her eyes and thought of George and Junie. Were they happy? George wasn't good with letters, but maybe with more schooling he would write to her at Marchmont and Miss Ellen would forward the letters so she could write back. After all, they came from the same close on the same street, they knew each other's mothers, they had to stay in touch, they were like family.

The devil on the wallpaper grew a tail as a palm frond that trailed the rose in daytime now curled out from behind the devil's large belly. Beryl could see his smile, leering like some of the men she used to have – especially the one who didn't want anything other than a hand job and made her smile while she did it. He'd said she had to smile or he wouldn't pay.

Beryl shut her eyes again and tried to sleep. Instead, she saw her mother's face. She was crying, like she did when the rent was due and there was no money. But this time, Beryl knew, the tears were for her daughters. Guilt rose like a wave. Beryl knew she should have talked to her mother more, explained how much she'd hated that first man – that she'd been too young and that they couldn't do that to Ruby. There were other ways to raise cash. Other people worked with their hands – like George's family. They could have made matchboxes. And maybe Miss Constance could have given them a place in the Home of Industry.

This was all a mistake. She shouldn't have run away. Her mother wasn't able to take care of herself. She might even be in the Lock Hospital by now. Beryl decided she'd have Miss Constance help her write to her mother tomorrow. Tell her where they were, not to worry and that she would stay in touch. When she was earning, she might even be able to send some money home.

The idea of a letter made Beryl feel better. She turned away from the wallpaper so that she faced Ruby and closed her eyes.

*

Lawrence's voice came crisp with each word he read from his favourite book.

"*September 30, 1659. I, poor miserable Robinson Crusoe, being shipwrecked during a dreadful storm in the offing, came on shore on this dismal, unfortunate island, which I called 'The Island of Despair'; all the rest of the ship's company being drowned, and myself almost dead.*"

Beryl looked down on Ruby, who lay asleep on the grass. Ruby's eyes were rested and dry. She'd spent days crying after Junie left, sobbing to herself with the ragged Victoria pulled tight to her chest. Ruby still hadn't let the doll go. Its soft, stained body was still damp from tears. But Lawrence's gentle voice seemed to have soothed her.

Out on the grass, the other children played at tag, letting out screams of delight as they evaded capture. Beryl watched the small Dora running through the trees as Hannah grew close. Their numbers had halved over the past week. Beryl had been asked to go with several families, but they'd all changed their minds when she said her young sister must come along too.

On the back porch of the house Miss Constance stood with the rich couple who had visited the day George and Junie were taken away. Beryl watched as they looked over the heads of the children at play. The woman's gaze took in Ruby and watched as Beryl stroked her sister's curls, but then the woman moved slowly, following her husband and Miss Constance indoors.

Lawrence's voice slowed, and Beryl felt herself grow sleepy. Miss Ellen stepped from the house and hurried toward them in the small spot beneath the trees. Beryl sat up a little at her approach. Lawrence stopped reading.

"Beryl," Miss Ellen called out. "Miss Constance would like to have a quiet word with you."

Beryl gently edged Ruby's sleepy head onto the grass. Her heart raced just a little as she wondered what she'd done wrong. But in the small office at the front of Marchmont House, Miss Constance gave such a beaming smile that Beryl realised the news had to be good.

Miss Constance pointed to a chair, while she and Miss Ellen sat on a long couch. "Beryl, I have just had the most wonderful offer from one of the area's most Christian families." She paused briefly before rushing on. "James MacDougal is a lawyer here, his father was one of the earliest settlers and the family now own huge swathes of farmland. They donate a great deal of food to Marchmont House and, if truth be told, I doubt we could function as well as we do without their help."

Beryl gazed at Miss Constance's thin face, wondering where this was leading but hoping it meant a nice home for her and Ruby.

Constance smiled eagerly at the girl. "Well, Beryl, like all that is good in the world, God offers up challenges to ensure we are worthy of his love." She coughed and cleared her throat. "Mr and Mrs MacDougal have had a great deal of prosperity in their lives, but they have not been fortunate in begetting children of their own. This brings such sorrow to Mrs MacDougal that the couple would now like to adopt a child into their home to treat as their own."

Beryl heard the words "a child". She wasn't going to leave Ruby behind.

"The good news, Beryl, is that Mrs MacDougal has become quite taken by Ruby. I think you will remember that they talked briefly on our first open day, and Mr MacDougal says his wife has not stopped talking about your little sister ever since."

Beryl felt a pulse in her ears as Constance's thin voice talked on.

"Now, I know, that you and your sister quite understandably would like to stay together, but I think you can understand what an opportunity this is. To be adopted by Mr and Mrs MacDougal would offer Ruby a life beyond the dreams of most children in Belleville, let alone Marchmont House. She would be loved and cared for in a home that is not only Christian but wealthy enough to share its fortune with others. Ruby would be a most fortunate child indeed."

Beryl waited for Miss Constance's thin lips to say that she could go with her sister to this most fortunate home. Instead Miss Constance gazed at her with a wide smile.

Miss Ellen coughed. "I understand, Beryl, that you would like to stay with your sister and continue to care for her in the wonderful way that you have. But I think perhaps you should think about what this opportunity might mean for Ruby. Most of the children here, as you are well aware, will be workers and servants in homes. If Ruby is adopted by Mr and Mrs MacDougal, she will escape servitude, become well-schooled and quite probably grow up to marry a gentleman and have her own house and staff."

A sob caught in Beryl's throat.

Miss Constance leaned forward. "Beryl, this is the very best opportunity any of our children could wish for."

Miss Ellen's voice was a little softer. "Beryl, I would not recommend you separate from your sister under any other circumstances, but with this offer you must think of what is best for your sister – a life as a junior servant in someone's home or a life as a little mistress growing up loved and adored by a couple who would cherish her."

Beryl, head still bowed, gave a barely perceptible nod, knowing she couldn't argue.

*

James and Hannah MacDougal collected Ruby within the hour. Miss Constance had woken Ruby as she lay on the grass, and Beryl watched as she'd gathered Ruby's small canvas bag and took her out to the porch. Still sleepy, Ruby didn't ask where she was going.

Beryl and Lawrence watched as the MacDougal's carriage slowed at the steps. Ruby was lifted aboard, and her small body disappeared into the darkness of the carriage.

A deep retch crept up through Beryl's chest at the sound of the horses' hooves. She watched the billowing dust settle across the dirt track, and then Ruby was gone.

Lawrence took Beryl's hand and squeezed, the boy's own face tracked with tears. "Why did she have to go so quickly?"

Beryl let loose a high-pitched cry.

Constance smiled at them both. "Now, children, Ruby is truly fortunate, and I'm sure you both wish her well. This should be no time for tears."

Beryl let out another short sharp cry, and Miss Ellen gathered the girl into a tight hug. "Let's go down to the kitchen." She pulled Lawrence into her other arm. "Let us see what we can find to ease your poor, troubled faces."

But downstairs Beryl sobbed until her face grew bloated and Constance worried she might grow sick. "Please, Beryl, calm yourself. Ruby will be well cared for. Mr and Mrs MacDougal are good people."

Beryl's head moved in a stiff nod as she let loose another cry. "It's not just Ruby – it's me ma. What's become of her?" A high-pitched squeak grew out of Beryl's throat and she shook her head. "I should have stayed and taken care of her."

Constance wrapped her arm around the girl. "Now, Beryl, you know what type of work that would have involved. I'm sure your mother is doing fine."

Beryl shook her head. "We shouldn't have done it. Me ma doesn't know where we are, and now Ruby's gone off to a new family, how will we ever find each other again?"

Constance's face flushed. She sat up straight and looked down into Beryl's face. "Now, look, you saved your little sister from that sinful trade. You knew what your Ruby was in for and you did a very brave thing for her. Now, she's saved – well and truly. Mr and Mrs MacDougal will treat her as their own. Your job now is to help yourself. Find a good home where you can work and learn, for you're a goodly girl, Beryl, and who knows what opportunity there is for you in this new land."

Beryl's sobs had ceased, but her red-ringed eyes gazed at Constance. "Will you promise me something, Miss Constance?"

Constance nodded. "What is it?"

Beryl looked like she was about to cry again, but she swallowed and held herself in check. "When you go back to London, will you go to my ma and tell her where we are? Tell her it was me – I wanted to go. But tell her about Ruby with Mr and Mrs MacDougal, and tell her we are both fine and I'll find her when I'm grown."

Constance swallowed. Beryl's mother might be a drunk, but she would surely wonder how her daughters got sent to Canada.

*

As the haze of sleep lifted, Ruby realised that Beryl was no longer with her. Instead a strange woman was pulling her into a hug. Ruby felt the stiff lace of the woman's dress scratch her face and, as she pulled herself free, a dark-haired man smelling of cigars leaned forward.

"Please don't fret, child. We're taking you home. You'll be happy with us."

Ruby yelled like she had never yelled before. She screamed out for Beryl, her small legs pushing off the seat to kick at the door.

The carriage slowed, but the man knocked against the carriage window.

"It's alright, Charles, just a little shock from the child. You can keep going."

Ruby pulled at the door handle, trying to free its latch while the woman leaned forward, tugging Ruby's hand in her own. "Please, Ruby, don't be scared. We want to love you."

Ruby stilled for a moment as she wondered what this meant. Then, as the woman pulled her back toward the seat, Ruby screamed and pushed at the woman's arms, chest and shoulders to get free.

By the time they reached Edgefield House, Ruby's face was swollen with hysterical tears. A butler carried her out of the carriage, sending her into even greater wails of fear.

Hannah MacDougal climbed down from the carriage feeling that she had brought home a wild bear cub. She knelt down on the grass so her face was level with the screaming Ruby and gazed at the child that was now hers. The honey curls were now damp and limp. The fair complexion was as ruddy as any farmer's and the beautiful grey eyes had grown blood-shot from tears.

After a few moments that allowed the child to grow familiar with Hannah MacDougal's own pretty features, the crying lessened.

Hannah kept her voice slow and soft. "Ruby, we like you very much."

As the child took in these few words, Hannah thought about how to follow them up. "We want to take care of you – play with you – see you go to school – we want you to live with us."

Hannah watched questions cross Ruby's face while the tears and sobs ebbed just a little.

"Now, we don't want to make you scared. But I would like you to let us try and make you happy."

A last small sob hiccupped out of Ruby's chest as she listened to what Hannah MacDougal had to say.

"If, at the end of four weeks, you are still scared and unhappy, we promise to take you back to Marchmont House. How does that sound?"

Ruby peered at the woman before her, as if waiting for more.

"Now doesn't that sound fair?" Hannah MacDougal asked again.

Ruby gave a barely perceptible nod. Hannah MacDougal smiled at the success of it.

*

Beryl left Marchmont House the next day. A huge man, taller and wider than any man Beryl had ever seen, arrived at the house bearing a letter from his preacher and saying that his wife needed help around the house.

Constance showed him Beryl. She knew an immediate placement would stop the girl from thinking of her sister.

But Beryl thought of nothing but her sister as she climbed aboard the flat-backed wagon. Bill Grouver flicked the reins at the horses and the wagon moved forward. Beryl stared back at Lawrence, Miss Ellen and Miss Constance through a mist of tears.

Bill Grouver's deep voice made her turn. "So, how long you been out here?"

Beryl couldn't think about time. She shrugged.

"Any family?"

Beryl let out a cry and fell into sobs that silenced her new master.

The wagon moved slowly out of town with Beryl looking deep into the lap of her blue serge skirt.

"You're a quiet one," Bill Grouver said. "My wife'll be happy about that. The last girl we had talked up a hurricane so that it seemed the house was never silent, and my wife, with six boys in the house, I'm sure you can appreciate, likes the occasional bit of silence."

The sun was high in the sky, bringing warmth that was occasionally whipped away by a cold wind from the north. Bill pointed toward a double rise of hillsides ahead. "You might want to put on your cape. It'll get chilly when we move through the pass."

His words made Beryl realise she was cold already, but she shrugged off his suggestion.

"Well, if you don't want to talk about your family, then let me tell you about mine." He paused. "Our oldest boy is Bill Junior,

173

he's fourteen and wants to move west as soon as he's old enough and take up his own homestead. I can't think why he would want to do that – our place is big enough – but, I guess, my wife says he's like me – wants to strike out on his own. He's a good boy – strong-willed in a way that can bring grief to parents but a streak that we all want in a boy."

Bill Grouver spat out onto the dirt track as the wagon moved slowly. "Our next son is Malky – Malcolm is his Christian name – he's also a good boy, more studious than his older brother, says he wants to go into business, maybe open a store. But who knows if that's just fanciful talk. Dougie and Craigie come next. They're twins and stick together like you would expect them to – but it sure is strange to watch them – barely exchange a word sometimes but they go along together like it was all planned out."

He glanced at Beryl to see if she had anything to say about this, but her gaze was still buried in her skirts. Her silence made him a little uncomfortable. He wondered if he should have looked at other girls rather than let that skinny English woman make the decision for him.

"Anyways, our second youngest is Andy. I think he's about five. A bit of loner, always peering at things, like he's trying to figure out the ways of the world and how it all works. He's not a great talker, so you and he should get along well."

He looked at her again for a sign that she might be listening. Her stiffness across the shoulders and the pitch of her back told him she wasn't asleep.

"Our youngest is Seth. Now, by the time he came along my wife was really hoping for a girl, as you can well imagine. All these boys make us blessed, as everyone keeps telling her, but I know she'd really like a girl for company as she gets older. I've told her not to fret. Every time I takes her, I tell her this might be us making that girl."

Bill let out a deep laugh and glanced at the girl beside him. Beryl felt the glance and pulled her thighs tight together under her skirts.

"You're a strange one, but I hope the wife likes you because if she don't, it'll be my life that's strung out. Raising six boys in a cabin ain't no fun for any woman, and she gets tired of all that work. I hope you're good with a scrubbing board because that's my

174

wife's most hated chore. You should hear her on laundry days – in our house with all those boys you can't keep washing to one day a week – me and the boys learned to stay out of sight when she brings out those tubs and that soap."

He glanced at Beryl again. "I sure do hope you like laundry."

*

George and Junie settled into a weary cycle of work. George looked after the cows, their milking, taking them to new pastures, often having to run in circles to keep the herd together and repeatedly counting to ensure none were lost. Junie tried to do what was asked. She turned the crank on the churner for hours on end and peeled potatoes. Her peelings had grown slimmer as slaps from Mrs Severn taught her the right way. But Junie struggled with drawing water from the well. Her arms and shoulders just weren't strong enough to pull up a full bucket. Mrs Severn would push her aside saying she was as good as a wart on a hog.

The best job, as far as Junie was concerned, was taking care of baby Ann. The baby had only started walking, and Mrs Severn didn't want her getting into any danger so she often set Junie to babysitting. Junie loved playing peek-a-boo and singing songs with the tot. She loved to hear the baby laugh, often joining in so that they both squealed with delight and shattered the silence that stilled the house. But once the infant fell asleep, Junie was ordered to wash clothes, scrub pots or peel more potatoes.

Junie grew to hate potatoes – and bread. Other vegetables grew on the farm – peas, beets and onions. But they were all for market, Mrs Severn said: "They're not for us."

Both children ate all their bread and potato at the end of each day, even though its dryness stuck to the roof of the mouth.

One evening George sighed before taking a first bite.

Mrs Severn sat up so she could peer down at him. "It's good enough for you. I don't know what you were expecting when you came here, but it shouldn't have been no meat and gravy."

He spoke quickly, without thought. "We expected schooling – and church school on Sundays."

The slap that landed on his cheek burned through to his jaw. George tried to move his face but it felt numb. After a few moments, he was able to squeeze his cheeks to his eyelids to shut out tears. He even tried to open his mouth to shovel in a first mouthful of potato, but his tongue wouldn't chew.

Junie leaned toward him, wrapping her small arm around his back.

Mrs Severn glared at her. "And you can stop that. You do something in this house and you take your punishment. He don't need you getting involved unless you want some too."

Junie pulled her arm back from her brother.

Mr Severn continued spooning potato and bread into his mouth, swallowing each mouthful as the next spoonful was raised, never changing his rhythm.

But in bed that night George cried as the children snuggled together. "Why did we come here?" he whispered as the tears crept into Junie's hair.

Junie stared out at the night sky through the slats and shook her head. "Mrs Considerance said it was good."

George shook his head gently, knowing he would normally laugh at Junie's twist on Miss Constance's name. This time it just wasn't funny.

*

Mary Trupper led her kids through the small alley and out onto Whitechapel. Rose, almost as tall as her mother, pulled at Maggie, who led Tommy by the hand. Maggie gave Tommy a quizzical glance; their mother never took them anywhere, but Tommy was too tired to notice. His jacket weighed down his breathing, making him almost gasp at the fast pace.

"Ma!" called out Rose. "Where are we going?"

Mary turned with a smile. "You'll find out soon enough – it's a treat."

Rose grinned. Her mother halted her step. "I just think you work hard, and you might like to see something funny." She hurried on past a trader holding up a dozen rabbits, all held by their rear legs and weighted down by their dead heads.

Tommy stared at the creatures, his legs slowing so that Maggie had to pull him. The Truppers wound their way past a man selling fly papers. His hat was covered in sticky paper heavily spotted with flies. Another trader hawked stewed eels, while another offered to sharpen knives.

Rose, Maggie and Tommy stared at them all. Each day they hurried between home and the Beehive, taking a route that was mostly narrow alleyways, so this view was new and striking.

A barrel organ could be heard, and Maggie's and Tommy's eyes widened as they grew close to a crowd, where a small brown creature leapt onto a bystander's shoulder. The crowd laughed, and Tommy stopped walking to gaze at the monkey wearing a waistcoat and hat.

Maggie grinned, until the creature leapt into her arms and she screamed. The small monkey leapt in fright, landing in Tommy's hands and sending him off into a wail.

Mary raised her arm to strike the beast. "Be off with you!"

The music stopped. "Leave my monkey alone!" called the organ grinder.

The monkey leapt onto his owner's shoulders, and Mary turned to her children. "Are you alright?"

Tommy let out a long breath in relief, while Maggie still whimpered. Mary turned to the organ grinder. "Keep that creature under control – you can't let it go attacking innocent children."

But the organ grinder had struck up a tune, he couldn't afford to lose any bystanders before it was time to pass the hat.

Mary led the children further on.

"Where are we going?" asked Rose again.

Mary glanced over her shoulder. "To a puppet show."

The children glanced at each other, Maggie and Tommy letting out broad smiles. Their mother had never taken them to see puppets before. She'd always said it was a waste of money. Rose remembered George telling his mother that they didn't have to pay until the end and that they could always scarper before then. But his mother had given him a dirty look. "We can't enjoy what we can't pay for," she'd told him.

Rose wondered, as she did every day, what kind of life George and Junie were living. Part of her, a growing part, wished she'd been allowed to go. Miss Annie said it was God's own

177

country where a young person could make a good life. Rose didn't want to be making matchstick boxes forever.

"Hurry," her mother called out from ahead. "It's started – look." She ushered her three children ahead of her and pointed to a large striped box where two puppets were already at play.

"Where have you been?" asked Judy.

Punch fell onto the floor of the stage and began to snore.

"You've been drinking, haven't you?" called out Judy.

Punch snored.

"Haven't you?" yelled Judy even louder. "And I bet you spent all of our money and now we can't pay the rent or buy food." She began to wail.

Punch woke up. "What's all this noise? Can't a man get a bit of sleep?"

But Judy wailed even louder, until Punch lifted his large stick and began to pound Judy again and again. Judy's cries got quieter and quieter until she cried no more.

Punch dropped his stick and wailed in sorrow until the doctor arrived and declared Judy dead.

"Ahhhh," called out the audience.

But Punch called the doctor a "Quack" and set about hitting him with his big stick. The doctor fought back, and the two puppets wrestled until the doctor lay dead.

"Ohhhh," called out the audience.

Mary glanced down to see wide smiles on the faces of her children. She snuggled up close to them and wished George and Junie were there. George always wanted to see the whole of the puppet show, and this time she had three farthings to put in the hat at the end.

A police puppet dragged Punch before the Judge.

"Mr Punch, you are a very naughty man," called out the Judge.

"Oh no, I'm not," said Punch.

"Oh, yes you are!" called out the audience.

Mary heard Tommy's voice above the crowd.

"Mr Punch, I sentence you to be hanged!"

"Ohhhh!" called out the audience.

Gallows are pushed onto the small stage, complete with noose.

"Mr Punch, are you ready?" called out the hangman.

Mr Punch nodded his head.

"Then let's begin, Mr Punch. Place your head inside the rope."

Mr Punch put his arm inside."

"No, no," called the hangman.

Mr Punch put his other arm inside. "Like this?"

The children erupted in laughter.

"No, no, your head!"

Mr Punch put his head under the noose.

More laughter.

"No, no, your head!"

Mr Punch put his head above the noose.

Tommy laughed so loud he spluttered.

"No, no! Let me show you," called the hangman, who proceeded to put his head into the noose. Mr Punch gave him a kick so he hung from the gallows.

The crowd fell into uproarious laughter, with Tommy and Maggie's faces red with mirth.

As they walked slowly home, they giggled over Mr Punch while Rose argued that he was a villain. "He is a bad character. I don't know why we should find him funny."

As they turned the corner into their alley, they saw a small crowd gathered at the bottom of their stairs. Mary thought immediately of the bailiffs and she wondered if she really had paid the rent. She'd given it to the factor, but maybe he'd pocketed it and now they'd be turned out onto the street. A sharp pain caught in her chest.

"Look, Ma, it's Mrs Brown!"

Mary stepped closer as three heavy men bundled a woman down the steps. She was tied up in strips of old sheet with her arms tight at her side, even her legs were strapped together so that her feet could only shuffle. Her mouth was bound shut with a bandage wrapped under her chin and tied at the top of her head.

Mary ran close enough to see Jean Brown's face flushed red as though she'd been in a struggle.

A voice called out from the crowd. "Take the mad bitch and burn her."

The sanitary man shook his head and climbed the steps of the wagon. He looked down at the crowd until he had their attention.

"This woman has been spreading disease. She's been working these streets – some of you might even have been her customers. Well, now she's off to the Lock Hospital and I advise you all to be careful about where you stick your wick – or you could end up diseased like her."

The crowd let out a small cheer.

"The poor woman!" Mary muttered.

"What did she do wrong?" Maggie asked.

Mary shook her head.

*

Beryl's arms ached from carrying tubs of boiled water out from the stove, and scrubbing the stains on the boys' shirts with a bristle brush and tallow. The mud came out fairly easily, but the dried-in dyes used on the sheep and the fruit spilled at meals might have been etched in. Beryl's arm muscles quivered, and she feared wearing a hole through one of the shirts with her scrubbing. She stopped to catch her breath and decided to rinse the shirt and hope it came out while drying. Her hands grew chilled as she rinsed the clothes in freezing water pulled from the spring. With the soap poured free, she guided the clothes, item by item, through the mangle. Laundry had one good point, it freed her from the eyes of Maisie Grouver.

Maisie watched everything Beryl did – from preparing breakfast to cleaning dishes to scrubbing the kitchen floor. Beryl knew Maisie wanted to see her steal food. She felt it as the mistress counted the chicken pieces in the stew, comparing it to the number that had been cut from the bird in the pantry, and gauging the bread left after each meal.

Doing laundry also gave her some peace and quiet so she could think of her little sister. Beryl imagined Ruby in a tall bed with lots of cushions and pillows, a bedcover of green satin and a maid to bring her meals. She smiled as she pictured the maid stirring Ruby's food when it was too hot.

"You!"

Beryl jumped at the sound and turned to see Maisie Grouver with a large wedge of cheese in her arms.

"We've cheese missing – don't say there isn't, 'cos I knows it." She dropped the cheese on the table and picked up a large wooden spoon. A gleam grew as she stepped forward, the wooden spoon raised to strike.

"I knew you were a thief the minute you stepped through that door and wouldn't look at us, hiding your eyes from us, keeping that devil mark out of sight."

Beryl, her hands chilled from the laundry, stepped back. "I didn't take any cheese, Mrs Grouver, I promise."

But Maisie had her prey in sight. She stepped forward.

"Mother!" Malky yelled out from the doorway. "The twins took the cheese – said they were heading out for rabbit baiting."

Maisie let her glare fall to the floor and threw the wooden spoon onto the table.

Beryl waited for an apology, an acknowledgement that she'd been wrongly accused. But Maisie took up a knife and began slicing at the cheese. "Get those clothes washed and hurry! The chickens need feedin'."

*

Ellen Bilbrough looked across her desk at Lawrence and wished someone else were there to advise her. Annie was further west seeking new distribution homes for orphans, while Constance had left for London to gather a new troupe of children.

Ellen looked from Lawrence's small, pale face to the letter that lay before her:

To Whom It May Concern:

I am a female farmer and recently heard about your venture in orphans. I don't get out much as the farm is large and keeps me hard at toil. But I would truly appreciate receiving one of your boys. I can promise hard work, but I run a Christian home and there would be none of the temptations of town life. I can't promise regular schooling as the nearest schoolhouse is more than two hours by horse, but I myself know more than the three Rs and

would be happy to help with any teaching. I can't get away to
Belleville to pick up any boy, but, if you can put him on the train,
our station porter, Chuck Clark, says he would bring him to me.

A letter with testimony from our preacher is enclosed.

Sincerely yours

Agnes Findlay

Instinct told Ellen that Lawrence was the wrong boy for Miss
Findlay, but he was their last child. She looked down at Lawrence's
awkward foot. His limp was unpopular with the local farmers, no
matter how much she'd talked up his education.

Ellen read again the letter from Miss Findlay's preacher.

To Whom It May Concern:

Miss Findlay is a true Christian woman who lets nothing halt
her path as she ploughs her isolated farm alone and with no help
from anyone. For many around these parts, she is a formidable
woman who is redeemed and respected. I have no doubt she will
offer a shining example of hard work and fortitude to any young
man you choose to put in her care.

May the Lord be with you,

Pastor Aaron Crane

Ellen looked at the small, pale boy before her. Maybe Miss
Findlay could offer Lawrence what he had never had, guidance in
physical labour. She was obviously strong-willed, and she may be
just the mentor Lawrence needed.

She smiled at the boy's worried face. "Lawrence, I think
we've found you a home."

*

Helen watched her daughter gulp hurriedly at her soup, the spoon
moving from bowl to mouth with a fast rhythm. Constance was
thinner than ever. Motherly instincts made her hesitant about
criticising her daughter, but they needed to talk.

She took a sip of her tea, as though no part of the conversation was planned. "So was Canada as perfect as you were led to believe?"

Constance nodded. She was ready to eat more, but enthusiasm to talk of her mission forced her to leave the spoon in the bowl. "Even more so, Mother. Our children were so well received that I cannot believe we haven't taken this path before. So many people there are keen to welcome them into their homes."

"Did you see all the children delivered safely?"

Constance shook her head. "Poor Lawrence – his limp was not favoured, but I have asked dear Ellen to keep him close – soon, we will find a family in need of his learning."

"And what now?"

Constance had taken a large spoonful of soup, and Helen smiled until, finally, Constance could answer.

"Mother, we must continue with this migration. We have so many children who are needy – and so many families in Canada who can offer them homes. Annie MacPherson and I talked in Quebec before I boarded my ship. She had just arrived with a group of one hundred and twenty children and within four hours of arrival she had found homes for fifteen!"

"Constance ..."

"No, Mother, I know what you are going to say, but we must continue."

Helen stood. "Yes, we must continue with our teaching of the orphans at the Home of Industry. We must continue with our work with the matchstick makers at the Beehive, and we must continue with our fundraising so that maybe we can open a second Home of Industry – that is the way we should be moving."

Constance shook her head. "No, Mother, it is agreed. I am to round up one hundred more children and accompany them to Canada. Annie MacPherson has been offered a new distribution home further inland – a place called Galt, and I'm to take these children there."

Helen's chest puffed up so that she felt fit to burst. She stepped away from the table but then turned quickly back again. "Harry Twistle – have you forgotten him? I had to tell his poor mother that he was dead – the woman is already in the Workhouse,

183

has life not been cruel enough to her? But you take her only son and …"

"Mother, it was an accident."

"Accident or not, she would have her son with her, bringing her some comfort through the misery of the workhouse if you hadn't persuaded her to send him to Canada – this woman trusted you."

Constance's hand fell to her chest. "There was nothing I could have done!"

Helen sat down so that her face was only inches from her daughter. "She's a mother and she trusted you with her most precious gift. How do you think she feels now?"

Close to tears, Constance shook her head.

"Now, before you even think of gathering more children for a trek to the homes of strangers, I suggest you go and visit Mrs Twistle in the workhouse – tell her something that will bring her comfort, offer her some hope that her son, at least, died happy."

"But, Mother, what could I possibly say?"

Helen glared, her eyes piercing so that her daughter had to look away.

But Helen wasn't setting her free. "And while you are out, I suggest you stop by and see Mary Trupper. She's keen to hear about her children – asks me for news every time I see her."

Constance sat up and pushed her half-eaten soup away. "I will visit both women this afternoon." She paused. "Harry was happy before he died. He and Lawrence became firm friends."

"And while you're visiting Mary Trupper, stop by and see her neighbour – Jean Brown. You took her daughters to Canada, but the woman remembers nothing about it. She's distraught and drinking even more than she used to, according to Mary."

Constance rose from the table, her face colouring. "I will go now."

She lifted her cloak and left, her boots clattering on the stairs as she hurried to the front door. If her mother could only see Canada and its wide open spaces she might be less resistant.

As she hurried down Great Eastern Street, Constance couldn't help but compare it to the spacious cleanliness of Belleville with its wide gardens and the fresh air that made you want to puff your chest with enjoyment. You could see to the other side of the road and no one coughed or rasped from frequent fogs.

Constance decided to stop and see Mary Trupper first. It was always easier to give good news than bad, and she was keen to tell Mary that she had found George and Junie a good home together. And she was sure Jean Brown would be happy to hear about Ruby's adoption by a wealthy lawyer. Even Beryl must be happy – Bill Grouver seemed such a friendly chap, happy to receive a nice girl like Beryl to help his wife.

Constance turned into the Truppers' alleyway and stepped over a dead dog – its innards ransacked, only the head and long bones giving it recognition. She raced upstairs to the Truppers' attic. The curtain had been replaced by a wood door. Constance knocked hesitatingly. Her mother hadn't said anything about the Trupper family moving.

"Come in!"

Hearing Mary Trupper's voice, Constance smiled. She put her head around the door. "Remember me?"

Mary's face changed from tired to joy. She rose from pasting matchboxes. "Oh, Miss Constance, your mother said you'd be home soon, and I've been so keen to hear news of George and Junie." She stopped to give Constance the chance to talk.

Constance paused, unsure of where to start and then smiled. "They are both well – they withstood the journey admirably ..."

"But where are they now? Are they with good people?"

Constance nodded. "Yes, yes, they are together on a farm. I believe George takes care of the cows, while Junie helps the woman of the house."

Mary stood back, a tear in her eye. She rubbed it away. "I miss them so much."

Constance sat down on the bed and bid Mary join her. "Truly, they are well. The homes in Canada are large and warm, the food so bountiful that no one ever goes hungry – I can say, truly, that George and Junie are in good hands."

Tears tracked Mary's face as she nodded. "I believe you, Miss Constance, but it is difficult thinking of them so far away and in the care of people I don't know."

Constance patted her arm. "But what about you? You have a door – no more curtain!"

Mary smiled. "Yes, I spoke to the landlord and, with the rent all paid, he had no reason to say no."

"Your other children are well?"

Mary nodded. "Tommy still fights against his jacket, but I think he knows it is for his own good." She looked at the floor and then up at Constance. "You know, Miss Constance, I really bless the day you came into our lives. I was suspicious at first – as well you know – but I don't know where we would be without you."

Constance blushed, uncomfortable with praise. "And what of your neighbour? I bring good news of her daughters."

Mary frowned. "She's gone, poor woman."

"Gone! Where?"

Mary nodded out toward the city. "The Sanitary man came for her – took three of them to tie her up and get her down the stairs. I doubt she'll see the outside again. She's at the Lock Hospital."

Constance let out a long sigh. It wasn't information she wanted to take to Beryl.

At the workhouse, the news wasn't any better.

"Betty Twistle killed herself!" Mr Marsh said when Constance asked to see her. "Drank the lye I gave her – she was supposed to be scrubbing those stairs with it." He pointed behind him. "She was in agony before she died – all those sins she must have committed. We get what we sow, don't we? Isn't that what the good Lord says?"

Constance stepped back from Mr Marsh and hurried back out the heavy gate.

*

Back at home, Helen was stoking the range. She wanted to bake a plum pie, Constance's favourite. She'd grown so thin. It was all the excitement of the mission, and she got carried away so easily. She'd always been the same. As a child, she would accompany Helen to visit the poor and, while Helen would carry a basket of bread, Constance would sneak in bits of bun, cake or any other bit of luxury they might have in their home.

As Helen pulled the sack of flour from the pantry, she pinched out the beetles that sat at its top and then spooned the flour into her mixing bowl.

Geeta came in the back door carrying the goods she'd bought at market.

"I hope you found some good plums," Helen told her.

Geeta placed her grocery sack on the table and pulled out a handful of small fruit. "Oh, yes, Mrs Petrie. These are extra sweet plums – a delicacy, the fruit man said, and a bargain at three farthings."

Helen stared at the fruit in Geeta's hand. "They're currants!"

But Geeta shook her head. "No, Mrs Petrie, the man said they are extra small plums – more flavour, he said."

Helen rolled her eyes. "Geeta, he lied to you. They're currants – trust me, I know a currant from a plum." She tugged impatiently at the grocery bag. "So, what else did he sell you? Turnips instead of potatoes?"

But Geeta's hands were already in front of her face in shame. "Oh, Mrs Petrie, I have let you down again. But the man was so sure – and even when I said they were not like the plums in India, he said they were extra special English plums."

She looked up, the tears staining her face. "I am sorry, Mrs Petrie, please, I will pay for the plums myself."

But Helen shook her head. Geeta was saving for her fare back to India. "Don't worry, I'll use the currants and make a bun."

But as she measured out the milk and butter, Helen wondered how Geeta had fared as a nanny. Maybe the family who had abandoned her at London docks had found fault with her work, although abandoning the poor girl in a foreign country was unforgivable. Helen frequently thought that if she was ever to meet the Mr and Mrs Parker she would give them a piece of her mind.

Helen dropped the currants into the bowl and was stirring the thick mix into a heavy cream when there was a knock at the door.

Winifred stood in her outside cape, a letter in her hand. She leaned forward, putting it straight into Helen's hand like it was something very precious. "It came this morning, and I know you love news of him – it's from Africa."

Helen slit the envelope open so fast that she cut her finger on the knife.

187

Dear Mother,

I write with great joy to tell you that our work here is almost complete. Our last box of Bibles is almost empty. The people we are with now seem happy to receive us and take Our Lord's word with little question. Sometimes I wonder if they truly understand what we bring, but they are good people with large hearts and like to be merry. Roger and I went out with some of the native men and saw a grand sight that few have seen before us. The natives call it the "Smoke that Thunders" and, Mother, that is truly a most appropriate description. From a distance you can hear the sound of the sky in a thunder storm while, over the heads of the trees, a heavy smoke flows up into the sky. But as we grew close, Roger and I were astonished to find a massive waterfall so wide we could barely see the other side, and so deep that the crashing water sent out the thunderous noise we had heard in the distance and threw up such massive sprays of water that it had looked like smoke. Mother, I truly wish I could have drawn such a scene. David Livingstone has named these waterfalls after our blessed Queen but, Mother, I cannot help but believe the Smoke That Thunders is a name more apt.

Soon, I should be able to tell you about all our adventures, for we are turning toward the homeward stretch. As we wind our way back to the Cape, we will stop at a few small villages to spread the word, but my heart is full because now I know our route is toward home. I will send this letter with a trader who is taking a more direct route to the coast. But know soon, Mother, that I will be journeying home.

Your loving son,
Mathew

A tear grew in Helen's eye as she smiled. Her boy was coming home.

*

Lawrence sat alone at the train window, listening as the steam engine beat a rhythm of *"further away, further away"* as it sped along the tracks. The land stretched out as though it were a vast ocean, and Lawrence thought of Robinson Crusoe looking out across the sea and seeing nothing that might offer rescue. He wondered if his father would ever find him out here.

Miss Ellen said it was unusual to send a child out to a home without first meeting the family, but these were unusual circumstances. The farm was at least one hundred miles north, and Miss Findlay couldn't take days away to travel to Belleville to collect him. But Miss Ellen had smiled a lot and told him to learn all he could and that there was more to the world than book learning. He'd packed only his copy of *Robinson Crusoe* and old letters from his father, for he hadn't received any new ones since he'd arrived in Canada.

Lawrence had asked Miss Ellen if he could take paper and envelopes with him so he could write to his father, but she'd pulled her mouth tight and said that maybe it would be best if he just got along with his work on the farm. Lawrence wondered if Miss Findlay might give him paper so he could tell his father about this huge, wide landscape and how it was good for agriculture. Maybe his father would see opportunity here and come out so they could be together.

Lawrence looked up to see the conductor weave toward him. This was the only passenger carriage and it was empty of all but Lawrence. The other carriages carried farm supplies.

The thin man gave him a nod. "This one's for you."

Lawrence felt the train slow ever so slightly. The beat of *"further away, further away"* relaxed. He stood and lifted his canvas satchel.

"Someone meeting you?" the conductor asked.

Lawrence smiled. "Miss Findlay. She's going to teach me to farm."

The conductor patted his shoulder. "Well, you've come to the right place. There won't be much else to learn around here."

The train slowed more quickly, pushing Lawrence into the conductor. The man held Lawrence's thin shoulder until the train came to a complete stop and then patted the boy toward the exit.

There were no steps to the platform and Lawrence was forced to jump, landing awkwardly on his misshapen foot. He limped as he looked around the platform for Miss Findlay. He wasn't sure what she would look like but he pictured her tall – because a small woman couldn't work a farm alone – and slim because of all her hard work.

All he could see was a station porter unloading sacks. He stood beside the man while keeping a watchful eye out for Miss Findlay.

"Boy, I'll get to you in just a minute," the elderly porter muttered.

Lawrence watched the man drag heavy sacks from the train and drop them in a long line.

"Let me help," Lawrence said as he placed his canvas satchel on the ground.

The older man stood aside to let the boy pull a sack from the train and then laughed as Lawrence's face turned red at the weight and he was forced to drop the sack at the platform's edge.

"This is man's work, boy," the porter said. "Get over there and sit like a girl while I finish."

Lawrence's chest felt like he'd been punched with a large stick and his arms tingled from the brief weight of the sack. He sat where he was bidden and watched until the older man had done his work. The conductor blew the train whistle and the engine changed from gentle idle to a slow *"further away, further away."*

"Take care out there," the conductor yelled at him as the train moved off.

Lawrence waved.

The station porter, his back stooped after the heavy load, stepped toward him. "Now, Miss Findlay sent a note that I was to take you to her place. Let me finish here and we'll be gone."

Lawrence was thirsty but didn't dare ask for water. He watched as the porter dragged his sacks into a room, locked it and then walked off. Lawrence's tongue grew sticky with thirst and he thought about sucking a rock, anything to get rid of the dryness.

He stood as the attendant approached. "Sir, may I please have a sup of water?"

The man laughed. "There's a water bucket and ladle not six feet from you, boy." He pointed to a wooden bucket concealed under a black iron lid.

Lawrence blushed as he dipped the ladle and brought the water up to his mouth to drink, again and again.

"That's enough, boy. Let's be off. I don't want to be travelling home in the dark."

As they made their way in the small cart, a cold wind blew from behind and Lawrence pulled his collar up around his neck, feeling glad that they weren't travelling into the wind.

"Aye, it's a harsh wind that comes from the east," the stationmaster said, then gave a small laugh. "It's also a harsh wind that comes out of the west. There's no shelter out here for those who feel the cold easily."

Lawrence shrank into his coat trying to stay warm.

"So, what type of farm work you used to?" The man's face looked blue in the dusky light.

Lawrence shook his head. "None, Sir."

The man gave him a firm stare. "Surely, you've worked on mowing and milking before?"

Lawrence reddened. "No, but our teacher in London gave us lessons. It was very interesting. But I'm hoping Miss Findlay needs help with letters and accounts because I read and write better than most older people."

The older man laughed, let the laughter die down and then snorted and let out another bellow of sniggering. "Oh, Miss Findlay, is going to like you. Forty acres she works off her own back, and they send her a boy who's good at books."

They turned off the track and into a hollow pass. Heavy black smoke could be seen ahead.

"Not far to go now," the porter said. "Miss Findlay might have a nice supper ready for you and maybe she'll ask you to read to her." A snort of laughter erupted again, and Lawrence gave him a puzzled look.

Agnes Findlay stood outside her low-lying cottage. She was taller than any woman Lawrence had ever seen. As they grew closer he could see a broad chin that reminded him of a caricature he'd once seen in a London newspaper. Only the grey hair pulled into a top knot gave Agnes Findlay the look of a woman.

She peered at Lawrence. "He's too small!"

"Not much for me to do about it. This is the one they sent you. I'm just making the delivery." The stationmaster slowed the cart to a stop and reached back for Lawrence's canvas bag.

"There you go, young man. I'm sure Miss Findlay will appreciate all your classroom learning."

Lawrence jumped from the cart, losing his balance as he landed so that he rolled into the dirt at Agnes Findlay's feet.

She looked up at the porter. "He can't even walk on two feet."

The porter laughed. Lawrence pulled himself to standing. "I'm sorry, Miss, it was just a bit of stiffness after that long journey. I'm keen to learn all I can, you'll see."

Agnes Findlay took her eyes from his earnest face and cast them down his body and to the foot that was raised from the ground to keep Lawrence standing level. "This boy's a cripple!" she yelled to the porter who was already turning his cart to head back toward the station.

His laughter rang through the cold air.

Agnes Findlay gave Lawrence a push that sent him back to the ground. "I need the cows milked, and you'd better be quick at it."

Lawrence scrambled to stand. "But where will I put my things, my coat, my bag? Can you show me my room?"

Helen cast her eyes down to the canvas bag. "There's no one here to steal anything, so leave that there and get moving. The milk barn lies at the back of the house."

Lawrence hurried, conscious that his limp was being scrutinised but keen to show it didn't hold him back. He tried to remember Mr Pascal's lessons on milking. Did he use his thumbs or not?

The barn was warm. Lawrence found the milk pail and began to work on the first cow. He was amazed when the milk spurted through to his pail and he smiled at his success. As the milk flow lessened, he moved to the next cow, then the next, until his pail was full.

Lawrence stood and looked for another pail. He had no idea what he should do with the full one, but he didn't want to see Miss Findlay until he could tell her that all the cows were milked.

A large wood bucket lay in the corner, and Lawrence took this to use for milking the next cow. The bucket was large and didn't fill until Lawrence had worked his way through all the cows. He ran off to find Miss Findlay, keen to tell her of his success.

"Keep a little for the house jug," she told him, "but put the rest in the churner – add to it with each pail you fill."

Lawrence smiled. "But, Miss, I found a large bucket and used that. It holds almost the entire milk."

Agnes Findlay's mouth open fell so that her chin hit her bodice. "What do you mean – that large bucket?"

"The big bucket that sat in the corner of the barn – it's a perfect size. I could tell from my math lessons that it would hold enough."

Agnes Findlay's hand swept Lawrence off his feet and back into the dust. "Boy, that bucket was for making pig feed." She kicked him as he lay on the ground. "That's the whole milking you just cost me."

As she reached down, Lawrence stumbled, his body unsure if he should pull back or take her assistance.

She pushed him again. "Now, get that bucket of milk and mix it with the feed at the back of the cottage – it can go to the pigs, although I don't like spoiling them with good milk."

Lawrence ran to the back of the cottage hoping he would recognise the pig feed.

That night Lawrence didn't read *Robinson Crusoe*. Instead, his small body fell into a deep sleep. The straw mattress was comfortable, and the attic roof was tight with no draughts.

But in the morning, it was Agnes Findlay's screech that wakened him. "Is that piss I smell." Her heavy feet clamoured up the ladder. Lawrence opened his eyes to see Agnes Findlay throw a tin chamber pot at him. "Don't you know what this is for? Don't those folks over in England know what to do with it – or do they all piss their beds?"

Lawrence felt the cold moisture that made his trousers cling to his skin. He shut his eyes tight. "I'm sorry, Miss," he whispered.

Agnes Findlay crouched above him, her head narrowly scraping the roof timber. She picked up the chamber pot and threw it again so it landed on Lawrence's chest. He groaned loudly at the impact.

"You learn to use the pot. I'm not laying anymore straw up here, not when I've got animals that're cleaner than you are."

"I'm sorry, Miss," Lawrence said again.

She shook her head at him. "You'd better be. Now get down those stairs. I've got plenty of work waiting for you."

*

Baby Ann cried without rest. Mrs Severn tied the infant to her back and tried to weed the vegetable garden, but the baby wouldn't sleep like she usually did.

Junie watched Mrs Severn bob up and down trying to soothe the child, until Mrs Severn draw her a sharp look and she remembered her chores. She reached down and pulled a weed, twisting its leaves so she got a good pull on the root, just like Mrs Severn had shown her. But really she hoped she would be told to watch the baby. The feel of the child's soft skin and the gurgling noises gave Junie so much pleasure, far more than she ever got from her old doll Victoria.

Mrs Severn walked the length of the vegetable patch, rocking from side to side in an effort to settle the baby. But Ann pushed furiously against her mother's back with thwarted anger. The mother muttered soothing noises as she rocked to see if that would quieten the child, but the baby wailed louder and Mrs Severn's face grew red with frustration.

"You!" she called out to Junie. "Finish weeding this entire patch – no shirking – while I take this one inside and settle her."

Junie looked the length of the vegetable patch. It was bigger than the garden at Marchmont House, but she knew Mrs Severn's mood. If she didn't get the work done she'd face a beating. Junie pulled at the next weed, its roots a little deeper than usual, and she twirled and twirled the stalk and leaves until she felt she could pull out the entire root. She thought about Ruby and Victoria as she moved forward, pulling at weeds. George said Ruby would take care of Victoria until Miss Considerance could put her in the mail. He sounded very sure when he said this, but Junie was worried that Ruby might not want to give Victoria up or maybe Ruby had already left the home and taken Victoria with her.

Ruby sucked at her thumb, the dirt from the weeds giving it a warm, tart taste. She worked up the line of vegetables, finding lots of weeds at the far end. She had to use her sucking thumb for these, as it took two hands to haul the orange roots from the ground. Her back felt tight and her legs ached with bending. Maybe Mrs Severn would let her play with the baby if she finished the work quickly.

Noises from behind made her turn. Mr Severn's face twisted into a growl and he was running at her. "What the hell are you doing?"

Junie stood and looked at the weeds spilling out of the bucket beside her, their small orange roots bringing colour to the dirt.

"That's carrots you've been pulling at – young carrots!" Severn's hand came down, catching Junie across the head and sweeping her down so she hit her head on the bucket, sending the contents out onto the vegetable garden.

Severn picked up one of the orange roots. "That's not weeds. That's our carrot seedlings you pulled up."

George heard him yell from up on the pasture. He sprinted to the top of the hill so he could get a good look at the house. Junie lay on the ground with Severn slapping at her again and again. George ran downhill, his legs catching momentum as he saw Severn step away and return with a wooden pole.

Junie lay curled so her back took all the blows. Mrs Severn came onto the earthen porch. Her husband beckoned her, pointed to the bucket so his wife could see what the girl had picked. The woman shook her head and raised her own hand to strike the girl.

George caught Mrs Severn's hand before she could hit Junie, but Mr Severn gave George a blow across the head that sent him straight onto his sister.

George huddled over Junie's back to protect her. Severn reached down, lifted the boy by his shoulders and threw him to the side.

"You get up that hill and take care of them cows."

George stared at his owner, and then darted back to cover Junie.

The man took a breath. "The girl had to be punished. Now, it's over so you get back to work."

George watched him, ready to pounce if Tom Severn moved toward his sister.

"It's over!" Severn yelled.

George stayed watching Severn for any sudden movement. Junie lifted her head just a little. George motioned to her. "You can get up now, Junie."

Severn pointed to the uphill pasture. "Get back to them cows, right now!"

George turned and ran, his heart pummelling his chest as he ran uphill. He looked back and saw Junie standing, facing the couple. He saw their heads move as they yelled. Assured that there would be no more beating, he ran further uphill looking for the cows. He caught sight of three in a ditch. The others were further uphill. George took out his whip and ran at the three cows, switching at their rears to push them uphill toward the rest of the herd.

Down at the house, Junie was given only moments of quiet before her canvas bag was thrown at her and she was lifted onto the back of Tom Severn's horse. Mrs Severn didn't wave as they moved off, instead she just shook her head and shuffled into the house. Tom Severn dug into the horse's side so she would gather speed, and Junie was forced to cling to a loose fold of his shirt. She was afraid of falling but she didn't want to get too close to the man. Her back and head hurt from the beating, and she tried not to think about where they were going. She hoped George would come after her. George always knew what to do. He would take her back to Ma, and Junie decided she would work harder at matchboxes and wouldn't let her mind wander. She would listen more to Rosie about folding the creases and making sure they stuck.

A cry from a large bird made her look up.

"Hang on, dammit," Tom Severn yelled. "This ain't no time to go gawping."

Junie held his shirt a little tighter. She wished again that she knew where she was going. Maybe he would abandon her in the woods like that story Lawrence had told her. She would have to wander for days, hoping a nice woodsman or fairy found her.

The sound of cartwheels came from ahead. Junie couldn't see anything as Tom Severn's back blocked her view, but she heard a cheery voice as Severn pulled the horse to a stop.

"Good day to you neighbour! And where are you off to?"

Tom Severn shrugged. "Belleville. I took in some of those English orphans a while back and I'm taking this one back. She ain't worth the food she takes."

Junie relaxed when she heard they were going back to the orphanage.

The round face of an elderly man leaned forward to peer at her. "Looks awful young," he said.

"Well, their parents can't wait to be rid of them – breed them like rats over there," Tom Severn said.

Junie felt the horse move forward and sat up straight now she knew where they were heading. She couldn't wait to see Ruby and Victoria and Beryl and Lawrence. And she would tell Miss Considerance to go and get George, rescue him from that horrible house.

The countryside rose and fell with the horse's movement until the track widened and they entered Belleville. Junie's heart raced as she peered past Tom Severn for a sight of Marchmont House.

"Sit back, you little bitch," he called over his shoulder.

Junie sat back and watched the passing homes, trying to catch sight of Marchmont. Tom Severn pulled the horse to a stop outside a tavern.

He climbed down, tied up the reins and lifted her roughly, almost throwing her off the horse. "I'm sure you know the way from here."

Without a look, he hurried into the bar.

Junie felt the cold of the evening settle across her shoulders. She looked around but saw nothing familiar.

A large man with a big muscled faced stopped in front of her, his huge eyes wandering across her face and then down her chest and body. Sensing danger, Junie stepped back and ran, her canvas bag weighing down heavy on her shoulders.

A woman with a small child stood at a street corner ahead. Junie ran to catch up with them. "Ma'am, Ma'am!"

The woman turned and threw Junie a scornful glare. "Get away, you little beggar."

Junie stopped and watched the woman pull the small girl across the road. The street was lined with shops. Junie knew Marchmont House was near other large homes and she walked the length of the street looking for a familiar side street. She hurried down one, stopping at other side streets for a sight of Marchmont House. It was getting dark, and she was thirsty, hungry and her feet hurt when she finally saw the high trees that surrounded the home. She hurried up the path unable to believe that she would see Ruby, Victoria, Beryl and Lawrence again.

At the top of the steps, Junie stretched up toward the doorbell, her toes digging into the wood flooring for extra reach. But her fingers couldn't reach the bell, and Junie felt tears of frustration at being so close to her old friends. She pounded her fist on the door and then, when no one answered, she gave it a kick.

When Miss Ellen finally answered, Junie ran into her skirts and burrowed herself there, tears taking over all other emotions.

"Child, what are you doing back here?" Ellen Bilbrough pulled Junie into the house and hurried her down into the kitchen. She poured a tall glass of lemonade, stirring in extra sugar because the girl looked even smaller than she remembered.

"Take something to drink and then you can tell me what happened."

Junie sobbed a little more and then turned her tear-streaked face to Miss Ellen. "It was horrible there and the mister brought me back. He dropped me off the horse outside the tavern and told me to find my own way here. I didn't know the way and a man looked at me and then a woman called me a beggar, and poor George is still back there. And they beat me because I picked out the wrong weeds, and it was cold and we was always hungry. I want to stay here now – or go back to me ma – but I don't want to go with no new family, Miss Ellen. Please tell Miss Considerance that – she'll listen to you."

Ellen smiled. "Hush, child, you're fine now."

Junie grabbed the woman's hand. "Will you tell Miss Considerance to go and get George?"

Ellen pulled the small hand to her. "Miss Constance is back in London right now, but don't worry, I'll tell her to go and see him."

*

Several hours later, George drove the cows back to the farm for milking. He noticed the horse was missing and George hoped that

Severn would be home late and they wouldn't have to sit together at the table.

He lined the cows up for milking and took the first bucket down to the house for Junie to churn. But outside the house, the potatoes sat in the bucket unpeeled. The skin on George's neck rose at the silence of the place.

"Junie!" he called out as he hurried toward the earthen porch.

Mrs Severn met him at the entrance. George looked behind her, expecting to see Junie playing on the blanket with the baby or at work at the stove.

"She ain't here."

George stared at the woman, too scared to ask but waiting to be told.

"She's no good to us. He's taken her back to that home."

George shook his head. "But she's my sister. I promised me ma. I said I'd take care of her."

Mrs Severn shrugged. "You'd better hurry with the milking because now she's gone you need to see to the churning."

*

Ruby pulled open the door to the doll house and placed Rebecca in her favourite chair. The doll was too big for the miniature sitting room, but Ruby didn't care. She put the best plates before Rebecca, tiny crockery with a miniscule floral pattern, and decided that Rebecca should dine on duck, for that was Ruby's favourite food. Cook always put extra aside for her, saying the fat would keep Ruby's skin fair and plump.

A small knock on the door brought in the governess carrying books.

Ruby gave her most pleading look. "Please can I play a little longer? Rebecca is still at supper, and then I must put her to bed."

Miss Emmerson smiled. "Ruby, we must give time to our lessons. You can return to play with Rebecca later."

Ruby's plump mouth turned downward.

Miss Emmerson pulled a book from her bag. "Let's begin with a chapter from *Little Women* – you'll like that story."

As Miss Emmerson read, Ruby heard about the March girls and their neighbour, Theodore Lawrence. She'd known a Lawrence once – he was dark-haired and had a limp, but very sweet – he'd read to her as well. She remembered playing with him at a lake, and Beryl was there – Beryl had once looked after her. Ruby tried to remember her face, but could only see fair hair like her own, the face hazy except for a dark mole on her cheek.

Miss Emmerson's clear voice interrupted her thoughts: *'Thank you, Mr Laurence; but I am not Miss March, I'm only Jo,'* *returned the young lady.*

As Ruby drew further into the story, the hazy image of Beryl faded and was replaced by the March girls all dressed up for the party at the Laurence house.

*

Junie lay in bed wishing George, Ruby or Beryl were with her. But they'd all been sent to new homes. Even Victoria couldn't be found. Miss Ellen said she remembered seeing her, but didn't know where.

A small sobbing sound came from one of the girls on the other side of the room. Someone else snored, while another whistled through sleep. Junie tried to close her eyes and think of nice things like George, her ma, Tommy, Ruby and Victoria, but she kept wondering where she would be sent next. Miss Ellen said she couldn't go home. She said there were too many nice people in Canada who wanted her to stay with them.

"Just because you found one bad apple, we can't throw away the whole pot," Miss Ellen said.

Junie didn't understand what apples had to do with going to another family, but Miss Ellen was nice. She'd let Junie sit beside her at dinner even though lots of other children wanted to sit there.

The sobbing girl at the other side of the room quietened, and finally Junie's eyes grew heavy.

Over breakfast Junie sat with a tall girl who looked a little like Beryl except there was no mole on her cheek. They didn't talk much as the girl had other friends, but Junie was happy to sit and eat porridge topped with sugar and milk. She'd forgotten how good it tasted. At the end of the table a group of small girls giggled over breakfast. Junie watched one of them pull a soft doll from under the table. The wool hair was thinner than before, but Junie recognised her immediately.

"Victoria!" she called out as she tipped up her chair and ran to the top of the table. Junie grabbed her doll, but the girl pulled it back. As Junie tugged at Victoria's legs, Miss Ellen placed both hands over the doll's head.

"We do not fight!" she said loudly.

"But, Miss, it's my doll – it's Victoria. I brought her from home."

The other girl gave the doll a tug. "No, she isn't. I found her in the playbox."

"She came from my house. She's always been mine."

"But I love her!"

"So do I."

"Girls!" called out Miss Ellen.

"Miss, it's Victoria. Me ma says I got him from me da, and I left her when that bad man took me and George out of here. I didn't mean to leave her."

The other girl silently weighed up Junie's claim. "But I found her all alone in the playbox."

Junie shook her head. "I wouldn't have left her in the playbox."

Miss Ellen crouched between them. "Can't you both play with her?"

The girls looked at each other.

"I used to share her with my friend Ruby, but she's not here anymore," Junie said.

The girl smiled and shunted along the bench to make room for Junie.

*

George woke up at dawn with a cold wind coming through the slats in the door. He'd slept with his father's shirt over his clothes. He took it off and hid it under the straw. If the Severns could take Junie away, they could surely take his father's shirt. He hurried out to do the milking, sweep the barn, carry the turds out to the vegetable garden, feed the chickens, gather the eggs and then run inside for a quick breakfast of bread with a small cup of milk.

The table was quiet except for Severn and his wife swallowing and gulping at their food. Even baby Ann made little noise. George ate as silently as possible, moving his jaw slowly and giving the couple no reason to look at him.

It was always a relief when the last of the bread was gone, the milk cup emptied and he could flee uphill to take the cows to fresh pasture. The wind whipped icily. But even with the cold biting through his ragged clothes, George preferred to be on the vast hills with only the noise of the wind for company. Up there he could think of his mother, sisters and brother without fear that he'd be slapped for laziness.

As George led the cows across to fresher grassland they'd not visited for weeks, he tried to imagine where Junie was now. He hoped she was being taken back to London by Miss Constance and, after she'd been delivered safely to their mother, then Miss Constance would return to rescue him.

Miss Constance had said they could write if they weren't happy. But there was nothing to write on at the Severns' home. Not that George could write a letter that would make any sense. And how would he get it to Marchmont?

George shook his head and led one of the cows away from a bog that surrounded a low stream.

*

Lawrence raised the axe as high as he could before letting it fall and sending a few chips of bark spraying from the log. He lifted the axe again, his arms quivering with effort but, again, he only chipped at the bark. His stomach growled, and he knew he would work better if only he could have some food. But Miss Findlay blamed him for the hens not laying yesterday so there'd been no supper for him last night and no breakfast this morning.

"And there'll be no food until you learn to pull your weight, Imbecile," Miss Findlay said.

That was her name for him. "Imbecile!"

Small tears welled at his lids as Lawrence lifted the axe as high as he could. He tensed his muscles to bring it down with great force, but the axe didn't move. Lawrence pulled, feeling a weight pull back. He grunted with effort, and then a dry laugh from behind made him turn and see Miss Findlay's strong arms holding the axe head.

She spat then curled her mouth as though about to swear. "Boy, leave the chopping to me and go see to the pigs. You're as much help here as a cow with no udders."

She pulled the axe from Lawrence's hands, but he held on. "No, Miss, let me try. I'm only learning and I will get better. Probably if I'd had some dinner or breakfast I'd be fine. I'm just so terribly hungry and it's making me weak."

Agnes Findlay's eyes narrowed. "That's all you want from me, isn't it? Free meals and a bed to piss in because you're too damn lazy to get up in the night. Well, there's no free food here. Get a job done, and then I'll be generous."

Lawrence kept a firm hold on the axe handle. "But, Miss, please, I really want to try. I promised my father I would learn all about farm life so when he arrives we can work together. So, you see, I need to learn to chop wood."

Agnes Findlay laughed. "Your father isn't coming anywhere near Canada. They don't let degenerates like him in here."

Lawrence's breath stopped as he dropped the axe handle and lurched at Agnes Findlay. "My father is not a degenerate." His small fists gave a brief pummel to Agnes Findlay's chest before she caught his arms and swung him down against the ground, holding him there with her boot. She lifted the axe and held the blade two feet from his face.

"Now, this here will take the head from your neck quicker than a knife to one of them hens. Now, you ever lunge after me like that again, and there'll be no mercy."

She brought the axe slowly toward Lawrence's neck so that he saw the nicks and stains on its metal grow out of focus.

Agnes Findlay laughed, a deep guffaw that reminded Lawrence of how his father sounded when he was on a winning streak at cards. And then she lifted the axe and brought it down on the log, chopping it cleanly in two.

Lawrence felt a warm wet spot between his legs and knew he'd disgraced himself yet again.

*

Junie's hands worked faster than the other girls as she helped scrub the potatoes for dinner. She held up her slim peelings. "Mine are longer than yours."

The other girl held up a stumpy peel and laughed. "Mine'll get better."

Between them Victoria lay on the workbench, her padding flat and her wool hair sparse.

Heavy steps on the stairs made both girls look up. A large boy hurried in saying Miss Ellen wanted to see Junie immediately. Junie grabbed Victoria and hurried upstairs. Outside Miss Ellen's room she paused – maybe George was inside, or maybe even her ma.

But inside the room was the fattest woman Junie had ever seen. Her chin fell onto her chest and her body seemed to fill the entire space between the guest chair and Miss Ellen's desk. Junie stared, unable to take her eyes away.

Miss Ellen held her hand out toward her guest. "Junie, I would like you to meet Mrs Gemmel. She's the housekeeper at a large house near Toronto and she's looking for a housemaid to learn the trade – that includes housekeeping, laundry and kitchen duties."

Junie wondered what this had to do with her.

The round woman scrutinised Junie from the roots of her thin hair to the toes of her recently polished boots.

Miss Ellen smiled. "Junie, I thought it might be something you would like to do."

Junie thought of scrubbing potatoes. She'd hated using Mrs Severn's old rusty peeler, but here at Marchmont, working with other girls, it could be fun.

Mrs Gemmel wheezed as she spoke. "Do you have experience?"

Junie looked down at her boots. She didn't want to leave Marchmont again. "No, Ma'am."

Miss Ellen's voice rose in tone. "Oh, come now, Junie, don't be modest. You worked hard in the kitchen at your previous home, and you often volunteer here for kitchen duty."

Junie nodded. She couldn't deny this.

"Miss Ellen here speaks very highly of you." Mrs Gemmel ran out of breath at the end of the sentence.

Junie nodded more vigorously.

"Well, Junie, I suggest," Mrs Gemmel paused, "we give you a trial as kitchen maid." She took a deep breath. "At Bagthorne House you'll get training," she paused for another breath. "A free uniform and a salary once you turn fourteen." The woman's head bowed as she drew in more air.

Miss Ellen smiled. "Well, I think that's a wonderful arrangement."

Junie shook her head, her own chest breathless as she wondered how to stop it all from happening."

Mrs Gemmel smiled at her. "Then we should see you Monday week." She took a long draw of breath.

Miss Ellen gave Junie a final smile. "Now run along dear, I'm sure they need your help in our kitchen."

Junie kept her eyes dry until she reached the kitchen and then she erupted into tears. Enid, the girl who looked like Beryl, came and put her arm around her.

"I don't want to go. I want to stay here," Junie sobbed.

Enid sat Junie down. "You must see that this is good news. You don't want to end up with a bad family again."

"And if this cook was fat, then that means the house has plenty of food," said another girl.

"And if they give you a good training, you'll have all types of jobs open to you when you finish," said another.

Junie couldn't see any good side. "What if my brother comes to look for me?"

"Miss Ellen will tell him where you are," Enid said.

Junie hugged Victoria. This time she wouldn't be leaving her doll behind.

*

On the blackboard behind Helen were drawn rows of neatly sized apples. She pointed her ruler as the children chanted in unison: *Two plus one is three; Two plus two is four; Two plus three is five; Two plus ...*

Upstairs Constance taught a group of girls about fish kettles. The group of 46 would be accompanying Constance on her next trip to Canada. They gazed at their teacher in puzzlement as she held up first a turbot kettle and then a kettle for cooking salmon.

One girl finally gained the courage to raise her hand. "Miss, why does a turbot need a different kettle from a salmon?"

Constance's mouth turned stiff as she searched for a suitable answer. "I myself am unsure of the merits of these pans. But, you must understand, the people who created these pans know the reason for their creation otherwise they wouldn't have made the salmon kettle square-shaped and the turbot kettle more oblong."

The girl who'd asked the question nodded cautiously. Constance knew she wasn't truly satisfied. "Sometimes, we have to accept the way things are done because it is a higher power than ours that created it."

She moved swiftly on to churning butter, and the girls followed her movements as she picked up the milk pan and patted the milk churner.

"Girls, those of you who end up on farms will grow to know your milk churner. Every single day, no matter how many other chores you have, you will skim your cream until it thickens. And, when the cream is suitably thick, it should be warmed near a coal fire and then poured into a butter churner."

The bell sounded time for lunch. The children filed out of the classroom and down to the lunchroom. Constance followed, catching up with her mother on the stairs.

"Mother, you know I am off to Canada in two days," Constance whispered.

Helen shook her head like a fly had whisked too close. "I trust you had a good class this morning."

"Mother, please let us discuss this. I believe it is the right thing to do. As does Annie MacPherson, who is no naive girl when it comes to finding ways to help the poor – this Home of Industry would be an empty ruin without her vision."

Helen walked more slowly downstairs, meeting Winifred on her way. "There is a letter for you. It's on your desk," Winifred whispered.

Helen's chest rose as she hurried back upstairs. This was surely a letter from Mathew and he was surely on his way home.

The letter on Helen's desk was from Africa, but the handwriting was not her son's. She pulled at the flap on the envelope.

Dear Mrs Petrie,

I write a letter that I know will not be well received. Your son Mathew is ill with fever. We were moving downriver when he suffered the shakes. Two days later a fever the likes of which I have never come across before fired up his entire body. But Mathew's fortitude is great, and he continued the slow march down the trail even though he desperately wanted to rest. We are now at the Cape and he is receiving aid from the Catholic Sisters, but his state is dire. He has not been conscious for five days and is unable to drink or eat. I found a ship able to take us home, but I have been told that he would likely not survive the journey in his current condition. The best hope is to wait for recovery here at the mission. So I send this letter in our stead and hope the next missive I send brings news of Mathew's recovery. I have grown close to your son throughout this journey, and we have shared hard times together. But we have also shared cheer and success. I know he was hugely fond of you, Mrs Petrie. He talked of his childhood with great warmth and, I know he looked forward to his return home.

I will keep you posted.

Yours at this time of need,

Roger Simonds

Helen pulled her cape from its stand and fled down the steps of the Home of Industry. As she ran through the streets of the East End, she felt chased by images of her son walking through fever and chills, growing tired and weak, but pushing on toward home. She would join him, she would nurse him, surely she could save him.

*

Constance arrived home to find her mother packing a trunk. Geeta was folding small items while shawls, corsets and skirts littered the bed. Helen paced the floor pulling out yet more clothes.

"Constance, run down to the shipping office and find out when the next boat to Cape Town leaves."

Constance scanned the confusion, feeling her mother had gone mad.

"Constance, hurry, your brother might be ..." Helen stopped and thrust Roger Simonds' letter into her hands.

As Constance read, Helen and Geeta filled the trunk with clothes.

"Mathew ..." Constance couldn't think of anything else to say. She watched her mother lift her grooming set from the dresser and several hats from the stand. "Mother, you can't go to Africa now."

"Why not?" Helen turned so quickly that Constance jumped.

"Well, Mathew might be well – he might already be on his way home."

Helen gave her a searching look.

Constance kept her gaze steady. "Roger Simonds might have put him on the next ship home, and you would surely cross mid-sea."

Helen sat quietly, and then stood and began packing again. "But what if he isn't? What if he needs me?"

"Mother, it sounds like he's being taken care of – those Catholic Sisters are probably very able when it comes to African fevers. He's in good hands."

Helen threw up her hands. "Then what am I supposed to do?"

Constance pulled her back down onto the bed. The two women sat thoughtful for a few moments. "Mother, we must keep busy and we must pray – Mathew is in His hands."

The two women sat in silence. Helen thinking of her son, feverish and thirsty; Constance picturing him rising from his bed.

Geeta watched both women, waiting for her next instruction.

Finally, Constance pulled on her mother's hand. "Come, we must be busy. If we sit and think too much, we will only fret."

She took her mother's favourite shawl from the trunk and wrapped it around Helen's shoulders. As she tugged on her mother's arm, Helen paused. "Geeta, please go to the docks and find out about the next ship to Cape Town."

Constance shook her head and hurried her mother through the London streets and back to the Home of Industry. Lunch was over, so Constance led her mother into the kitchen where the two women washed dishes and scrubbed pots. It wasn't their usual work, but they needed to be busy.

As she scrubbed at a burned pot, Constance thought about her father. His death had come very quickly. He'd been with them for breakfast, bade them a cheery farewell and they never saw him again. His blood stopped, the doctor said, and he died in the street outside his church. She'd been nine, Mathew six. Her mother had stayed busy making cakes for parishioners who visited to say what a good man he was.

Constance watched her mother scour a pot and knew that she was doing the same thing now – staying busy.

The two women worked until late in the evening. When the orphans were in bed and there was no more work to be done, they headed home. As they turned from Commercial Street, Helen asked the question Constance had dreaded: "Did you ever visit Mrs Brown?"

Constance shook her head. "Mother, she is in the Lock Hospital – the sanitary man caught up with her."

"And Mrs Twistle?"

Constance's silence made Helen uneasy.

She stopped walking and pulled her daughter to a halt. Her voice grew angry as she thought of Mathew and how much she wanted to be near him. "Constance, she was the child's mother – she needs to know something more than her child is dead. She needs to know if he was happy – that he'd had some joy from the world. Please, Constance, you must go and talk to her."

Constance shook her head. "I can't, Mother …"

"But you must – it's your responsibility."

"Mother, she has poisoned herself – she is dead of grief."

Helen turned her face to the soot blackened wall and wept.

*

209

Beryl lay on her back trying to ease her shoulders which ached from scrubbing the kitchen floor. She had scrubbed it four times, but each time Maisie had found a stain to complain about. She stretched out her legs in an effort to sleep, but damp cold bit through the wool of her socks. She pulled her legs up and sighed. She had to be up first in the morning and get the fires started and then pull water from the well. Thankfully there were biscuits left over from supper, so breakfast would be easy.

Her mind buzzed as she thought about the round of baking, sewing, scrubbing and cleaning she would do after breakfast. The hardest part was keeping a pot of water on the boil. Hot water was always needed but it was so easy to forget and find the pot burned dry. Maisie had hit her with the burnt pot once, singeing Beryl's hands as they flew up to protect her face. Bill had slapped his wife and then plunged Beryl's hand into cold water. Maisie had drawn her threatening looks for a week after that.

The only good thing was that Ruby was safe and well, at least Beryl hoped she was. Miss Constance had promised them so much, and while it hadn't worked out for Beryl, she felt sure that Ruby was living the life that had been promised. She wondered if her little sister ever thought about her. And her mother – where was she? She hoped Miss Constance visited her but she knew what type of reception her mother would give. Probably a few swear words and maybe even a slap.

A small tear crept to Beryl's eye as she thought about her mother. She wasn't a bad woman – it was just the drink. If she'd been more like George's mother, they could have worked at matchstick boxes and all would have been fine.

*

When she boarded the steamship *Sarmation*, Constance felt better prepared than before. In her bag she carried ginger to treat sea sickness and she had packed a large map so that, with the Captain's help, she could help the children track their passage and reduce the boredom that had beset her first group of immigrants.

The *Sarmation* wasn't as big as the *S.S. Sardinian*, and when they stepped below deck Constance found the area was communal and her children would be on constant view.

"Children," she announced, "this is a great day. We are taking this ship toward our new destiny – our promised land – and I think we should pray."

As she led the children in prayer, Constance could hear no sound from the other passengers. She peeked ever so briefly from one eye and couldn't help but smile when she saw all of the passengers had joined them in prayer.

"Amen!" the children called out.

Constance gave the other passengers her most appealing smile. "Do feel free to join us in prayer or singing at any time."

A woman nearby smiled back, while her husband busied himself with the rolled up blanket that held their belongings.

A tiny girl tugged on Constance's dress. "Miss Constance, is this where we find my relatives?"

Constance shook her head. "Milly, as I said before, I'm not sure we will find your relatives, but we will find a nice family who will love you."

The girl gave a lopsided grin that showed blackened teeth. "My da said my relatives would get me, he promised."

Constance rolled her eyes, quietly angry at the father who made a false promise to his daughter. There were no relatives in Canada. Constance had even visited him to check this out. He was a widower and said the only way he could send his daughter to Canada was by telling her she was going to relatives. He'd cried when he said this, but poor Milly kept her faith in him.

"Milly, we're going to go up on deck and will find a good spot to wave goodbye to England. Are you ready?"

The little girl nodded, and Constance directed her one hundred children onto the deck. She led with the same song she had sung with her first group of migrants:

"What a friend we have in Jesus,
All our sins and griefs to bear
In his arms he'll take and shield you
You will find a solace there ..."

211

The children sang heartily, although Constance looked around to ensure no other missionary had come aboard with children. The ticket clerk had said there would be no other large parties aboard the ship, but Constance wanted to be sure.

"Children, this will be our special place on deck. The journey is long – two weeks." She unfolded the map she had brought along and pointed to one boy to hold a top corner while she took the other.

She pointed to a black etched shape at the right-hand corner. "This is England – while this," she moved her finger across a swathe of emptiness to a larger shape, "is Canada!"

The children peered forward. One or two glanced back out to sea and then at the map again.

"But, Miss, how can that be England – it's too small. And the sea we have to cross doesn't look big at all."

Constance shook her head. "This is small because it's made of paper. We can't have a real image because it would stretch all across the sea." She pointed again to the small shape. "London is down here and all through the night on that train we travelled to Liverpool – here." She moved her pointer ever so slightly.

"So now you can see, we really do have a long way to go."

The younger children were already chattering and a few were tagging each other as if ready to give chase.

Constance folded the map away. "Children, let us sing. Let us raise our voices up to heaven for we are going to the promised land."

"Jesus bids us shine like a pure clear light
Like a little candle burning in the night."

*

Mrs Gemmel told Junie to work with Alice. Junie watched the girl warily, she was about the same age as Beryl but with heavy black hair and a large mouth that flopped open when she wasn't using it.

After Alice helped Junie into a dark grey dress and a white apron, she stood back and then readjusted the apron, pinning it tightly around Junie's thin waist.

"Now, your uniform has to be kept clean. Even if you have to wash it at night and wear it damp in the morning, it has to be clean," Alice said.

Junie nodded. "Yes, Ma'am."

Alice giggled. "You don't have to 'Ma'am' me – I'm just another servant like you."

Junie blushed at her mistake.

"Now let's start upstairs, shall we? I'll work with you for the first few days, and then Mrs Gemmel says you've to move to the kitchen."

Junie followed Alice upstairs. Another set of feet could be heard coming. Junie looked up to see who it was, but before she could find out Alice had pulled her into a dark cupboard. Junie felt the back of her head hit a metal pipe. "Why did you do that?"

"Shhh," Alice whispered.

The two girls listened as heavy slow feet passed by. Alice opened the cupboard door and peeked out. She beckoned Junie forward.

Alice spoke a little louder, her jaw moving deliberately slowly. "That was Mr Bagthorne and we're not allowed to let him see us."

"Why not?"

"Mrs Gemmel says so. She says the man of the house should never see the underservants." Alice spoke with a long lilt to the end of each word. It was a bit like Mrs Severn, but nicer – softer.

Junie still wondered why, but Alice had moved down the hallway so she hurried after her.

Alice opened a door off the hallway, and Junie hurried in keen to see the family's rooms. Dresses of every colour and flounce were draped over the chairs and hung from the open doors of the wardrobe. Junie's mouth opened in delight.

"This is the mistress's room," Alice said. "Miss Ragweed takes care of her, but we have to sweep out the fireplace, dust and make sure the floor is well swept."

Junie touched a shiny gown that hung from a door, its green sheen beckoning like a lure.

"Don't!" called out Alice. "Only Miss Ragweed handles the dresses."

Junie stepped back.

"Here, you sweep while I do the fireplace. And don't forget to go under the bed and dresser," Alice said.

Junie ran the broom across the floor, picking up small balls of fluff, a little dust and a few grey sequins.

"Does Mrs Bagthorne want these back?" Junie pointed to the sequins that squinted out from the dustpan. She would love to sew them on Victoria.

Alice shook her head. "It's best to leave them on the dresser and let Miss Ragweed decide."

Junie finished sweeping the floor and then began dusting. The furniture was already so shiny and smooth that Junie could see the shape of her face reflected in the wood. She polished a little bit more, rubbing extra hard at a blemish.

"This is such a nice room," she said. "Are all the rooms like this?"

Alice looked up from the fireplace and smiled. "This is the nicest – especially if you're a girl. Mr Bagthorne, he has stuffed animals and allsorts in his that I don't even like to look at never mind dust. And their son, James, he keeps lots of tiny bugs in small dishes. Mrs Gemmel says he's studying them. I don't know – it all looks very cruel to me."

"What about Mrs Gemmel? Does she have a nice room like Mrs Bagthorne?"

Alice shook her head. "No, it's nice though – down from the attic and bigger than ours."

"What about Mr Gemmel?"

Alice giggled. "There is no Mr Gemmel – the housekeeper isn't married."

"But we call her …"

"I know, it's silly, but that's what we call her. It's tradition – I don't know why."

Junie rubbed her rag into the finely carved legs of the dresser. It was nice work – not like matchbox making and certainly not like peeling potatoes with a rusty knife. Junie wondered again about George and hoped Miss Considerance had rescued him.

*

Constance edged away as Pastor Clarke leaned close. She turned her head from his as though his sudden closeness was purely an accident and she stared out on the green Ontario countryside, avoiding his gaze.

Pastor Clarke pulled a little on the horse's reins. "Aye, it's a good deed you've done us. Those children you've brought are like manna from heaven for the folks around here. Farming these lands needs keen hands."

Constance nodded. "Well, I believe The Lord led us by his very own hand. It truly is a Garden of Eden. I have never seen land so vast and colourful." She breathed in, smelling the pine carried downwind from the low hillsides. "I truly never believed God's earth could be so beautiful."

As she said the words, Constance thought about her mother. She'd hated leaving her in London waiting for news of Mathew, but what else could she do. Annie MacPherson was already journeying back to London, and she had expected Constance to be en route with the next party of children.

Pastor Clarke leaned close again, pushing Constance toward the edge of the seat. "Aye, well, I'm sure all those children you brought appreciate the great bounty of this land. But we could do with a few more young women – wives for the men, about your age, I'd say."

Constance sat a little straighter, her voice turning formal. "So, tell me about Mr and Mrs Severn. Junie seemed to say they were bad people. And Ellen Bilbrough said her back was bruised from beatings."

Pastor Clarke raised an eyebrow. "How old did you say the girl was?"

Constance thought for a moment. "Eight – or maybe seven – I can't truly remember."

"Aye, well, it's a bit young to be taken on to a farm, but from what Tom Severn said, she pulled up their entire crop of carrots."

"It was a mistake," Constance said.

"Oh, no doubt, but when you work like these people do, mistakes can make or break a homestead." He paused. "Now, maybe Tom Severn was a little heavy-handed, but they are good people although not blessed with patience. Tom Severn was a prospector and gambler out west, but he found the Lord, took a wife and moved north, buying up a rough homestead that no one else wanted."

He smiled at Constance. "You know taking a wife can change a man."

Constance turned quickly to look back out onto the countryside, not willing to give his fleshy face any hint that she understood. "But you wrote their reference. Do you think they are worthy of our children?"

The minister gave a small laugh. "More than worthy. I mean, they're not people who laugh a good deal – or give smiles easily – but there's plenty men out there who smile too much and do nothing but evil."

Constance sat back against the leather seat of the cart drawing crisp air deep into her lungs as she watched the low rise hills around them. After the dank smells of London with little to see beyond steep sooty walls, Constance smiled at the goodness of it all. They were rescuing children not just from the poverty and vice of their parents but from the death and disease that plagued their homeland.

As they approached a slow-moving creek, Pastor Clarke slowed the horses to a stop. He climbed down from the cart and hurried around to help Constance from her seat.

She looked around a little puzzled. "Are we here? I see no house."

Pastor Clarke laughed, his plump hand keeping a tight hold on Constance's arm after helping her from the cart. "My dear, I thought you might like a little walk, break up our journey. I would like to show you the beauty we can offer so that you might be tempted to take up a more permanent offer."

Constance's throat grew tight as she blushed, but she pulled her arm from Pastor Clarke's and turned quickly to climb aboard the cart. "Pastor Clarke, we are on a mission here – a mission for Our Lord – and I would be grateful if we could continue with our journey.

Pastor Clarke moved sullenly to his seat and took up the reins. They travelled in silence, moving uphill on land that was clearly rocky with soil barely covering the huge outcrops. Pastor Clarke pointed into the distance where Constance could see an earthen mound with a dark doorway etched into its centre.

"A sod home," Pastor Clarke said. "Many settlers live in these at the beginning. They're fast to build and warm to live in – especially in winter."

As they moved closer Constance could see the small porched entrance to the Severn house. Nearby was a barn made of wood so warped and worn that it looked as though a harsh wind might sweep it across the land. A few chickens pecked at the dried earth around the entrance.

Pastor Clarke pulled up the cart and helped Constance down. A tiny woman with a small worn face came out onto the porch carrying a pale sleeping baby, a wary look across her face.

Pastor Clarke's voice turned hearty. "Mrs Severn, how are you doing this fine day?"

The woman nodded quickly and looked behind her. "I'm sorry but Tom is up fencing today."

"That's all good, Mrs Severn. But we really came to see the boy, George." He took Constance's arm again and felt her stiffen at his touch. "This here is Constance Petrie who brought all those orphans out from London."

Mrs Severn gave Constance a darting glance and looked down at her baby. "He's up with the cows – with the snow due, it's the last days for pasture."

Pastor Clarke nodded. "I understand and don't you worry about it." He coughed. "It's just that the boy's sister made some comments – they probably weren't very fair to you – but she seemed to suggest that the children slept in a cold cave and were beaten."

Mrs Severn kept her gaze on the ground.

The pastor smiled. "I've told Miss Constance here that the child probably has fits of fancy and assured her that you and your husband are the solid bricks on which the fortitude of this fair land is based."

The woman looked up quickly to see if this meant trouble. She looked down when she saw Pastor Clarke's smile.

"But I hope that you won't mind showing Miss Constance around. She is returning to London soon and would like to take a good report to the boy's mother."

Constance followed the woman through the porch and into the earthen room. Only the dim glow from the stove provided any

217

light. Constance looked around for curtains that might be drawn to provide light and realised that there were no windows.

"I've just swept out," Mrs Severn said.

Constance looked down to see a dried earthen floor. "You cook in here?" she asked.

The woman nodded. "And there's a well outside."

A still silence stood as Constance peered through the dark, seeing carpets pushed against the mud walls and holes plugged shut with sacking.

Pastor Clarke coughed. "And the boy, is he well?"

Mrs Severn nodded.

"Does he go to school and Sunday church?" Constance asked.

The woman looked to Pastor Clarke.

"Well," said the minister, "it's common for homesteader families to visit church only in the winter. The rest of year, the farm is seven days a week or these people just wouldn't survive. Same with schooling – many families send the children only in the winter months." He looked at Mrs Severn. "So, I'm sure we'll be seeing the boy once the cows are in the barn."

She nodded. The three stood in silence.

Finally, Constance spoke. "That's a pretty baby."

Mrs Severn looked down as though forgetting she even held Ann.

"Is she well?" asked Constance.

The woman nodded.

"Well," said Pastor Clarke, raising his hat in retreat. "I think, Mrs Severn, we can let you get on with your work here. I trust you will tell the boy we called."

The woman nodded quickly and followed them out to the cart.

As they drove off, Pastor Clarke leaned over, his closeness pushing Constance further away. "So, what did you think?"

Constance glanced back at the sod house. "Well, they are certainly humble. The poor woman looked scared that we might take George away – and that's a good sign. They must be fond of him."

"Aye, well these people don't like to show their emotions. But I have no doubt you're right. A humble abode, but a happy one."

Constance thought of her mother. She hoped she would approve of George's new home. "Pastor Clarke, my mother awaits news of my brother ill in Africa and I would like to return home as soon as possible. Can I ask you to visit the remainder of my children? I intended to visit them all, but the distances are so far, it would take me months."

She looked up to see Pastor Clarke smile down at her. She didn't like his look and certainly didn't want to give him any encouragement, but if he could bring reports of her children. "Would you see that they are well treated and send news of them all to Marchmont House?"

Pastor Clarke nodded his head. "I can see to those in my district – which is certainly wide – but I know some of the children have been sent even further – for them and for you, I will write to my colleagues of the cloth – give me a list of names, farms, districts, and I will ensure the job is done."

Constance smiled up at him. She would keep her promise to her mother, someone would check up on all the children.

*

After milking, George shut the cows in the barn, the bulls in the pen and the chickens in the shed. It was starting to snow and George hurried into the warmth of the house.

Mrs Severn carried a pot of potatoes from the stove. "A woman came to see you today."

George knew immediately it was Miss Constance. "What did she say? Did she come to get me?"

Mrs Severn shook her head. "She asked some questions. I think your sister gave us some bad mouth."

George leapt forward in his seat. "But what did she say? Is she taking me to Junie?"

Mrs Severn gave him a hard glare. "She said we was just fine – said to tell you she called."

George slumped down onto his seat. A lump rose into his throat and suddenly he had no energy to do anything other than cry. How could Miss Constance leave, thinking he was happy here? Didn't she listen to anything Junie told her?

Mrs Severn ladled potatoes on his plate. George looked away, gazing at the floor, not seeing or hearing anything until Tom

Severn came in, his figure casting a shadow from the candle behind him.

"You need to be up early tomorrow, boy. This snow could be the last those cows'll see pasture – so that shed's gonna need a good shovelling first thing."

George kept his gaze on the ground.

"You hearing me, boy?"

George nodded. He picked at his potatoes, taking small bites and then wrapped a spoonful of potato into a slice of bread and shoved it deep into his pocket. Miss Constance might think this was a good home, but he would tell her.

He ate the rest of his dinner and then went to his own earthen room. The cold winter wind had blown snow across his bedding. George dug his father's shirt out from under the straw and put it on. He then wrapped himself in the blanket the Severns had given him and waited until he could hear no sounds from the house.

Tying the blanket tight like a large shawl, George set off toward Belleville and Marchmont House. Falling snow meant there was no moon, but George knew the way down to the track at the bottom of the hill and from there he would trust in his instincts. He remembered a little of the journey that brought him to the Severn's house, and that would help.

He walked quickly and then ran, stumbling at the occasional warren hole, but soon he was sweating and by the time he'd reached the bottom of the hill he was breathless. He pondered which direction he should follow. To the right was dark, while in the other direction he could see a small glow in the night sky. Also the snow outlined a deep indent of cart-tracks that might belong to Miss Constance. He began to run again, following the tracks through a small forest. The blanket was now to warm to wear so he carried it close to his chest. His pace slowed as his legs grew tired. He stopped a few times as he heard branches snap under the weight of snow and feared someone might be following him. Then he picked up his pace and ran again until his chest threatened to burst, and his legs quivered with weariness.

Through the trees he saw the dark outline of a farm in the snow. George crept close and found a small sheltered hayloft. He sat down heavily and let his breath slow. Below, he heard the cows shuffle at his noise and a horse snort before going back to sleep.

George lay down, resting his legs and feet on a higher bale of hay. He smiled at the thought of telling Miss Constance that he didn't like Canada and she should send him and Junie back to their ma. His eyes closed in contentment.

He awoke to a jab in the ribs and a large plump face above him. "You there! Who do you think you are?"

George looked up into the fleshy mouth of the man, who jabbed him again with a stick. George stuttered as he struggled for the right words. "I just thought I would stop for a rest. I'm going to Belleville. I'm going home."

The man's face grew angrier. "You're one of those Homekids, aren't you? One of those beggars they brought out from London – I always said that was a bad idea. We don't need any of your bad blood here."

He moved closer to George, pulled away his blanket and held it out like it was evidence of a crime. "I suppose you've stolen this from the good folks who took you in?"

George shook his head.

"Who you with anyway?"

"Tom Severn," George answered quietly.

"Good folks – hard working! So what else you stole from them?"

George shook his head again. "Nothing! I was running away because ... I didn't like it and I miss my ma."

"Work shy – bloody lazy, the lot of you. Whoever thought this was a good idea should be shot and made to work a farm like we do."

"But, Sir, I did work hard. But they sent my sister away after promising to keep us together, and then they didn't feed me much and I had to work from dawn until dark and they would never talk to me or even use my real name."

The man stood upright as though growing more clear in his cause. "They wouldn't use your name and made you work – well, that sounds like a good reason to run off in the night and go stealing into my barn."

"Sir, I didn't steal."

The man lunged at the bulge in George's pocket and pulled out the bread and potato. "What's this? Looks like good food to me."

"Sir, it's me last night's dinner. I kept it for the journey."

"Stole it, more like. Now, I'll drive you back to Tom Severn's place so he don't miss your work today. Those good folks don't need to be let down by the likes of you."

George stood. "But, Sir, I don't want to go back. I want to go to me ma."

"Well, you should have thought of that before you let the Severn folks give you a good home."

George felt his arm pulled so hard it sent a searing pain though his shoulder. He was thrust onto the back of a horse for return to the Severn's farm. As he watched the dark mound of the Severn's home grow close, George felt tears freeze his cheeks. Tom Severn thanked the farmer, who turned tail toward his own farm with any further word.

George walked heavily toward the barn to begin his work. He felt Tom Severn's glare behind him, heard a few steps and then a fast motion made him turn. A whip's lashes flared through the air and, in moments, George felt their sting across his chest and the blow propelled him to the ground. He rolled onto his stomach and the whip came back down across his shoulders. He heard the whip's lashes crack and, moments later, his arms and legs caught its searing pain. George lifted his head for an escape. He saw the house and ran while the whip cracked behind him, catching around his legs and pulling him to the ground. He wriggled free and ran again toward the porch door. Mrs Severn stepped out and George screamed at her to move as the whip sounded behind him. He lunged at the doorway, expecting to see her move and let him bolt for refuge into the house. Instead, she folded her arms across her chest to block his way.

George screamed as he turned toward the barn. Another crack of the whip sounded closer than before and George saw the lashes come down like black ropes from the sky and wrap around his face and chest. George curled down into the snow, and felt the sting of the whip as it was brought down again and again until he could feel it no more.

*

As Agnes Findlay mowed the hay, Lawrence walked behind, pulling the sheaves together and tying them tight. Agnes Findlay paused frequently and yelled at Lawrence to catch up. But his arms ached and the pitchfork he had to carry felt too heavy to lift.

He spread his arms wide and dragged together what he could, hoping that with this small effort he could gather enough hay to form a sheaf. He didn't notice Agnes Findlay behind him until she'd grabbed the pitchfork from his hands and held it at his throat.

"I ain't feeding you so you can stand around daydreaming."

Lawrence shook his head as much as he could without catching his neck on the prongs of the pitchfork. "Sorry, Miss, sorry."

"You'll be damned sorry." She pushed him away and then gave him a kick that sent the boy face down onto the ground.

Lawrence lay there grateful for the brief rest.

"Now, get up and gather those sheafs. This ain't no time for no resting."

Lawrence rose onto his hands and knees, pausing just for a few moments until the sound of a huge "Heelllooo!" sounded across the pasture.

"Now, who in the hell can that be? Don't they know everyone's busy this time of year." Agnes Findlay hurried up the slope so she could see the cottage on the other side.

"It's the pastor," she called back. "Now, you get up and get gathering while I go and see what he's needing."

Lawrence sat back on his knees, gazing at all the hay around him. It lay so thick it felt like he was being asked to gather the very sand from a beach. Slowly he reached out and began pulling together the stalks. It grew and he pulled it neatly into a smaller sheaf.

"Hey, you, Imbecile!"

Lawrence looked up to see Agnes Findlay standing on the rise. "Get down to the cottage quick – it's you Pastor Crane wants to see."

Lawrence dropped the hay and hurried uphill with more energy than he'd felt in a long time. The pastor must be taking him home, or back to Marchmont, or maybe it was his father, he was on his way to find him. A deep pain caught Lawrence in the chest and he stumbled as he reached the top of the rise.

Agnes Findlay spoke through thin lips. "You're happy here. Tell the Pastor anything else and you'll never speak again."

Lawrence stumbled ahead, lifting his heel high off the ground so he could run away from Agnes Findlay and down to the cottage where an outsider waited to rescue him.

Pastor Aaron Crane sat at the kitchen table, a cup of hot broth in his hands and a slice of Agnes Findlay's bread and jam before him. He put his cup down when Lawrence ran into the room.

"So, you're the boy who can read and write as well as most scholars." His mouth turned downward as he scanned Lawrence's small figure. "I must say you don't look like much of a specimen. Come here until I get a better view of you."

Lawrence hurried forward. "Sir, did my father send you? Have you come to take me away?"

The pastor laughed. "No such news, my boy. Just a visit to check that you're being well cared for."

All breath left Lawrence's chest, and he felt himself sink until the pastor's thick fingers prodded him back up to standing. "You eating well, boy?"

Before Lawrence could say anything about the meals he'd been missing, Agnes Findlay's voice came from behind.

"He's a weak child. Not much he likes to eat. You'd think that after all that starving those kids did in England they'd appreciate good food."

Pastor Crane peered at the large bruise on Lawrence's cheek, the one he'd got for asking for more food when he hadn't finished his chores. "What's this, boy? Does it hurt?"

Agnes Findlay stood at the pastor's side. "He falls a lot. A clumsy boy like you've never seen, Pastor."

"And what about these cuts to his fingers? They look like they could turn troublesome."

Agnes Findlay shook her head. "He won't have any solution to them – says it stings and runs a mile when I even mention it."

Lawrence shook his head. His heart raced as he felt his face grow flushed. "Sir," his voice croaked and he said it again. "Sir, I wondered if I might talk to you privately."

He felt Agnes Findlay move forward. "What would you want to do that for? Anything is fine in front of me."

Lawrence looked at the pastor, gazed at his eyes hoping the man might see his fear. "Sir, I think I might like to say my prayers with you alone."

Pastor Crane sat back in his seat with a soft grin. "Well, of course, my boy. I'd be delighted. Not too many of your fellow immigrants are so keen on prayer." He looked at his host. "Might you leave us for a short time, Miss Findlay?"

As soon as she'd closed the door, and Lawrence had heard its familiar latch, he stepped forward to the pastor. "Please, Sir, you must take me away from here. Miss Findlay is most cruel, she beats me and starves me and then yells that I cannot do my work."

The pastor coughed and sat back in his seat so he could see the boy better. "Well, young Sir, I can only assume you do something to deserve such punishment. I have known Miss Findlay since she was a young woman who lost her parents, and the goodly soul has struggled alone with this land for at least two decades. She is not an ungodly woman."

Lawrence knelt down at the pastor's knees as though in prayer. "But, Sir, please, I fear that if you do not help me then no one will and I will perish here alone and never again set eyes on my father."

Pastor let out a heavy sigh. "Boy, Miss Findlay took you in and gave you a home when no one else would – not even any stranger in your own birth land. Now, I believe you should show her some gratitude rather than coming up with fanciful stories of starvation and beatings."

Lawrence's legs shook, tears filled his eyes and he held his bony hands out in prayer. "Please, Sir, believe me, Miss Findlay is not a charitable woman. She calls me Imbecile and ..."

Pastor Crane swatted Lawrence's hands apart. "Enough, boy, you are unchristian in these allegations. Now, let us pray that you learn how to receive charity. Your desperate aspersions on Miss Findlay's character are a sin that only God can forgive."

The pastor stood to say his prayer. Lawrence cried as he muttered an accompaniment.

*

Ruby stroked the kitten's fur, her eyes bright with delight. "Is she really all mine?"

Hannah MacDougal's own eyes sparkled. "Why, dear Ruby, of course she is yours." She watched Ruby's hand, perfect in its plumpness, as it touched the grey fur of the kitten's ears, face and back, and then move down to the white fur of her paws.

"Mama, it looks like she's wearing socks."

Hannah pulled Ruby in a tight hug, a flicker of joy passing through her chest at the word "Mama". It didn't matter how often she heard it, the joy was more than she'd ever felt before.

"Mama, what will we call her?"

Hannah released her daughter and smoothed a loose curl from her forehead. "I don't know, my sweet. Do you have a name that is your favourite?"

Ruby looked up at the carved ceiling as though seeking inspiration, and then a small smile crept onto her face. "I like the name Junie. I think that's probably my favourite."

Hannah let out a sigh of relief that it wasn't Beryl's name she'd chosen. "Then we shall call your kitten Junie."

A knock brought Effie, the housemaid, into the room "Ma'am, it's Minister Clarke to see you."

Hannah rose to greet the minister.

"Mrs MacDougal, it is such a pleasure to see you again."

Hannah pointed to the tall armchair at the fireplace where a hefty stack of logs threw out welcome heat. "Please, Minister, take a seat."

The minister stopped on his passage across the room to pat Ruby's curls. "And you have a kitten," he said. "One of God's most precious creatures."

Hannah wondered about the purpose of the visit. She, James and Ruby visited church every Sunday, but it was rare for the minister to visit them at home. Even when it came to donations, the minister would always visit James's office.

"So what can we do for you, Minister Clarke?" Hannah asked.

He smiled. "It's actually the young Ruby I have come to see."

Hannah's chest filled with pain. The adoption papers had all been signed, but what if there had been an error?

The minister saw her look of fear. "Don't worry yourself, Mrs MacDougal, Marchmont House ask us to visit all the Home

Children and report their wellbeing. I don't believe you and Ruby have anything to fear, she looks the picture of happiness."

Ruby looked up from stroking Junie and gave him a wide smile.

"Aye," he said. "She looks the picture of health and happiness."

*

Helen arrived at the Home of Industry before the orphans rose for breakfast. It had been her routine since Constance left for Canada. She slept little and found work easier than worrying over Mathew lying in a hospital bed and being cared for by strangers.

She would have liked her daughter to have stayed home, forsaken Canada to await news of her brother. But Constance had been strident in her mission. "Annie MacPherson is depending on me."

Helen had wanted to remind her that her brother lay in Africa – and the news could be bad. But Helen hadn't wanted to put her own fears into words. Instead, she had given her daughter a tight hug in farewell and then filled her days with work. She knew that if the news was bad, she should tell herself that she was lucky to have had such a beautiful son. For that is what Pastor Birt would say. Do not mourn his loss but celebrate the brief time she had had with her son.

The letter when it came was brief:

My Dear Mrs Petrie,

It is with deep regret that I must tell you that Mathew died this morning. He did not regain consciousness, but he left this world with little suffering. I will return on the next ship with his belongings.

Yours, in great sadness,
Roger Simonds

*

Beryl was standing at the range boiling the cheese cloths and mixing the stew when a loud knock on the door made her turn.

A preacher, tall and slim with a white collar that looked too large for his thin neck, stood there. "Miss Beryl Brown, I presume?"

Beryl hesitated and then nodded her head.

Maisie appeared from the back bedroom. "Pastor Harris, this is a good day when it brings a visit from you." She pulled a chair out from the kitchen table. "A cup of coffee for you, I'm sure the girl here can find you some biscuits with honey."

Beryl hurriedly dried her reddened hands.

The preacher smiled at her. "It's your young lady here I've come to see."

Beryl's heart raced in her chest. Miss Constance must have sent this man to collect her. She must have learned the truth about Maisie Grouver and now Miss Constance was taking her back to Marchmont. Beryl's hand shook as she poured the coffee.

Pastor Harris leaned back in his chair. "A letter from Marchmont House requests that I visit all the Home Children in my district and see that they are well. You know, I'm sure they can't all end up in such good homes as yours, Mrs Grouver."

Maisie smiled like Beryl had never seen her smile, wide so that it showed gaps where her missing teeth would have been. "Oh, I think she's happy enough here. It can't have been a good place they came from, not when their families are keen to see them go so far."

"Well, quite … Those poor children, but I suppose it's the ones who are left behind we should really feel sorry for."

Maisie nodded and then turned to Beryl, giving her a darted stare. "Well, I'm sure the girl will tell you herself how happy she is to be here – although she doesn't always show it. Quite ungrateful most of the time."

Beryl felt her heart pause as the preacher smiled. "And, Beryl, may we hear from your own lips that you are happy in your new home?"

The girl felt Maisie's glare, and words faded from her mind.

The preacher's voice was soft. "Come, child, I'm sure you can tell of the kindness you have received here."

Beryl's mouth moved, but she only stuttered a few noises as she felt Maisie's threatening stare.

Maisie broke the silence. "She's a quiet one, don't ever have a lot to say. At first I was pleased to have another female around the house – thought it would be company like – but she don't offer much in the way of companionship."

"Well, being quiet has its blessings." The preacher took a long drink of his coffee.

He stood. "Well, I can write that all is well for Miss Beryl Brown at the Grouver household." He paused, turning to Maisie herself. "Although, I must say I have noticed the absence of your family at church on Sundays. You know, all your children, including this young orphan here, should receive the scripture if they are to appreciate the Lord's blessings."

Maisie blushed. "I am sorry, but I will tell Bill when he gets home. Now that harvest is over, I am sure we will be there on Sunday, I promise."

"And this young lady – is she attending school?"

Maisie hesitated only a moment. "No, Pastor Clarke, she's quite far behind and our Malky is getting her caught up." She blushed heavily at the lie.

The preacher nodded, satisfied at bringing strays back to his flock.

*

George spoke no more to the Severns. He followed their instructions silently while all he could think of was getting through each day. Winter brought the long frozen nights, and the gate on his earthen cave let in snow and wind. Some nights, George thought he would freeze to death, but he didn't complain. Instead he took his blanket out to the barn and slept amidst the cows, their body warmth keeping the chill out. Tom Severn knew where George slept but said nothing.

An early thaw showed the tips of long grasses, and Tom Severn sent George to take the cows to pasture. George felt his chest lighten a little as he hurried uphill. The cows, eager for grass, needed little encouragement.

Although only half a mile from the sod home, George felt flickers of joy in his chest. As the cows grazed, he lay across a flattened rock and watched the light clouds as they drifted across the blue sky. He wondered if they were moving toward Marchmont. He remembered that when they'd travelled from Belleville, they'd moved in the direction of the setting sun. So, to return to Belleville and Junie, he would have to travel back toward the rising sun.

George sat up in excitement. He stared downhill with the realisation that he knew the way to Marchmont.

A long "moo" from behind made him turn. The cows all faced up hill, their heads down in feeding. George scanned their rears, counting slowly. They were three short. He looked again, running from one edge of the plateau to the other before glancing down into a dell and seeing the missing cows. George ran, his whip raised ready to herd them back onto the plateau. But, as he got close, water clogged into his boots, sucking them down into the mushy mud. George threw himself back so that he gripped the solid earth. He wriggled free of his sinking boots and pulled himself back onto solid ground. The three trapped cows let out short panicked sounds as they sank further into the marsh.

George looked around to see if he could get closer and pull them out. He ran to the closest cow and pulled at its tail. The cow shook, its cry turning into a hiccup of moans. George let go and ran downhill toward the barn.

"Come quickly!" he yelled before he'd even seen Tom Severn.

The farmer dropped the axe he was using to cut firewood.

"It's the cows, three of them are stuck in the marsh!" George's voice was high in panic.

Tom Severn ran without waiting for more information. George sprinted after him, arriving at the dell as the cows' rumps were disappearing from view and the creatures' large eyes stared in desperation.

Tom Severn hovered around the marsh, trying to get closer, like he thought he could pull them out by their necks. Finally, as the deepest cow threatened to sink, he looked at George like he might throw him in after them.

George knew the look and ran. He took off down the hill with Tom Severn behind him. He didn't know where he was going but he wouldn't stop at the sod home, he was heading down to the track and he would follow it toward the rising sun and Belleville.

But a blow to the back of the head sent George tumbling downhill. He didn't know what hit him. He lay dazed until he felt the shadow of Tom Severn above him. George opened his eyes. The farmer held out the castrate cutters. George's eyes grew wide. He knew what they were and he'd seen Tom Severn use them on young steers. He rolled ready to run again, but Severn grabbed him by the hair and pushed him back onto the ground. The farmer held the castrate cutters close to George's face. "See these?"

He gave George's groin a telling look and George turned onto his stomach and sobbed like he had never sobbed before, and when he stopped, he ran. Taking the same path he had taken before, George ran downhill, stumbling into holes and falling over bracken but each time he fell he got straight back up and continued running.

He heard Severn call out behind him, but he didn't turn. When he reached the cart track he ran in the direction of the rising sun and didn't feel the ache in his legs or the pain in his chest until he reached a low lying lake that he'd passed on the road from Marchmont. The sight made him stop and smile like he was seeing the house itself. He stopped, resting with his hands tight to his knees and seeing finally that he was barefoot. His boots had been gobbled in the mire with the cows.

He hurried on walking briskly, letting his breathing slow down. Occasionally, he looked behind him, anxious that Tom Severn might come from behind or that some neighbouring farmer might take him back. But the road stayed quiet until dusk when George saw a horse rider come across the hill. Thick gorse bushes lay off the track and George hid there until the rider had passed. As the moon appeared in the sky, George's stomach began to cramp with hunger, but the boy kept going, ignoring the wood smoke of distant farm-houses where food might be on offer.

A cloudless sky and a moon close to full kept the cart track well lit, and George walked because he couldn't think about stopping. Any pause might mean getting caught, and he couldn't go back to the Severns' farm.

By dawn, every step was like walking on pins, but George kept going. He saw a log cabin close to a small wood, where the farmer had hailed Tom Severn only to be ignored. George passed by.

But the farmer's wife called out to him. "Good morning to you!"

George pretended not to hear, although the smell of bacon made his stomach growl.

Her voice grew closer. "Would you like some breakfast?"

George paused. "I can't pay for it."

She shrugged. "You look like you've been on the road for some time."

George turned back to the road and began to walk. He couldn't risk her taking him back to Tom Severn.

"Where you going?" she called out.

"Belleville – I have family there," he lied.

"Well, you might want to something to eat, it's another ten miles or so."

George stopped again. "I told you, I can't pay."

The woman looked a little like his ma – thin with brown hair pulled back into a knot at her neck. "That's no matter in this house."

George followed her into the log cabin. Its warmth wrapped his chill so that he just wanted to lie down and let it soak in. The woman bid him sit at the table where three young children ate eggs, bacon and bread.

"Two eggs for you?" the woman asked.

He nodded. "My name's George."

"Well, George – this here is Andrew, Duncan and our little Agnes. They'll be out doing their chores soon and maybe you can take a rest in their bed."

George stood quickly. "No, no, Ma'am, I can't take any rest. I have to keep going. You see, my family, they're expecting me in Belleville today."

The woman stepped closer to him, resting her hand on his shoulder. "George, you're tired – even a child like these can see that. Now, you won't make Belleville today without a few hours' rest. How long you been walking, anyway?"

"Only since yesterday," he said.

"And you went all through the night – no food, I guess?"

George shrugged like it was no feat.

"Well, sit and get some food into you." She scooped two fried eggs onto a plate, added bacon crisp from the oven and placed it on the table.

George sat, unable to argue anymore. He ate, while the woman buttered him two slices of thick bread. George nodded thanks but didn't stop eating until his plate was clean.

"Want some more?"

George's eyes smiled, and she grinned at him. "The name's Senga MacGrory. My husband owns this homestead. He's out with the bulls right now."

At the mention of bulls, George turned pale.

"You had a bad experience with bulls?" Senga MacGrory asked.

George shrugged and began to eat his second plate of bacon and eggs.

"So what were you doing out west?"

George shrugged again, his mouth full of food.

"Look, I'm no Inquisition. I'm just a nosy woman who likes to know the business of strangers. We don't get too many visitors around here."

George swallowed his bacon. "I was on a homestead, but it didn't work out."

Senga sat at the table to her own plate of breakfast. "Some of those homesteaders can be pretty hard-nosed. You get a bad one?"

George nodded.

"Well, maybe after some rest, the world won't seem like such a bad place."

*

George slept in the large bed belonging to Andrew, Duncan and Agnes. He awoke to the smell of boiled ham and stretched out, feeling every muscle in his legs cry out in pain. The soles of his feet had broken out in sores. George hobbled into the kitchen where Senga MacGrory watched her children write their letters.

She smiled to see George. "A good rest?" she asked him.

George nodded as he walked to the door. He looked outside to see the sun heading toward dusk. "I think I slept too long."

Senga MacGrory shook her head. "You were tired, and I suggest you stay here for dinner, have another good sleep – I can rig you up a bed on the floor – and then you can set out for Belleville in the morning. My husband might even be able to take you on the horse part-way."

At the mention of the husband, George shook his head. "No, no – maybe I should just leave now. I can walk through the night and be there in the morning." He remembered his fictitious family in Belleville. "My parents will be out looking for me."

Senga MacGrory put a cup of hot broth before him. "Look, George, you don't need to lie to me. I know from the look of you that you're running away – and you're afraid my husband might take you back. Well, don't be. He's a good Christian man who's all too willing to give everyone their say."

George let out a long sigh, wanting to cry.

"So, what brought you out here? You're accent still so English, you ain't been here long?"

George told Senga MacGrory the story of making matchboxes, Miss Constance bringing him to Canada and losing his sister back to Marchmont. The MacGrory children stopped writing to listen, especially when he talked about saying goodbye to his mother and getting on the omnibus. They watched George's mouth as he talked about the ship journey and losing Harry overboard, and then being taken by Tom Severn and his sister being returned to Belleville without even a goodbye after she'd picked carrots instead of weeds.

"How fast did the omnibus go?" asked Duncan.

George stopped, unsure of what he meant.

"The omnibus – did it go so fast your head spun?" the six-year-old asked.

Andrew gave Duncan a nudge for asking the wrong question.

George shook his head. "I don't remember. I was crying for my ma." Tears came to his eyes, and Senga MacGrory held him in a tight hug. The feel of her arms around him made George cry even more and soon sobs churned through his chest.

He was being held like this when Gordon MacGrory stepped in, muttering about drainage and clogged pipes. He saw his wife hugging a strange boy and stopped talking. On a firm stare from his wife, he tiptoed to the table and, as George quietened, she introduced them.

Gordon held out his hand. "Please to meet you, young man."

George's hand hesitated before reaching out in a handshake. He kept his head down, embarrassed about the tears that stained his cheeks and the snot that now plugged up his nose. Senga handed him a rag and he gave his nose a good blow.

Duncan spoke quickly. "George is from England and he came here on an omnibus."

Gordon laughed. "That's quite a story."

Senga's voice was more serious. "He's headed to Belleville – had a bad experience working for some homesteader out west."

Gordon nodded. "So, young man, how old are you?"

George swallowed. "I was eleven, Sir, but I think I became twelve over the winter."

"And did that homesteader out west break your nose?"

"No, no, Sir, that was a thief after my newspaper money." George began to cry again at the thought of newspaper selling. It sounded so safe now.

Gordon reached out and touched the boy's hand. "I didn't mean to upset you, George. I was just curious – some of those folks out west have fierce reputations."

The noise of Senga dishing out plates of ham, carrots and potatoes disturbed any further conversation. George ate slowly, keenly aware that he was a stranger in a very nice home.

"So, what do you expect to find in Belleville?" Gordon asked.

George quickly swallowed a carrot. He so enjoyed the tart taste that he was almost sorry to let it leave his mouth. "It's the home there. The people who brought us here – Miss Constance and Miss Ellen."

"And what do you think they'll do with you?"

George shrugged. "I don't know. I'd like to find my sister Junie."

Gordon sat forward in his seat, pushing his empty dinner plate away from him. "Well, how about this? I can do with some extra help around here – the boys aren't quite old enough to do the jobs I need. But if we promise to treat you like one of our own, send you to school and church – would you like to stay here with us?"

George grew pale and then flushed as his heart raced. These were surely good people, but he shook his head. "I have to find Junie. I have to see she is looked after."

Gordon nodded. "I understand – and it's to your credit that you want to see her cared for. So how about this – tomorrow, I ride you the first few miles to Belleville and you write to us if you want to take up my offer. I would hate to see you, or anyone, heading back to those folks out west."

George smiled as though he'd been offered a kingdom – or a future.

*

It was late evening when George entered Belleville and found the high-treed garden that surrounded Marchmont House. He grinned as he hurried up the path. Inside he could hear children laughing, and his heart raced at the thought of seeing Junie.

His ring was answered by an older boy who looked George up and down before saying. "They only take English kids 'ere."

George stepped into the hallway. "I am English, and I've been here before. Is Miss Constance around?"

The boy shook his head. "She brought us out and then went back to London."

George felt a little panic, he didn't want to be sent back to Tom Severn. "Is Miss Ellen here?"

The boy turned and George followed him through the house to where Miss Ellen sat over some accounting books. She looked up, startled, at the sight of George and then stood to greet him.

"Child, what happened? Have they sent you back?"

George shook his head. "I ran away – they were horrible. And …" he paused looking at the boy who had opened the door to him.

"Jack, why don't you go and supervise the younger boys?" Miss Ellen told him.

George waited until the boy was out of earshot and then stuttered just a little as tried not to cry. "He – he threatened to cut off me goolies."

Ellen Bilbrough looked at him puzzled.

"You know – me globes, me manhood," George said with a nod downward.

"Ahh," Miss Ellen blushed. "And how did you get here?"

"I walked." He looked through the window at the children at play, trying to catch a familiar face.

"Let's get you some refreshment," Miss Ellen said and led him down toward the kitchen. She turned to him as she walked. "This is rather embarrassing," she said. "But we've had so many children come through here over the last six months. I'm sorry, but you're going to have to tell me your name again."

George felt a rage flood up through his chest and his voice reached down the hall and into the many rooms upstairs and down. "You took me from my mother – promised us a better life. You gave me to a man who beat us and threatened ..." he paused, unable to say what Tom Severn was going to do. "And now you say you can't remember my name."

Upstairs and down, small faces came out to peer at him.

"It's not as bad as it sounds – I just need a small clue – trust me, George." She looked at him with a smile. "That's it, isn't it? You're George, big brother of Junie."

George grinned at the recognition.

"Well, come through to the kitchen, George, and let's get you some food."

*

Over dinner George learned that Junie had gone to a large household where she would learn to be a housemaid.

"They're nice people," Ellen Bilbrough said. "They wanted an older girl, but I persuaded them that Junie deserved the opportunity. I myself have been to see her several times, and she seems quite happy."

"Can I see her?" George asked.

Ellen Bilbrough gave him a long look. "I'm not sure that would be a good idea, George. It might upset her, make her want to be with you. This is a good opportunity for Junie – by the time she's seventeen and finished her service, she will be sure of a good position."

237

George sank into the chair. "But I just want to see her – see that she's happy – and let her know that I'm free from the Severns – don't ever let anyone else go to their place."

Ellen nodded. "After what you've told me, you can be sure of it."

The matter of seeing Junie was dropped as Ellen Bilbrough told George that Ruby had been adopted by a very rich couple. "They fell in love with her on the first visit and then came back several times. Of course, Beryl was against the idea at first, but Miss Constance persuaded her that this was the best possible outcome for her sister. She would grow up in a grand home and be well educated. Beryl herself was taken by a large family, the wife wanted help raising her large family of boys. Lawrence was here the longest. His foot turned people off, but finally a woman farmer who lives alone took him. I'm sure he's finding his way out there, although I've no doubt it will be hard for the poor boy."

George went to bed thinking about Junie working as a housemaid. Miss Ellen said the family had a lot of servants so the work wouldn't be too hard, and she'd have people to learn from.

As he closed his eyes, enjoying the warm safety of Marchmont House, he felt his bed shake. He looked up to see Jack, the boy who'd opened the door to him earlier.

"So what's it like out there? I heard you tell Miss Ellen that your family were horrible – and from the look of you, some of us were scared."

George sat up. "Yeah, they were horrible, but no one will be sent there, Miss Ellen promised."

Jack sat on the floor beside George's bed. "Yeah, but how do we know that none of us will go to other people like that?"

He stared at George for an answer. Other kids moved closer.

George shrugged. "I don't know. I've found another family, and they've offered me a home with them. They're really nice."

"Yeah, but there has to be something hasn't there – some way out if it doesn't work out?"

George thought for a moment. "A letter! Miss Constance promised me that if we weren't happy we were to write to Miss Ellen. Well, the house I stayed at didn't have ink, never mind paper – so I would say, take your own. That way you're prepared."

Jack nodded. "So how bad was it?"

George lay back down. "I'm tired," he said.

In the morning, George told Miss Ellen about the offer to stay with the MacGrory family.

"But George, we don't know them," she said.

George let out a sigh that made him seem so much older than his years.

Ellen Bilbrough thought for a moment. "It just doesn't fit in with the system. Miss Annie said we need reference letters from the local preacher before we let you go with anyone."

"Miss Ellen, you had a reference letter for Tom Severn, and look at how that turned out. The MacGrorys are good people. They fed me and took care of me when other farmers would have taken me back to Tom Severn."

Ellen Bilbrough shook her head. "Look, why don't you write to them? Ask them to furnish a letter from their preacher, and that will let me see that they're serious about caring for you."

*

Frost crunched lightly under Lawrence's naked feet, and the boy shook as he ran through the cold dawn air to the hen-house. He ran past the gap in the fence, thinking only of the hen-house that would provide a little temporary warmth. But as he unlatched the gate, a strange silence crept through the cold, making him stop. Feathers littered the earth, pulling Lawrence's gaze across the ground until he saw the gap. The loose slats he was supposed to fix had been torn apart.

She'd told him yesterday – he could still hear her voice: "Imbecile – that fence needs fixing before my hens go missing."

But he'd been so tired, especially after cleaning out the barn, and he'd left the job undone.

He thought of how to tell Miss Findlay and wished he could just write her a note and hide. A sour smell lifted into the air, and Lawrence looked down to see his feet in a pool of diarrhoea.

*

Constance sat on the deck of the ship feeling the cold wind blow strands of hair free from the pins. Her face welcomed the chill after the dark, dank berth below, and she felt a private thrill at the freedom of travelling alone, no children to guide, advise, teach or care for. She didn't resent the children, but it was so nice to finally be alone, to think and look back on all the Lord had given her. She was also finally able to think of her mother. She would be fretting over Mathew, although by now Mathew was probably on his way home with some rollicking great tales to tell them.

Below the ship's rail, the grey sea rocked the ship as white-tipped waves pushed them forward. Constance watched and wondered about little Harry Twistle and where he lay. She hated to think of Harry and knew she should not have allowed the boys to stay on deck alone. But, just like her mother said, she hadn't thought of all the dangers children could find. And now little Harry lay below her somewhere.

As the wind grew stronger, Constance felt a chill seep into her bones. She wrapped her arms around her shoulders, gaining some warmth, and then bobbed on the toes of her boots to keep from freezing.

"Poor Harry," she muttered. "May the Lord have you close to his side."

The smell of pipe smoke made her look round. The Captain of the *S.S. Sardinian* stood looking down at the sea. "Feeling well?" he asked her.

Constance nodded and smiled. "I think I got over my seasickness on the first voyage."

"Aye, most do." He stood in silence for a few moments. "And the children you've been escorting – are they doing well?"

Constance stood a little straighter. "I believe so. The people of Canada seem happy to receive them."

The Captain kept his eyes out to sea. "Do you visit them – those that have found families?"

Constance blushed despite the cold. "We try to, but the distances are so far."

"You must try to." As the Captain turned to look at her, his voice grew stern. "See all of them – and listen to them."

Constance shook her head, of course she would listen to them.

The Captain stepped a little further toward her. "Talk to them alone, and listen – don't care what the family tell you – listen to the child."

Constance stepped back. "But I do." As she said this she thought of Junie and her tales of beatings and realised she hadn't waited to hear George's story.

"When a child says they are being ill-treated, they're not making mischief. They're trusting in you."

Tears gathered at Constance's eyes, and it wasn't due to the wind. Junie wouldn't lie. She had no need to.

Constance sat back onto the bench realising she had been stupid. She shouldn't have listened to Pastor Clarke talk about how good the Severns were – she should have waited for George.

The Captain leaned a little further. "And keep an extra careful eye on the little ones – they always get hurt first."

Constance thought immediately of Lawrence. "How do you know all this?"

He gave a knowing look. "I grew up in an orphanage, and the parish sent me to so many foster homes that I saw the best and worst of humanity before I'd even grown my first whisker."

Constance let out a deep sigh, knowing she'd been too trusting.

*

Beryl opened her mouth silently. The songs had less tune than the ones Miss Constance had taught them, and Beryl couldn't catch any of the words. She looked around her. It felt so long since she'd seen anyone other than the Grouvers, that all the faces in church drew her eyes. The plump woman on the neighbouring aisle puffed out her cheeks as she sang like she was blowing into a dead fire. The man in front sang with a flat voice, and Beryl stared at the gleam that shone from his bald scalp. Everyone looked new and enticing, and Beryl felt herself drawn to them all, craving an exchange of words that might make her feel like she belonged.

The song faded and the congregation wriggled as they sat. Beryl squeezed into her seat between Maisie and Bill Junior. The

241

tall, thin preacher stood before them, his deep, flat voice filling the church.

"Blessed Parishioners, as we gather here today we must think of the prodigal ones."

Beryl had no idea who was prodigal, but she thought about Ruby and wondered what she was doing today. She would probably be at church with her new family and maybe wearing a nice dress with her hair in pretty curls. Beryl hoped Ruby's new family knew that she didn't like to have her hair brushed first thing in the morning, and that pulling on the tugs would make her cry, and that it was best to comb her hair with your fingers before bringing in a wide-toothed comb. Ruby hated to have her hair combed in a hurry.

As the piano keys struck up a new song, Maisie, Bill Junior and the rest of the congregation stood. Startled, Beryl jumped to standing, drawing a dark glare from Maisie. Beryl coloured, knowing she would face punishment for not paying attention. Seeking some favour, Beryl joined the voices as they rose in song. But her flat voice moved in contradiction.

Maisie dug an elbow into Beryl's chest. "Quit it!" she whispered.

Beryl silently opened and closed her mouth. She stared at the cross ahead and small tears glinted in her eyes. The music ended, and the preacher bid them drop their heads in prayer. Beryl felt the tears trickle down her cheeks and wished she were somewhere else or at least going home with someone other than Maisie Grouver.

"Go in peace!" the Preacher raised his hands high into the sky, and the congregation turned to file out through the aisle.

Beryl kept her head down. She didn't want Maisie or any of the other Grouvers to see her cry.

A heavy whisper, almost harsh, came from behind: "Beryl!"

Beryl turned quickly, the voice so familiar but from a distant past. The heavy woman puffed behind, her cheeks very red from effort, and then a tall couple with children followed. But then Beryl spotted the dark hair, pale eyes and twisted nose. "George!" she called out.

Maisie glared at her. "Stop your calling out."

But Beryl had stopped in the aisle, plugging up the exit as she stared at George. The heavy woman grunted as she squeezed past, but then the couple with the children stopped and George had to press past them.

He grabbed Beryl's hand. "I couldn't believe it when I turned around and saw you."

Beryl stared at his pale eyes and burst into tears. She tried to talk, tell him about Ruby, but words choked her and she blushed as she bubbled.

A woman had joined George. She wrapped her arms around the weeping Beryl but the kind touch made Beryl cry even more.

"It's all fine," whispered the woman, gently patting Beryl's shoulder.

But a nudge into Beryl's back made the tears stop. Bill Junior scowled at her. "Ma says to get going right away."

He turned quickly toward the church door. Beryl knew she had to follow him fast. She gripped George's hand tightly and hurried out after the Grouvers. Her tears flowed freely as they climbed into the wagon and the twins accused her of getting Jesus.

"She doesn't have Jesus. She just saw an old friend," Malky said.

Maisie glanced over her shoulder. "Well, that's no reason to go giving us a showing up at church."

Beryl wiped her face with the sleeve of her dress, but then she thought of George and images of her mother and the street and the smell on their stairs and the tears came all over again.

"That's the last time we'll take her to church," Maisie said. "Too highly strung, she'll need that beaten out of her."

Bill Grouver pulled his eyes off the track ahead and stared down at his wife.

Slowly Maisie turned away. "Well, we ain't taking her back there anyways," she said a little more softly.

Beryl could still feel the spot where the woman with George had held her, the place across her shoulder still prickled at the contact.

*

Dear Father,

I don't know if you'll ever receive these words. I have no parchment so I am using this blank page from Robinson Crusoe. And I feel so strong an urge to contact you that I'm using chicken blood I've saved in a cup as Miss Findlay doesn't have any ink and wouldn't let me use it even if she did.

Father, I am so unhappy here. Please, you must come and rescue me. I don't know how you might receive this letter as I have no way of reaching any post, but I appeal to you, Father, please rescue me fro ...

The chicken blood dried up and Lawrence dropped his head so that it rested on the flyleaf of his favourite book.

*

Maisie had been in bed ill for three days now. Beryl didn't know what was wrong – "women's troubles" was all Bill said. He rolled his eyes when he said it like it was something he would never understand. For Beryl, Maisie's illness meant more work as she took over the care of Seth and tried to keep up with her other chores. Seth fretted for his ma, no matter how Beryl tried to amuse him. Of course, the child didn't like being out in the cold while Beryl hung up the laundry, but Bill had warned her not to disturb Maisie. So Beryl tried to make it into a game by asking Seth to throw her the clothes pegs so she could hang up the linen. It had worked for about eight pegs then Seth grew bored and she'd had to let him cry while she pinned up the rest of laundry and hurried him indoors.

That night Beryl lay in bed feeling too tired for sleep. Her shoulders ached and a deep throb pulsed in her forehead. She took a deep breath and tried to relax her back onto the straw mattress. A cold dampness eased through her shawl. She rolled over, pulling her blanket tighter around her shoulders, and wriggled to find a warm spot. But footsteps, padded in socks, came from the base of the ladder.

She lay suddenly still. The ladder groaned from a weight. Beryl sat up and lay down quickly as Bill's head came into view.

He grinned. "Aye, lass, it's cold up here, but I'll soon bring some warmth to your cheeks."

Beryl hated the feel of Bill, although he'd been kinder than some of her old customers, and she had been a bit warmer when he'd climbed out from the blanket and sneaked back downstairs.

"You're too young for motherhood, so we're safe there," he'd told her.

But the next morning Maisie was out of bed, and Beryl felt her glare as she scrubbed the kitchen table.

"You're spilling suds, you stupid girl," she yelled as she held Seth on her knee. "And make sure you keep that water for the floor. We can't go wasting soap, you know."

*

Constance hurried down to the underground train at St Pancras. She had only travelled on it once before and had forgotten how smoky it could be. When she emerged at Liverpool Street her cape was covered in soot. She dusted it off and coughed as the heavy smog and dust filled her nose and throat. Already she missed Canada and its clean fresh air that let you see across vast fields. Here she could barely see the brewery on the other side of the street.

She crossed the road and hurried up Bishopsgate, passing a newspaper seller.

"New book says apes are our cousins," yelled the young boy.

Constance gave him a farthing, and couldn't help but smile when she thought about finding George on this very spot. She would visit him on her next visit to Canada, and she would listen to all he had to say.

On previous trips from Canada Constance had gone straight to the Home of Industry, keen to give her report on the children she had housed. But this time, she wanted to see her mother. She hurried, thinking of seeing her brother again – watching his dark grey eyes smile as they told of his adventures. She had to admit she'd been jealous when he'd set off for Africa, but that was a long time ago and now she had her own mission to tell him about.

But as she crossed the street toward the house, a dark shape on the door made her stop. She peered through the fog, slowly discerning the black ribbon of mourning.

Constance dropped her bag, her breath sharp in her chest. Mathew was too good, too young. She ran to the front door, leaving her bag on the street behind her. Winifred opened at the first knock, and Constance suddenly feared it was her mother herself who was dead.

But Helen sat in the darkened drawing room clad in black crepe, one of Mathew's old letters in her hands.

Constance fell upon her mother's chair, causing the letter to fall to the floor. "Oh, Mother, I am so sorry, I shouldn't have left. I just didn't believe this would happen – not to Mathew ..."

Helen stroked her daughter's head. "Calm yourself, child. He is in good hands – nothing can hurt him now."

Through the dim light Constance looked up to see the lines etched more deeply into her mother's face, and the hair greyer than she ever remembered. She threw herself back into Helen's tight embrace, thrusting her face into her mother's neck. "Mother, I am sorry, I should have been here with you. I chose the children, I chose work – I am sorry, I will not leave you ever again."

Helen shook her head, brushing Constance's cheek with her own. "You were busy, seeing the children, ensuring their welfare – it's what Mathew would have wanted."

Constance shook her head. She hadn't really seen to the children. She hadn't been as thorough as she should have been.

Helen's voice was a gentle whisper. "You know your brother would have been proud of you. I know I disagreed at times, but Mathew would have told you to take all the children – as many as you could fit on the boat. That's what your brother would have said."

Constance sobbed as the gentle arms of her mother held her. She wanted to say that she hadn't really seen to each child's welfare – she'd visited George but not spoken to him. And the rest, even Lawrence, she'd left to Pastor Clarke.

Constance's tears turned to incoherent blubs as she tried to tell her mother the truth. "I'm sorry, Mother, I ..."

Helen pulled her tighter to her chest. "Don't fret now, child."

Constance cried into her mother's shoulder, knowing she would go back to Canada and visit all her children – George, Junie, Beryl, Ruby – but she'd start with Lawrence because he was her first – and her smallest.

*

Lawrence lay on the straw matting, small breaths pushing through his thin chest making him want to cough, but he was too tired. The latest bruising Agnes Findlay had given made the saliva hard to swallow. He heard a rustle in his throat that made him feel like he would drown – like Harry. He loved Harry. His cheeks eased a little but not to make a smile.

The diarrhoea that had plagued Lawrence made the air fetid, and he wriggled, trying to move until a gasp pushed his chest too far. Lawrence saw his father, then his mother, and then no more.

Acknowledgements

Long before Thomas Bernardo, there was Annie MacPherson – a Victorian missionary who began the work of taking children from the streets of London to new homes Canada. Much of her writing is now out of print, but further reading can be found in the British Library: *Canadian Homes for London Wanderers, The Christian Magazine*, 1870; *Summer in Canada, The Christian Magazine*, 1872; *God's Answers: A Record of Miss Annie MacPherson's Work at the Home of Industry, Spitalfields, London and in Canada*, 1882; *The Children's Home-Finder: The Story of Annie MacPherson and Louisa Birt*, 1913.

A Canadian journalist wrote of what became of these children, and the impact their migration had on Canadian society. Kenneth Bagnell's book, *The Little Immigrants: The Orphans Who Came to Canada*, 1980, is a very worthy read.

Lightning Source UK Ltd.
Milton Keynes UK
UKOW01f1921210916

283502UK00002B/7/P